The Hedgerow

A Novel By

Anne Leigh Parrish

To John, Bob, Lauren, Lacey, Sam, Frida, and Tsuga

Contents

The Hedgerow

Chapter One

Edith didn't have to read the return address to know the letter was from Walter. They'd been coming all summer, always on a Wednesday. The first paragraph would be about his law job and the cases he was assigned. The second paragraph would talk about his parents, or his sister, Kathleen, and the wild things she and her new husband were up to. Sometimes he wrote about someone he had lunch with, or a problem with his apartment the landlord was neglecting to address. The third would touch on current affairs, now all about the Koreans and the trouble they were stirring up. He'd close with *All Best,* as if they never married, never cared for each other, and never made a single plan together. Sometimes, when her heart softened, she thought he might sense how she'd fallen apart after moving out of their apartment. He could be trying to bolster her spirit with a cheery, neutral tone, as if to say, "I understand, you'll be fine, I'm fine, too." But usually, she thought not.

She took the letter from the silver tray in the hall where Henry's butler, Alistair, had left it, and went into her room. The door that connected it to Henry's was closed, but not locked.

There was something about having her own bed that was deliciously freeing. Henry was a good man, and a good lover, but she didn't like lying next to him all night. She thought it was civilized, this arrangement of separate yet connected bedrooms. His wife, Mary, had had her own room down the hall, one with no shared access. She wanted it that way. She had gone back to England last winter. Henry had asked her several times for a divorce since then, and she refused. It just didn't make sense. Two months before she left, she had an abortion. The pregnancy was kept secret from him, but she confessed it to Edith. It seemed that when a woman didn't want a man's baby, or the man himself, she should be willing to set him free unless her pride stood in the way, or fear of being a divorced woman, though now, in 1949, it was more accepted.

Far less accepted was an unmarried man and woman living together, though neither Henry nor Edith worried too much about that when he invited her to move in. She accepted because when she left Walter she had nowhere to go. It was pleasant at Henry's; she needed that comfort to heal and collect herself. Henry devoted himself to her, didn't talk about the past or the future, and seemed glad to just drift along with her in tow. Then, just the other day, he told her to tell Walter that it was time to divorce.

"You need an orderly life, my dear, and waiting for him to free you is disorderly," he said. They had just made love, and he was slipping on his robe to return to his room. The clock by the bed ticked quietly. Outside, Cambridge and the whole of Boston were asleep, pressed down by gentle, inky darkness. Henry stayed longer than usual, lying awake beside her.

Sometimes, she tried to time her breathing to his, willing her rhythm to match his, but it never did.

Edith put the letter in her drawer without reading it. She'd never done that before and took it as proof that Henry was right, the time had indeed come. She scratched out a hasty note to Walter at her writing desk. She asked him to find someone to handle the arrangements. She was about to close with "I'm sorry," but stopped herself. Why did she have to be sorry? She changed who she was for him, or at least gave up what she wanted. Her abandoned doctoral degree drifted past, yet for once she didn't grieve. She had the bookstore and it meant more to her than poetry ever had, but then she hadn't set foot in it for two months. She needed to return and pick up where she had left off.

She wrote Walter's address on the envelope, stamped it, and dropped it on the same silver tray where his letter to her had been before.

Next, she used the telephone in the library to call Patricia Wilkins, the manager at The Turned Page. She wanted an update on the sales for the week. Patricia gave her the numbers. Edith noted the small drop from the week before. Patricia explained that July was often slow, many people in Cambridge were away then. She, herself, was due to visit Cape Ann the following week, which meant leaving Jocelyn and Liza, the two college girls she hired, in charge. Edith asked Patricia if she thought the store would carry on without her for those few days, and Patricia was confident that it would. Edith said she hoped she'd have a lovely vacation and would speak with her again, soon.

She realized Henry was still out. They had lunch, then he had to run an errand. She assumed he'd be back within the hour, but he'd been gone for close to three. She went into the kitchen to find Alistair sitting at the table with the newspaper and a cigarette.

"Has His Lordship returned? I didn't hear the door," Alistair said.

"Not yet. Did he say where he was going?"

"Not to me, Madame."

"Alistair."

"Yes, Madame?"

"It's high time you called me Edith. I know you think we Americans are far too informal about everything, but I can't stand it another minute."

Alistair looked bemused. He was in his early fifties, with thinning hair and a second chin. He worked for Henry's father back in England, then later for Henry and Mary, and had been eager for the chance to come to the States with them. Edith wondered how he liked it here. She knew almost nothing about him, his personal life, or even what he did on his days off. Henry said something about his being a member of a club. She assumed he meant the kind of gentlemen's club to which Henry belonged where you could go and sit in deep leather armchairs and drink good whiskey, but Henry said, no, he meant a club with other domestic servants, a professional association he thought. It sounded like a chance to gossip about one's employer, and she hoped Alistair was always discreet.

She asked if he'd like a cup of tea.

"Madame?" he asked and got to his feet.

"Oh, sit back down. I'll make it. For us both."

She slipped on the apron Alistair wore when he cooked. It fell to mid-calf since he was a lot taller than she was. And wider. She had to wrap the ties around her waist twice. She hadn't worn an apron in a while and didn't mind the feel of it. She told Alistair she hoped that wasn't proof that she was just a housewife at heart.

"I'd say at heart you're a businesswoman," Alistair said and offered her a cigarette. She took one and allowed him to light it for her.

"Well, I was."

"If you'll permit me, I feel certain you'll be back in the thick of things in no time."

"I doubt it will be that easy."

So many changes, each more difficult than the last!

During the war, she had a job in Washington. Afterward, she enrolled in graduate school at Harvard when Walter began law school there. She completed her master's degree in American poetry, applied for the doctoral program, and on the same day that she was accepted, he told her to drop out. He'd been spotted as a young man with promise, one who needed a certain kind of wife. They fought bitterly. He refused to back down. Angry and miserable, she went to New York to live with Walter's Aunt Margaret and worked at the United Nations as a secretary. That was in June, a little over a year ago, and all that summer, Walter begged her to come back. In August, she did. Then Walter and Henry became friends, and Henry bought The Turned Page for Mary to have something to do. Edith became the manager when it was clear that Mary wasn't interested. Edith's father died, she came into a little money, and bought the store from Henry last spring. Things were fine until she learned Walter was having an affair. Her only choice had been to leave him.

The kettle whined, Edith turned off the flame and poured the water into a pot where a stuffed tea ball was waiting to steep. She arranged everything on a tray and brought it to the table. Alistair reached to take it from her, and she told him not to bother.

Edith sat and Alistair filled their cups. He poured cream into his, stirred, and smiled to himself. Edith asked him why. He said he was just considering how there she was, sitting with him in the kitchen when she had been so formal the first time she came to the apartment last Thanksgiving with Walter.

"Yes. I was as nervous as a cat. I think I was a little overwhelmed by how Henry and Mary lived," Edith said.

"Understandable."

"Of course, Walter was over the moon that he made friends with a real English lord."

"He sounds somewhat impressionable," Alistair said.

"Who, Walter? Oh, yes. And easily flattered."

Which is how that creature, Babs, got her hooks into him so easily. Babs was an ambitious woman and needed an ambitious husband. The one she had was a quiet man, a good law student and now a decent lawyer, Edith assumed, but Babs wanted more. And what Babs wanted Walter would be happy to provide, not like what Edith had wanted, her own career, for one. Babs would make Walter her career, which would suit him perfectly if they were still together. Walter never mentioned her in the letters.

The front door opened, and Alistair stood and slipped on the black jacket he'd removed and hung on the back of the chair. Before he got out of the kitchen, Henry appeared. His usually polished air had dulled. He'd been drinking.

"What a cozy scene!" he said. Edith got up and took off her apron. She asked Alistair to bring her tea into the library, and to make some for Lord Henry, too. Henry walked ahead, chatting about how awful the traffic had been around Beacon Hill, which was odd because he thought the place would have emptied for a while. It was summer. Didn't Americans take their holidays in summer?

"I think you stopped off somewhere," Edith said.

"My club."

"And had a couple."

"Well, yes."

"Any particular occasion?"

"Just got talking with a new member, Ethan Bradford, charming fellow. He wants to sell me a yacht."

"What?"

"A sailboat, really."

"Do you know how to sail?"

"No, but wouldn't it be smashing to learn?"

"Oh, Henry."

The semester ended in June and Henry decided not to continue with graduate school in the fall, leaving him at loose ends. He was wealthy and didn't have to work. Edith suspected he came to Harvard just for the fun of it. He could have easily attended an English university.

Edith sat down. Alistair arrived with the tea tray, set it on the table, and asked if they needed anything else. When Edith said they didn't, he left.

Henry looked skeptically at the tea Edith poured him. She could tell he wanted another drink. She stood up and got him a small glass of scotch from the liquor cart.

"You're a darling," he said and took the glass from her.

"I'm enabling what's becoming a bad habit."

"You sound peevish."

"I'm not. I was waiting for you, that's all."

"Please, don't be upset with me," Henry said.

"I'm mostly upset with myself."

"Why, for Heaven's sake?"

She said she'd taken refuge in his comfort for too long, then stressed that he mustn't misunderstand. He and Alistair had taken excellent care of her. All that time to lie in bed, all those lovely cups of tea delivered gently to her room. They lifted her from the low point the breakup of her marriage had caused, and she would be eternally grateful, but she wanted to get back to work now. Henry held his glass and didn't drink from it. His gaze, which had been soft, almost woozy, focused.

"Are you leaving me?" he asked.

"No, of course not."

"Good. Because I have a little something for you."

He put down his glass and removed a small velvet box from the inside of his jacket. He extended his hand as an invitation to take it. She did. The box held a ring with a large square-cut emerald. It was breathtaking. She slid it on her finger and found it fit perfectly.

"How did you know my size?" she asked.

"Alistair borrowed your discarded wedding band."

"He went through my things?"

"Only your jewelry box, which sits in plain sight on your dresser."

"Oh, Henry, I do wish you hadn't!"

"Don't you like it?"

The green color drew her in. She found it calming, almost soothing.

"I do, very much. It's exquisite and wholly undeserved," she said.

"Nonsense."

Emeralds were her favorite gemstone, though she'd never owned one. She must have mentioned that to Henry but couldn't recall when or where. He was generous but didn't buy her gifts. He had given her nothing since she moved in, until now.

"I don't suppose this means . . ."

"That I'm proposing? I'm afraid it does."

"I think Mrs. Tremaine finally got to you."

Edith referred to the neighbor at the far end of the hall, who had run into them several times in the elevator. Henry politely introduced Edith as his good friend. Then, when Edith's name went on the mailbox, Mrs. Tremaine paid them a visit to offer congratulations on their marriage. Edith told her that they weren't married. Henry, overhearing from the library, came to explain that Edith had her own bedroom, always had, and always would. Theirs wasn't that kind of relationship. Mrs. Tremaine, widowed, in her sixties, said she had no use for modern ideas and threatened to call the police, at which point Henry summoned Alistair and asked him to explain the sleeping arrangements to her. Alistair said he was prepared to swear in court that nothing untoward had ever taken place between Mrs. Sloan and Mr. McCormick, and he was in a position to know because his duties as butler required that he live in.

"She's a dreadful nuisance, but no, she's not the reason," Henry said.

"Why, then?"

"Oh, Edith, you can be quite exasperating! Don't you know I'm in love with you?"

"No, I didn't know."

That was a lie. It had been clear to her for months. It had begun to make her feel guilty because she didn't feel the same way toward him.

She thought about the advantages of accepting him. Money topped the list, though she had some of her own. Respect was a close second. She knew how people worked. Being married to an English lord would put her in a separate class, far above anything she'd have occupied as the wife of an up-and-coming lawyer. She didn't care about class, but about being able to make her own decisions without reproach. People didn't criticize you, at least not to your face, when they thought you were above them in some way.

Could she be happy as his wife? Was she inclined to accept only because he was kind to her, or was there truly a deeper connection? They were like-minded about many things, the value of literature, for instance. They both believed personal freedom was more important than social convention. He had his faults, of course, among them an overdeveloped fondness for alcohol, and impatience with what he thought was laziness in other people. Sometimes he was hard on Alistair, and she gently rebuked him for it. She asked him to imagine what it might be like to be at someone else's beck and call, and he responded that growing up his father had treated him like a servant. Not in terms of asking to be waited on, but to be attentive, and stand in silence to receive another lecture.

A wedding to look forward to would put an end to the limbo she floated in. But it was at an end already, wasn't it? The bookstore now occupied her thoughts the way it had in the beginning. The last item she addressed before she fell in on herself was a plan to host author readings. Then there was the press she wanted to establish. As a husband, would Henry help or hinder? She had a feeling it might be the latter, that he might turn out to be needy, or feel deep down that women had no place in business, though there was no hint of this. She could give back the ring, but she couldn't go on living there if she did. They had crossed a frontier and there was no turning back. They must move forward together or not at all. This proposal was merely an extension of the path they'd been on for some time. There were worse reasons to marry someone. She had married Walter because everyone expected her to. Now the only souls involved were hers and Henry's. That made things much more intimate and simpler.

"Yes," she said and extended her hand. He approached, joined her on the couch, and took her in his arms. They kissed for a long time, then pulled gently apart. As always, she felt safe with him, comfortable.

"May I ask why you agreed, given that you're not in love with me?" he asked.

"I'm not being mercenary if that's what worries you."

"I know you're not."

She said they proved they could live together, were good together in bed, and well, she had gotten used to him.

"I hope that doesn't disappoint you," she said.

"Not at all."

She could see it did, though. She reminded him she never promised him love. He said that sometimes love snuck up on you when you least expected it.

"I'm sure you're right," she said. She looked at the tea tray and asked Henry if he'd make her a drink. He asked if she preferred sherry or scotch. She was in the mood for sherry.

As he got it for her, she told him about the letter she had just written to Walter.

"Was it difficult?" he asked.

"Not really."

"Such a brave woman."

"I'm not brave, just practical."

"Highly."

"And speaking of practicalities . . ."

"Mary," he said.

"Pay her off."

"I've already offered far more than she'd get as a settlement."

"Then what does she want?"

"To see me."

"What?"

"I'm to ask her in person. On bended knee, knowing her," he said.

"You have to go to England?"

"Unless she's moved somewhere else."

"Oh, for Heaven's sake! How long have you known about this?"

"Not long."

Edith didn't press him. He wouldn't yield if he didn't want to. She asked him if the timing of his proposal to her had anything to do with Mary's request to see him.

"I'm afraid I don't follow," he said.

"Perhaps you wanted me in your pocket for ammunition, as it were. To strengthen your request."

"You mustn't think that."

She asked when he was leaving.

"We sail on the fifth," he said.

"We?"

"I booked you a stateroom if you care to come."

"To England?"

"Yes, to England."

"You're full of surprises today, Henry."

"I hope your passport is in order."

"It is, which I suspect you already knew. And I promise to think about it."

Henry summoned Alistair with his infernal handbell, and when he arrived, Henry asked him to make a dinner reservation for them at Parkers. They were to celebrate their engagement.

"Very good, milord, and may I offer my congratulations," Alistair said.

"Thank you. And Alistair? The next time you want to rummage through my things, please ask me, first," Edith said.

Both Alistair and Henry stared at her.

"I'm not angry, I'm just saying," she said.

When Alistair left, taking the tea tray with him, Edith leaned back and kicked off her shoes. Henry smiled. He said before it must be a uniquely American habit because he never saw an English woman do that. Edith was sure Henry never spent time with Englishwomen in the lower classes, and if he had, he'd have seen plenty of stocking feet.

After another moment, Henry stood and went to the window to take in the view, something he did when his mind was full. Edith thought she should go to him, be loving, and thank him again for her gorgeous ring but couldn't. She worried that Walter would refuse her request for the divorce. It might be all over with Babs, letting him harbor some notion that he and Edith would get back together. Walter could be both stubborn and unrealistic, a difficult combination. She told Henry her concern.

"In that case, I think I should crack his skull," he said.

"I can't tell if you're joking."

"I'm not."

"Oh, Henry, that's not like you."

"Blame it on the liquor then."

"Why don't you leave off until we have dinner?"

"Just as you say." He put his glass on the table. She noticed it was almost empty. There were beads of perspiration on his forehead, and she didn't like looking at them, so she studied his shoes. Their high polish struck her as fussy and overdone.

She lifted her eyes and found him watching her.

"You said something about needing to get back to work. I assume you mean the bookstore," he said.

"Yes."

"I thought you had second thoughts about it."

"Not at all. I meant to ask you; how long will you be away?"

"About a month."

She could get a lot done in a month. The two college girls who helped must know a slew of local writers. Patricia would, too. A sign could be placed in the window inviting them to send a note if they were interested in giving a reading. Until a schedule could be drawn up, she could offer a Saturday afternoon children's story time. But who would host it? She supposed she could, or one of the girls. Perhaps some over-eager local mother would want to take that on. The store had two main rooms, one in front and one in back. The back was a perfect spot. She'd have to round up a colorful, cheerful rug for the children to sit on, as well as some small, inoffensive snacks. Nothing should cost too much. The idea was to make a modest investment and bring in mothers who would leave them to be entertained while they browsed the shelves. But what if they weren't dedicated readers, but just housewives looking for an hour away from their children? They might bolt out the door the minute they handed over their Jimmy or Jane.

As to the press itself, she'd written to a local printing company soon after she arrived at Henry's. The reply gave printing prices per copy up to a certain number. The per-unit cost dropped as the order size increased. Choosing a typeface was key. Some were more difficult and thus more expensive to work with. She needed to schedule a visit to meet with the manager, look at the various typefaces, and discuss paper stock, another complex issue. And she'd only contacted one press. There were several others she wanted to speak to.

But Henry had just proposed marriage, given her a gorgeous ring, and invited her to sail with him to England. Was she really thinking of not going? His feelings would be hurt if she stayed behind. And hadn't she longed for a trip like this?

"It sounds perfect," she said.

"I'm sorry, what does?"

"An ocean voyage."

"You'll come?"

"I will."

"Jolly good! I think we'll have a marvelous time."

He laid out the itinerary after they docked at South Hampton. They'd spend a couple of nights in London at Claridge's and then take the train north to Shropshire. It was a lovely ride. Did she have a camera? If not, there was still time to get one. He also advised her to take a trunk because she'd need clothes for all kinds of weather. And evening clothes, of course.

"Whatever for?" she asked.

"My parents are old-fashioned. We dress for dinner."

"Oh, I couldn't possibly do that. I'm allergic to evening clothes."

"I'm afraid you'll have to try."

"And I'm afraid I won't."

He held her gaze, then looked away.

"All right, my dear, I shan't press you," he said.

They repaired to separate rooms to change. Edith put on a pale green dress with a string of pearls. She studied her reflection in the mirror of her vanity table. Henry's parents would assume she was marrying him for his money. They probably assumed the same thing about Mary, but with her it would have mattered less, because she was a better fit. She was upper crust, dressed impeccably, spoke beautifully, and was witty and charming. And cold, as Edith supposed most upper-class British women were. Edith wasn't cold, but she was stubborn. Henry's parents might like that about her, or they might think it spelled trouble. Not dressing for dinner would prove nothing, except that she was a crass American. Well, she couldn't change who she was, could she?

Alistair drove them to the restaurant. He was a new driver, and unsure of himself, which put Edith on edge. Henry didn't seem to notice. He enjoyed the car, a late-model Cadillac, with its eight-cylinder motor and plush interior. He held her hand and said she'd love England, she really would. Oh, and Alistair would come with them, wasn't that grand?

"As your butler?" Edith asked.

Henry smiled indulgently. "No. Mother and Father still have old Carstairs, at least they did as of their last letter.

Doddering old wreck of a man, but still keen to serve, I expect. Alistair will be my valet."

"And am I to have a maid?" Edith asked.

"Of course. One of the parlor maids will do, I expect."

"Henry, I was joking."

A faint smile flashed across Alistair's lips in the rearview mirror then vanished as a nearby driver honked. Alistair swore under his breath. Edith had offered to help him practice his driving, but he always declined.

They arrived at Parker's and Henry asked Alistair to return around nine-thirty. If they weren't ready, he should circle the block until they came out, so he should make sure the gas tank was full. Alistair said it was, he'd taken care of that the other day.

After the first glass of wine, Edith's mood improved, but by the second, it soured. She felt like she was acting in a play, following a script, complimenting the duck she ordered which she found ridiculously heavy for summer. Henry's eyes were on her almost every moment and she tried casually to avoid his gaze until he asked her if she were well.

"I'm just thinking about the store," she said. The duck sat sullenly on her plate.

"Oh, Edith. Must you, at a time like this?"

"I think of the store quite a lot. Just because I've failed in my responsibility to it doesn't mean it's not always on my mind. I thought you understood that."

The couple at the table nearest them stopped talking, utensils in mid-air.

"You haven't failed in anything. I simply meant you should be enjoying yourself," Henry said and signaled the waiter to clear their plates.

He said he was sorry and blamed his remark on being anxious about going home and seeing his parents.

"Why anxious?" she asked.

"We've had our differences. They weren't keen on my coming here. And frankly, I don't know how they feel about divorce. There's nothing they can do to prevent anything, I have my own resources, as you know. I just don't want to have to suffer their thinly veiled disapproval."

"Well, I'll be there to help. I'm pretty good at weathering that kind of thing," she said.

He took her hand and gave it a gentle squeeze.

They declined dessert, paid the bill, and went outside to find Alistair waiting for them. He asked if they enjoyed their dinner, and Edith said they had, it was delightful, then asked him to drive them over to The Turned Page.

"At this time of night?" Henry asked.

"Why not?"

The streets were quiet and pleasant. Windows were softly lit, and the night sky was bright and clear. Edith loved Cambridge after taking a long time to warm to it. They passed the street she and Walter used to live on, and she was surprised to feel no pang at the memory of their shabby little walk-up. A light glowed in the front room of their former apartment and Edith was sure it belonged to another student, toiling away toward a brighter future and an easier life. She never faulted Walter for his ambition, only that he denied hers.

Harvard Square was more crowded than the side streets had been, yet people walked in a gentle, unhurried way. Edith directed Alistair to the store. He couldn't park in front, so she asked him to let them out, then to find a parking spot and join them, if he liked.

The door was locked but the lights were on. It took Edith a moment to locate her key inside her handbag, then she had trouble getting it to work, and Henry helped her. Inside, Patricia was unpacking a small crate of books. Straw had spilled onto the floor.

"Patricia! Why are you here so late?" Edith asked.

"Edith, my goodness, I didn't know you were dropping by!"

"Just a surprise visit. We were dining out."

Patricia and Henry had met before, and they said hello to one another as Patricia pushed up loose strands of gray hair that had escaped her bun.

"Some orders came in and just sat. I told Liza about them, and she put them there in the corner. How does that look to customers? Anyway, I decided to stay and just get the whole thing taken care of," Patricia said.

"You're wonderful! Is there more to unpack?"

"This is the last."

"I'll help."

Henry lit a cigarette and wandered around, bored. Edith ignored him and lifted copies of Graham Greene's *The Third Man* from the box. She put three with the new releases on the central table in the front room and said the others should go into the storage area in the basement. The shelving system down there had finally been completed. There was some ridiculous delay because the floor wasn't level, the wall wasn't plumb, and the overhead bulb was so dim that doing anything accurately was a challenge until the carpenter installed a standing light connected to a long extension cord. Edith was furious when she discovered he left it burning for an entire weekend, having forgotten about it the Friday before when he quit for the day. Also in the crate were copies of Shirley Jackson's story collection, *The Lottery*. Edith ordered them despite Patricia's concern that they wouldn't sell, given the macabre nature of Jackson's work. Edith said even though Harvard was highbrow in the extreme, and many would look on Jackson as a writer of cheap horror, a woman author taking on such a violent subject was important, and Edith wanted to support her. And, she stressed, Jackson's appearance the year before in *The New Yorker Magazine* meant she already had a mainstream audience. Edith thought Patricia was too timid and needed to be encouraged to recommend titles she was leery of. The first round of Orwell's *1984* had sold out and so had two subsequent orders. The only trouble was they had to be kept behind the counter so the censors, who always arrived unannounced, wouldn't see them.

There were new cards pinned to the shelves to indicate the category of titles found there, drawn by hand, and decorated with a charming border of flowers, vines, or even smiling moons for the small section on astrology. Edith asked who had designed them.

"La Gioconda," Patricia said, then explained this was her nickname for Jocelyn, the other college girl, who said little and always looked as though she had a lovely, yet terrible secret.

"She's talented."

"Art major."

"Didn't you say we should never hire art students?"

"I made an exception."

"What's the matter with art students?" Henry asked. He'd settled himself on a window seat and was flipping through a second-hand copy of *Robinson Crusoe*.

"Patricia thinks they're loose," Edith said.

"Well, all the more reason to engage them, I'd think."

"Oh, honestly, Henry."

Patricia said a letter came for her that morning and was in the office. Edith went in and noted how tidy everything was. Bills to be paid were in one stack; book orders were in another. When Edith had put herself on leave, Patricia drew up checks each week for her to sign and sent them to Henry's address. The bank statements were sent over, too. Edith reviewed the bookkeeping ledger and checkbook, both kept in the desk's drawer and found everything in excellent order.

The letter was under the telephone. The Florida postmark meant it was from Walter's sister, Kathleen. Kathleen's life had changed a lot recently, too. She had married and given up her job at Marshall Field and Company in Chicago to follow her husband to a small town in the Florida panhandle near a tung nut plantation he bought. Why tung nuts, Edith had no idea, but Dennis was a hustler, a "maker of deals," her mother called him, so obviously he smelled a financial opportunity there.

Dear Edie,

I'm sending this to your place of business because I misplaced your new address and couldn't very well ask Walter for it. These days, any mention of you sends him into a tizzy, and heaven knows, he's not in a good way as it is. Not that he's your problem anymore, I realize that. I understand completely your reasons for leaving him. Heck, if I ever catch Dennis with another woman . . . well, I leave the rest to your imagination. But that's neither here nor there. He sounds miserable—Walter, not Dennis, and I can't help but infer some dreadful regret over his decision to involve himself with what's-her-name. Again, not your problem, I just wanted you to know. If you hear from him, will you let me know how he seems? I guess I just feel so far away, down here in this wild, red-earth country. The locals are appalling, by the way. I can't understand a thing they're saying. Dennis, of course, is in hog heaven. As for me, I'm bored stiff and trying to persuade D to let me handle the accounting. That's what I'm trained for, right? The silly man seems to think I'm going to put on an apron and stay in the kitchen. He's got another thing coming. Hope you and what's-his-name, Lord Something or Other, are doing well. You, and an English peer. Who'd a thunk it?

Love,

Kathleen

Edith admired her lively spirit. They'd been friends for years, and Edith had worried that leaving Walter would change that. Obviously, it hadn't.

Henry leaned his head in.

"Anything interesting?" he asked.

"It's from Kathleen, you remember her." Walter and Henry had dinner with her when she came to Boston last winter. Edith hid out at home, faking a dreadful headache.

"I do. What has she to say for herself?"

"She's worried about Walter."

"Why?"

"She says he's unhappy."

"I should imagine."

Edith folded the letter and slipped it back into its envelope, which she shoved into her handbag.

Henry said Alistair was in front with the car, and they should be getting along. Edith left the office and told Patricia she had news.

"Henry and I are to be married, and we're going to England so I can meet his parents. We'll be gone about a month," Edith said.

"Oh, my, that's splendid!" Patricia hugged Edith, then rushed forward to shake Henry's hand. Henry turned pink, taken aback by her sudden effusion. Patricia was acting like any other old maid by displaying much more excitement over an engagement than she felt. A quizzical look came over Patricia then, and Edith suspected she was thinking about Edith's current marital state and the obstacle that presented. She asked to see Edith's ring, and when Edith extended her hand, Patricia gasped, then said an emerald was an unusual choice.

"Well, Henry's unusual, aren't you, dear?" Edith asked. Henry, now recovered, looked slightly peeved.

Edith explained she would let Patricia know how to reach her in England in case of an emergency, and that she'd have to hold all bills until Edith's return. She wanted to begin reviewing them again. She hoped the delay wouldn't cause a problem with any of the vendors. Patricia didn't think so, because they were prompt in making payments. Edith said once she returned from abroad, her presence would be on a regular basis. She thought Henry sighed quietly at this remark but couldn't be sure.

They all left together, and Patricia used her own key to lock the door.

On the ride home, Henry took Edith's hand and said, "You adore that place, don't you?"

"I do."

"Then I'm glad we stopped in."

Edith wished she hadn't said she'd go abroad with him. What felt right just a few hours before was now a burden. She'd much rather stay here and throw herself back into work than sightsee and be nice to a couple of people she had nothing in common with. Nothing besides their son, that is.

Edith rested her head on his shoulder and tried, without success, to put away the annoyances of the day. She let go of his hand and was grateful he didn't take it again.

Nothing ever timed out right in life, she thought.

Chapter Two

Walter's note saying they had to appear in court the next day came by messenger. How like him to tell her something important at the last minute! Edith signed for the note and gave the boy a fifty-cent tip. He looked at the coins in his hand and said she must have had some really great news.

She went to the library and stood in front of the window where the sky was knotted with the clouds of a slow-moving thunderstorm. Appropriate weather, she thought. Maybe Walter had arranged for that, too. Henry was in the living room discussing with Alistair the details of how to close the apartment in preparation for their departure, though that was still a few weeks off. He must have heard her heels on the wood floor next door because he appeared a moment later to ask who rang the bell and apologized for Alistair not answering it. She let him read the note.

"This is wonderful! Don't you agree?" he asked, after giving her an unwelcome embrace.

"Of course."

"You just wish he'd given you more time to prepare."

"For the hearing? What is there to prepare?"

"What you're going to say, of course."

"I don't follow."

"You have to give grounds."

"Oh, well, mental cruelty and incompatibility."

"Splendid."

Henry said he'd go with her, and Edith said it wasn't necessary. Henry insisted.

"Don't you trust me to handle myself properly?" she asked.

"Implicitly. It's Walter I don't trust."

"Well, being there won't change the outcome. You might as well do something else, something more fun. Go buy your boat."

"I thought you were against that."

"No, not really. I just find the idea, well, a little preposterous if you'll forgive me. If I were a member of the leisured class, it would be different. A boat isn't something I'd ever casually buy. I mean, it's not like a new hat, is it?"

Henry asked her to sit down for a moment because there was something he'd been meaning to say. She stared at him in irritation, Walter's note still in her hand. She tossed it into the fireplace, then realized the warm season meant it would stay there for many weeks until the next fire was lit, unless Alistair noticed it, which he no doubt would.

She dropped down onto the couch, kicked off her shoes, and put her feet on the coffee table next to an elaborately carved ivory box, a precious gift his uncle brought back after a diplomatic posting in India. Henry remained standing, and

Edith was reminded of her late father's stance in the moments before delivering a scalding rebuke.

"I've been sensing some . . . resistance from you ever since you accepted my proposal. Are you having second thoughts?" he asked.

"No."

"Good. Then help me to understand your, how shall I put it, hostility."

"I'm not hostile, I'm just trying to get my bearings. I'm a stranger in your world, Henry, you know that. I can imagine how glaring that will be when we visit your parents. They're going to wonder how on earth you became involved with me, and what you could have been thinking."

"There you go again, selling yourself short. What happened to all that confidence you had just a few days ago when you were telling me about your plans for the bookstore?"

"That's different. That's a matter of business. I feel comfortable thinking about that because I know it's what I'm born to do."

Edith nudged the box with her big toe. She became aware of a change in Henry's demeanor.

"What?" she asked.

"I envy you that, knowing where you belong."

"Oh, please, don't give me another 'poor little rich boy' speech."

His expression tightened.

"I'm sorry, that was unkind of me," she said.

"Won't you tell me what's got you upset? Is it Walter?"

"Oh, I don't know. I guess I dread seeing him again, even in a neutral setting."

"Then let me come with you!"

He helped himself to the other end of the couch, maintaining a respectful distance between them. The trouble was that he tried too hard. He wanted her to be all wrapped up in him, totally swept away, then in the same breath praised her cool objectivity, even in matters as mad as love. He was just making the best of her ambivalent nature. She couldn't help being that way. She never could.

"Did he send you a copy of the petition?" Henry asked.

"What petition?"

"For divorce! You have to draw up a petition to file with the court. It lays out all the terms you'll both have to agree to."

"No."

"Well, he jolly well ought to have. I have a mind to ring him up now and remind him it's best to play fair."

"Don't do that."

"Edith, my darling, you truly confound me."

She let him lean in and kiss her. She was glad for his comfort until she felt guilty for her harsh words only moments before.

At her request, she spent the night alone. She slept hard. She decided it was a sign she was ready to leave the past behind, once and for all. The bad weather had cleared, and the day was sunny and pleasantly cool for a New England July. Henry offered to have Alistair drive her to the courthouse, but she preferred to walk, saying it was only a little over half a mile and would take just a few minutes to bring her face to face with

Walter for the last time. Henry laughed at her turn of phrase, even as he looked her over critically. She wore her fanciest dress, pale pink with lace eyelets around the neck and cuffs. Below the red patent leather belt, the flared skirt swung saucily as she spun around for his benefit. Her hat was a smart red velvet beret. Henry said she looked like she was heading off to a cocktail party, not a divorce hearing. Why didn't she wear something more appropriate, like a dark suit?

"Because the clouds have lifted, in more ways than one," she said and pulled on her white gloves. She promised to telephone when it was all over. Mrs. Tremaine was waiting at the elevator when Edith got there; her terrier, Otto, wagged his tail at Edith and strained at the end of his leash until Mrs. Tremaine poked him with the toe of her heavy, sensible shoe. Edith commented on how threatening the weather had been yesterday, and how lovely it was today.

Mrs. Tremaine brought her handkerchief to her nose. They heard the elevator door open a couple of floors below and stay open an unusually long time. Edith speculated that one of the tenants must have held it for someone coming up the hall. Mrs. Tremaine agreed. She focused on Edith with mild disapproval.

"I'm getting divorced today," she said.

"Oh."

"And Lord Henry and I are to be married."

Edith slipped off the glove on her left hand to show Mrs. Tremaine her ring.

"Congratulations," Mrs. Tremaine said, as Otto sniffed the hem of Edith's dress.

The elevator didn't move. Edith looked at her watch and thought she might need to take the stairs down in another minute. Then the car approached, and the door opened. As Mrs. Tremaine stepped inside, hauling the reluctant dog with her, Edith said she forgot something, and that Mrs. Tremaine should go ahead without her. The look of relief on her face brought a wave of prickly irritation to the back of Edith's neck. Mrs. Tremaine didn't meet her eye. The door closed, and Edith's heels clicked loudly down the stairs as she held tightly to the dusty handrail that soiled the palm of her right glove.

Stupid woman, she thought, bursting out into the sun's overly cheerful glare.

The day was warmer than it had promised to be when she opened her bedroom window that morning. She removed her gloves, and then her hat. Her shoes pinched. There was a puddle on the sidewalk she managed to step in before realizing it was there. Now her feet were wet, but the sensation was cooling, if annoying.

In the park across the street, a couple stood in the shade of a giant elm. Their rough, sudden gestures caught Edith's eye. The woman waved her arms, and the man clutched his head for a moment, before reaching for her and holding her in place. The woman didn't move, then struggled to free herself. She wore a plain brown dress with a sweater thrown over her shoulders; the man's slacks were wrinkled, and the sleeves of his shirt were rolled up to reveal thick, muscular forearms. On a bench nearby a man went on tossing crumbs to the pigeons who strutted clumsily, bobbing their foolish heads; the young mother pushing the pram leaned down to check on her baby and paid no attention to their raised voices. Edith stopped and shaded her eyes for a clearer view. They embraced and kissed passionately. Just a lover's quarrel! She imagined she was watching the prelude to a permanent breakup. But why? Sometimes people pulled apart quietly, as if in a slow-moving dream. That's how it was for her and Walter.

So, why the letters? Without her there to reflect him, he just automatically put her where she'd so often been, on the receiving end of his thought process. He made it a point to let her know that he was candid at work about his altered living arrangement and often mentioned someone kind, who had him around for drinks and dinner. He was good at arousing sympathy. When she fled to New York and Aunt Margaret's wonderful apartment he told his classmates he was on his own then, too, no doubt so they'd take pity on him.

The courthouse came into view and Edith slowed her pace. It wouldn't do to arrive early. She wanted to sweep in at the last minute as if she had only just remembered the appointment.

As she climbed the white stone steps, she became uneasy, almost agitated, no longer defiant and self-assured. She wished Henry had come. Was it too late to call him? He'd rush over, but how would that look?

Inside the building, it was dark and cool, but Edith wasn't soothed. If anything, the cavernous space and the echo of her footsteps alarmed her further. She removed Walter's note from her purse. She saw she was to report to Courtroom C, and also that she was almost ten minutes late! How could she have lost track of time? She sped down the empty hallway, wondering where everyone else was, then realized that all hearings began promptly on the hour or half-hour. The room she wanted was at the end of the hall. As she pushed open one of the two closed doors, the overhead lights made her squint. In the chamber were the judge, a bailiff, and a court reporter. Walter and Babs sat at a table. Edith stopped, stunned. She wanted to leave before they saw her, but the judge already had.

"Your name?" he asked. He was old yet sat erect in his black robe. She approached the bench until she reached the barrier separating the front of the room from the rows of empty seats. She swung open the gate and went through it. Walter and Babs turned their heads and stared at her. She thought she detected a faint smile from Babs, but if so, it was gone in an instant.

"Your name?" the judge asked again, more firmly.

"Edith Sloan."

"The defendant. You're late. Please be seated."

The bailiff gestured to the other table before the bench. Edith sat.

The judge cleared his throat and said divorce proceedings were the most difficult matters over which he presided. Marriage was an honorable and sacred estate, undertaken by two people who made solemn vows to love, honor, and obey. Those vows had been broken, it was clear to him by whom, and he hoped the guilty party would in time repent and reflect on this sad behavior.

When he stopped speaking, Edith raised her hand.

"Yes?" the judge asked.

"You referred to me as the defendant."

"Which is what you are. Mr. Sloan brought the case against you."

"I'm sorry, what do you mean, against me?"

The judge removed his glasses and rubbed one side of his veined, blotchy nose. He cleaned them with the sleeve of his black robe and put them back on.

"Young woman. You seem to be of average intelligence, though I am the first person to concede that looks can be deceiving. Your husband is suing you for divorce. On the grounds of mental cruelty, incompatibility, and desertion."

"What do you mean, desertion? Walter, what's he mean?"

The judge banged his gavel.

"All remarks are made to the court and proceeded by 'Your Honor.' Is that clear?"

"Yes. Your Honor."

Walter looked at Edith with none of the malice she expected to see. He seemed exhausted. Though it was hard to tell for sure from where she sat, there appeared to be a stain on his tie, which was light blue for the warm season, as was his suit. Babs was dressed in black and wore no lipstick. Edith wanted to rub hers off. She had chosen a fiery red to match her outfit.

The judge continued. In his experience, a woman who ran away from her husband for no good reason other than being asked to do her duty to home and hearth wasn't much of a woman, and Mr. Sloan was better off without her. He didn't mind saying that he had a daughter, and when she married, if she did anything like what Edith had done so callously and remorselessly, he would disown her, even over the objections of his own beloved wife.

Edith raised her hand again. The judge nodded his permission for her to speak.

"Your Honor, I did not run away from my husband. My aunt—his aunt—was ill. I went to New York to be with her."

"Mrs. Sloan, your husband's aunt was not ill. That was a ruse. Mr. Sloan has stated clearly in his petition that this was an agreed-upon story told to cover your bad behavior."

"That's not true!"

"Was his aunt ill?"

"No."

"So, you abandoned him for no good reason."

"He told me to quit school, to stay home."

"That was his perfect right."

"It wasn't fair!"

"Mrs. Sloan, I will tolerate no further interruptions."

"Your Honor, my husband committed adultery with the woman now at his side," Edith blurted. Her face was burning.

"Have you proof?"

"He told me so. He told me everything."

"That is not proof. Your statement is therefore irrelevant."

The judge looked down at the paper on his bench. He took a long time with it. Edith hoped he was reconsidering the awful position she'd been put in. Babs was behind this, she was sure.

"There will be no settlement, no alimony payment. This should not prove a hardship to you, Mrs. Sloan. I understand you are the owner of a local bookstore?"

"Yes. Your Honor."

"In that case, and since your husband, soon-to-be ex-husband is just starting in his career, I order you to pay his legal fees, and yours, too, of course, though I see you did not file a response to his petition. Therefore, I will reduce your fees to a nominal amount."

"No one told me I had to file a response. I only got the notice to appear here yesterday!"

"Would time to prepare change your situation as it regards your husband?"

"No."

The judge again removed his glasses, cleaned them, and put them on.

"In the matter of Walter Sloan and Edith Sloan, married in the District of Columbia on the twenty-sixth day of February 1945, I declare the marriage dissolved."

Again, the gavel sounded.

The judge instructed Edith to stop by the clerk's office so that she could be notified of her expected payment. The bailiff asked everyone to rise. The judge stood and left the room by a door near the bench. The bailiff followed him. That left Edith, Walter, Babs, and the court reporter, who had stopped typing. She rolled up the paper spilling out of the machine and packed the whole thing away in a heavy leather case.

Edith walked up the aisle quickly, then felt Walter's hand on her arm.

"Wait," he said.

"For what?"

He escorted her out of the courtroom, still holding her arm, despite her attempts to shake him off.

"You could have gotten yourself in a lot of trouble back there. He could have held you in contempt of court, and ordered you to spend the night in jail," he said.

"What do you care?"

"I just do."

"Go to hell."

Walter dropped her arm. She looked at his tie. It *was* stained.

"Besides, Henry would have gotten me out," she said.

"I supposed he would."

Edith's head ached. She thought of Babs sitting there, smug as a crow in her black dress. That took some nerve, to show up at their divorce hearing. But then, Babs had nerve, a lot more than Walter did.

"Why did you send me those letters this summer? What was the point?" Edith asked as a woman passed, dabbing her eyes with a handkerchief.

"I don't know. I just felt like it, I guess. Did you read them?"

"No."

They went on standing, not looking at each other, held there out of habit, regret, or both, until she turned away and walked down the hall.

"I hear you're getting married," Walter said. Edith stopped and swung around.

"How?"

"From Henry, of course. He called me up with the news."

"I see."

"And I'm sure he told you Babs and I also plan to marry."

"Yes."

"Well, we should have a double wedding."

"That's not funny, Walter."

"No, I guess it isn't."

"Goodbye."

He said something she didn't hear. It couldn't possibly matter what it was. Edith presented herself to the clerk on her way out to ask what fee she must pay. The clerk looked up the case number in her file and handed Edith a slip of paper.

"Twenty-five dollars? Isn't that an awful lot?" Edith asked.

The clerk, who seemed to be about Edith's age but whose face showed the strain of greater years said some found it a bargain price to get out of a bad situation. Edith said she didn't have her checkbook with her. Might she send the payment in by mail? The clerk said it must be received within ten business days.

It wasn't until she was in the taxi heading back to Henry's that she realized she was free, but only to an extent. One ring off, one ring on. Like a revolving door, she thought. Convenient for everyone, except her.

At home, she went straight to the library and poured herself a large whiskey, though it wasn't yet noon. Then she took off her stupid hat and threw it on the couch along with her purse. She had a large swallow of her drink, sat on the couch, and kicked off her shoes. Henry entered the room. She leaned her head back and closed her eyes, willing herself elsewhere.

When she opened her eyes, Henry was watching her, and she thought of all the times she'd found him doing just that, like a cat watching a mouse it wanted to chase, capture, and rend.

"You went behind my back," she said.

"How so?"

"You talked to Walter."

"I had to. He had to know there was no chance you'd ever return to him."

"Don't you think that's my business?"

"Well, technically speaking, it's now our business."

"You still had no right."

"I was only trying to help."

"If you want to help, stop interfering."

Henry's eyes grew dark. He stared at the rug. She wished he'd sit down, or do anything but just stand there, looking like a scared little boy.

"I've offended you again. I must stop doing that," he said.

"The only thing you must do is stop thinking you know best about everything."

Alistair, hearing the strife in their tone, appeared discreetly in the doorway to ask if they required anything. Henry asked Edith if she cared for luncheon. She didn't. What she wanted was to sit and finish her drink if that were permitted.

"Yes, of course," Henry said, and Alistair discreetly withdrew.

They didn't speak, and Edith was grateful. Then, he asked how the proceeding had gone.

"Well, other than having to pay Walter's fees and mine, it was awful. He gave my deserting him as grounds."

"You're not serious."

"I'm completely serious."

"That bastard."

"Who? Walter, or the judge?"

"Walter, of course," Henry said.

"Well, why don't you call him up and give him a piece of your mind?"

"I deserved that."

Edith recalled Walter's face when he said he and Babs would be married, how unhappy he looked about it, about everything. And how had she looked when she said she and Henry were also planning to marry? Hardly overjoyed. And here was Henry, also looking miserable. What was wrong with everyone? They were all just trying to move forward in ways that made sense or had once made sense. If they no longer made sense, no one seemed to realize it.

The alcohol should have calmed her but only increased her agitation.

The room was bright and airy but to Edith, it felt stale and dark, a place where windows never opened, and the light never found its way into the corners.

She said she needed to make a telephone call, and asked Henry to excuse her for a moment, so she could be alone.

"Oh, of course, my dear. Perhaps you'll have some appetite when you're finished," Henry said.

"Go ahead and eat if you're hungry. I'll have a piece of toast or something later."

She asked Henry to close the door on his way out. She settled herself at Henry's desk, reflected on the fact that she had no telephone in her own room and wanted to remedy that, then lifted the receiver and dialed the operator.

"I want to place a person-to-person call to Mrs. Gloria Parry in Urbana, Illinois," Edith said, then realized the listing would be under Betty's name, so she instructed the operator to search for her, instead. Betty was her mother's lifelong friend. She wrote mystery novels, and after Edith's father died and the house was sold, her mother moved in with her. As she waited to be connected, Edith drifted west. The weather would be hot and muggy there, just as it was in Boston, but without the benefit of an occasional breeze smelling of the ocean. Her mother and Betty might be sitting on the back screened-in porch, enjoying a pitcher of lemonade, talking about the garden, or what to have for dinner later. Easy concerns, with easy answers.

"Hello?" Betty's voice came on the line, and the operator said whom Edith was calling for.

"Just a minute," Betty said. Another minute passed, and Edith thought about the expense involved, then didn't care because Henry would of course pay the phone bill without question.

The phone changed hands.

"Edie?" her mother asked, alarmed.

"It's all right, Mama, there's no emergency. I just called to say I'm coming home for a visit."

"Oh, that's wonderful!"

Edith laid out the facts about her divorce and engagement. Time to clear her head was what she needed now, time away from Boston. Her mother listened and seemed to hear what Edith didn't say. Edith promised to wire the date and time of her arrival and told her mother she would see her soon. They hung up.

Seconds after she put the receiver in the cradle there was a quiet knock on the door and Henry appeared. Edith said she was going home for a while; she didn't know for how long but would keep him posted.

"But why are you leaving?" he asked.

"Oh, Henry, if you don't know the answer to that, we have no hope."

"Will you come back?"

She said nothing and went into her room to be alone.

Chapter Three

In the dream, Edith argued that her situation was different. Yes, Henry was still married, but Mr. Rochester had concealed the fact of his wife's existence from Jane, whereas Edith knew all about Mary. And Edith was no poor governess, but a business owner, autonomous, now free of her first marriage. The person to whom she said this seemed to be a professor, someone seated behind a desk at the front of a large room. Whoever it was faded and was replaced by the cheerful wallpaper of Betty's tiny guestroom, which featured climbing rose vines that twisted, met others, ran free again, but kept ascending with lovely red and pink blossoms. Too busy a pattern, Edith thought as she focused, and recalled a short story by Virginia Woolf where an unhappy woman sits in a dining room also surrounded by overly detailed wallpaper, staring at it, trying to determine an underlying pattern and can't. She's teetering on the edge, and it's suggested that the wallpaper might be her undoing. Woolf expertly depicted Victorian sensibilities, especially as they pertained to trapped, miserable women. Who wouldn't have been miserable, then? Stuck at home while her husband was making his way out in the world, counting on her to be there when he returned.

Isn't that what Walter wanted of her? It didn't matter that he later changed his mind. The core belief of her inferiority never left him. Edith wondered how Babs felt about a woman's independence. She might see herself as the power behind the throne, and would subtly and cleverly direct Walter's career advancement, assuming she had any idea of how to go about it. When her imagination failed, she'd nag. Walter would hang his head and promise to do better because shame and regret were two things he responded to.

So did Henry, though it his case, it seemed as if anxiety drove those feelings in him, a deep sense of worthlessness, which shocked her at first. No heartthrob, he still was better-looking than most men, and far better off. He was witty and kind, though his kindness had suffered of late in the face of Edith's indecision. She seldom thought of his feelings for her, but now she considered the idea that he was deeply in love with her. It was hard to fathom because she'd never felt that way about anyone, and it struck her now as a dreadful fault. All this time she equated love and sex, assuming that splendid sex was enough of a bond—that and being in accord with the important things in life, like how people should be treated, what were good ambitions, and which ones spoke of greed or malice. Henry wanted his love returned; so had Walter. She'd tried her best with Walter, said the words, and later realized that for her romantic love was nothing more than being fond. What she felt for the poetry she once studied and sometimes still read, and for literature, in general, was passion. How could she ever feel that for a human being?

The smell of bacon frying reminded Edith that she hadn't eaten since the train stopped in Chicago the night before. She arrived late, spent a few minutes with her mother and Betty, promised to catch them up in the morning, then came up to this charming room and dug into Greene's *The Heart of The Matter*, which she had borrowed from The Turned Page on her way out of town (to be later sold at a discount, as was her policy), but soon tired of the wife's dreary life as a British colonial in West Africa, and her husband's desperate attempts to make her happy. Too much like her own life, she thought cynically as she put out the light.

She slipped on her bathrobe and came barefoot down the narrow stairs into the kitchen where her mother stood at the stove in a sleeveless cotton dress over which she wore a yellow apron. She turned and asked if Edith had slept well, then said she looked fancy. The robe was a gift from Henry, blue silk with lace on the collar and cuffs, perfect for warm weather and not much else. Edith helped herself to a chair at the table, and her mother poured her a cup of coffee from the percolator.

"Where's Betty?" Edith asked.

"Working."

Betty's bedroom doubled as her writing studio. Edith peeked in last night and saw the folding table neatly up against the wall, and her typewriter on the window seat. The room was on the other side of the house, which explained why the sound of typing didn't reach them.

Edith's mother put a plate of bacon and eggs on the table in front of Edith.

"Aren't you having any?" Edith asked, picking at the eggs with her fork.

"I ate earlier. We tend to meet the dawn around here."

"And what do you do while Betty spins her latest yarn?"

"Garden. Today I'll see what weeds need to go."

Edith's mother sat down across from her and lit herself a cigarette. Her eye fell on Edith's emerald ring. Edith extended her hand, so she could take a closer look.

"My, my, that's quite something," her mother said.

"It is that."

"You don't sound too happy about it."

Edith pushed her eggs around on her plate. Her mother sat, not exactly waiting, but not rushing, either. She occupied a neutral space Edith recognized from long ago and had come to appreciate as she grew older, a place to let things rest until they needed to shift.

"Mama, I'm in trouble," Edith said.

Edith's mother put out her cigarette and lit another one. She blew her smoke toward the ceiling.

"Not *that* kind of trouble," Edith said.

"It would be all right if it were."

"You're hoping for a grandchild."

"Not if you don't want to provide one."

Edith got herself a glass of water and sat down again.

"So, just what kind of trouble, then?" her mother asked.

"I've agreed to marry a man I don't love," Edith said.

"Does he know you don't love him?"

"Yes."

"And he still wants to marry you?"

"Yes."

"So, he's going into this with his eyes open."

"Again, yes."

"So, what's the problem?"

Edith told her about Henry calling Walter and telling him their plans, not saying anything to her, and letting her find out in that awful way. Her mother agreed it was harsh, but that it also spoke of desperation—fear—on Henry's part. Edith needed to consider that before making her final judgment.

"Final judgment as in deciding not to marry him?" Edith asked.

"Something like that."

"Oh, I'll marry him. I said I would. And his big mouth doesn't change anything. I suppose in a way, it's a small blessing. Now I know he's capable of doing stupid things and isn't perfect."

Her mother wanted to know if she'd believed that Henry was perfect before. Edith thought while she finished her eggs. She said no, she didn't think he was perfect, but confident, sure of himself, and in control. He was a man who knew what he wanted, except that now, after these months together, she saw that he only wanted her—or wanted her more than he wanted just about anything else.

"That's called love, dear," her mother said.

Edith nodded.

"And he's well off?"

"Very."

"Well, it's not hard for him to get what he wants, in a material sense. He knows money doesn't impress you. He's not used to people not caring about money. It makes him insecure."

"Yes, but it was still underhanded."

"It was."

"He apologized for it."

"As he should have."

Edith took a cigarette for herself.

"I've made a huge mess. I've been too slow to get back to work, and too fast to yes to Henry," she said.

"You needed time to get your bearings. You shouldn't feel bad about that. You'll pick up the store right where you left it if I know you. As for Henry, maybe you made up your mind to accept before he even brought it up. Sometimes we decide things without knowing we have."

Her mother was right. And Henry must have sensed that. He understood the inevitability of their situation, just as she did.

Edith saw him waking up in his four-poster bed, an absurd, creaky piece of furniture, and listening out of habit to any sound that might come to him from behind the closed door to her now empty room. He'd lie a little longer, thinking about the day ahead and how best to fill it. Then Alistair would knock and bring in a tray with coffee and the morning paper. There might be letters on the tray, but none from her; Henry would tell himself it was too soon for that, and that in any case, she would only write if her stay would be lengthy.

He had insisted on driving her to the station. They barely said a word in the car. He asked if she were going for her mother's sake, if something had happened, and Edith said he knew better. She just needed time to think. As Alistair swerved to avoid a crazed squirrel making for the verge, she realized she'd used the same words to Walter when she went to New York just a little over a year before. History was repeating itself. Henry took her decision with more dignity than Walter did, but she suspected it hurt him more. She regretted that.

Betty appeared wearing slacks and a loose-fitting smock. She had a pencil stuck behind one ear. She kissed Edith warmly on the cheek, just as she had last night, and asked how she was.

"Fine. Feeling a little like a brat for running away from my fiancé. But not so much I'm going to turn around and run right back to him."

"Good girl. Give yourself some time to think things through. You can stay here forever if you want."

"Oh, Betty. I would never impose that long."

They all chuckled.

Edith asked how the new book was coming along, and Betty got a distracted look for a moment.

"Fine, for the most part. I can't figure out how guilty my heroine should feel for killing off her husband. I think my readers want her to overflow with remorse, but I don't think she's like that," she said.

"What's she like, then?" Edith asked.

"A practical sort. Does what she has to do. In this case, getting rid of the philandering, booze-soaked loser she's chained to."

"Hear, hear."

Edith said her books sold well at The Turned Page, and that she'd love to have some autographed copies to display. Betty said she'd send her some.

After breakfast, Edith joined her mother outside, where she was pruning the clematis vine that rose in glorious chaos up the lattice on the back porch. She wore a wide-brimmed straw hat. She nodded to a pair of gardening gloves and told Edith she could yank the grass pushing up in her flower beds. Edith got started but soon found the sun uncomfortably warm, and said she'd move into the shade and trim the rose bushes. The white and red blossoms were deliciously fragrant. Sometimes she longed for a place in the country where it was quiet, and nature could come into her own. Years ago, her mother wanted to move out of town so they could have a larger yard for Edith to play in. Her father said she was being selfish; their home was perfect because it was near campus. He'd have to drive to work, and gas was expensive. He wasn't made of money. And she'd be stuck out there all day without a car, had she considered that? Edith stopped clipping. She should have known that before long, her father would find his way into her thoughts.

A little over an hour later, her mother suggested they take a break and have some lemonade. There was some already made in the icebox if Edith wanted to bring it out to the table on the porch. It was lovely to sit there in the shade, with the garden all around them, and when Edith mentioned this, her mother said, "Your father thought my interest in flowers was silly."

"He didn't know anything."

Her mother removed her hat, and sadness swept over her soft face.

"I miss him, you know. Despite everything. We had a lot of good years together," her mother said.

"Really?"

"Of course. He was quite charming in the beginning."

She said they met at the post office when she went in to mail a letter. The line was long, and he let her go ahead of him. She loved his courtly manner. Edith shifted uncomfortably in her chair. She'd heard this story before.

Her mother continued. Theirs was a quick courtship. Each was tired of being alone, though they never said as much. They didn't have to. They were delighted with each other, for a while, at least.

Children weren't for him; he was clear about that. He wanted to know all about her cycle, so that, well, things could be timed appropriately. Married women didn't have many options for preventing pregnancy then, other than to watch the calendar closely and hope.

"What about you? I assume you wanted me," Edith said.

"Of course! But I said otherwise, hoping he'd change his mind if something ever happened, which it did."

"Obviously."

He was angry, felt she betrayed him, and went back on her word. But she never promised, she just didn't disagree, and he took that to mean the same thing. He wanted her to see a doctor and get him to say she wasn't healthy enough to carry the pregnancy, that it would endanger her health.

"He wanted you to have an abortion."

"Yes."

"He always hated me, now I know why."

"He loved you when you were small."

Edith couldn't remember affection, only an absence of hostility. That must be what her mother meant. But her mother said her father adored her, pushed her in her pram, and sang her to sleep.

"Hard to believe," Edith said.

"I know, given how different he was later."

"What made him change?"

Her mother said an accumulation of disappointments. For instance, he wanted to be a physicist but found the subject too challenging.

Edith reflected that women were usually disappointed by what the world gave them or allowed them to have. Her father might not have gotten everything he wanted, but he'd done pretty well for himself. Any disappointment came from vanity, or an inflated sense of entitlement. She had no sympathy for him.

"And he often felt disrespected by his colleagues, even his students," her mother said.

Edith saw her mother's marriage as an endless process to shore up a fragile, childish ego. It must have been exhausting.

"I don't care that he didn't get what he thought he deserved. He was a monster," Edith said.

"He felt awful about it."

"About what? Hitting me? Sending me to bed without dinner for the smallest offense?"

"He knew he was going too far but couldn't back down. It was a matter of pride with him."

"At my expense."

"Yes. And mine."

A dog barked in the neighborhood, and someone told it to stop. A cooling breeze blew along the porch. The sky turned gray, and Edith sensed a thunderstorm was on the way.

"Why didn't you leave him?" she asked.

"Well, I decided to, there at the end. But when you were young, I didn't think it would be right for you to be raised without a father. Of course, I might have remarried, but there was no prospect of that at the time. Then you grew up, went to college, moved to Washington and by then I suppose I learned to work around his moods. It wasn't all bad. I always had Betty to talk to, even though he didn't like her."

"Why didn't he?"

"Because she made no bones about the fact that she thought he was a brute."

"Good for her!"

Thunder rumbled.

"Are you happy here?" Edith asked.

"Betty is wonderful, and the house is comfortable for me, but she's used to being on her own—she never married, as you know—and I think I crowd her a little."

"Surely she hasn't said so?"

"She never would."

Her mother said it would be easier if she'd made more friends. The people she knew had all been acquaintances of Edith's father, like Walter's family, for instance.

"I can't see you getting all chummy with them, at this point," Edith said.

"No."

"Join a garden club. You'd be welcomed with open arms."

"You know, that's not a bad idea."

Her mother fanned herself with her hat. She asked how the divorce proceeding had gone. Edith said it went fine, except for having her character assassinated in court.

"I think Walter chose that judge on purpose, because of his attitude, I mean. I bet someone from his firm pulled some strings and got the case assigned to him," she said.

Her mother shook her head. A few raindrops fell, smacking the wide leaves of the oak trees at the back of the yard. Edith loved thunderstorms and always had. Her father, she remembered suddenly, had been alarmed by them.

The wind lifted, and the trees swayed. Lightning flashed, and the thunder gradually became fainter. Even a small storm could drift for hours over that flat land. Edith recalled how the hills of Boston were a novelty when she first walked them. Even Washington wasn't as flat as Urbana.

Betty stuck her head out and asked if anyone were starting to think about lunch. Edith's mother said not quite yet, and Betty instantly withdrew, sensing the private nature of their conversation.

"I'm sorry to talk about myself so much," Edith's mother said.

"Don't be sorry. I'm glad."

Her mother asked if she thought Walter would marry the woman he was involved with.

"She came to court with him," Edith said.

"She didn't!"

"I think they deserve each other."

Her mother laughed, and Edith was glad her mood was sunnier.

Over lunch, Betty asked Edith about the press she wanted to establish. Edith said she had put that on the back burner for the moment, but wanted to get it up and running when she came back from abroad. She then had to explain about sailing to England in another two weeks, to which her mother said she didn't have much time to get ready for a long trip like that. Shouldn't she think about getting back home?

Edith didn't know.

By the end of the week, comfortably settled with her mother and Betty, Edith wrote to Henry to say she wasn't going to go to England with him. She would return to Boston and devote herself to The Turned Page. She would be fine on her own without Alistair, so he mustn't even think about not bringing him along if he wanted to go. Here, she paused. Being asked to consider the feelings of someone in his employ might not come easily to him. As to her feelings, Edith didn't speak of them. She didn't say she had changed her mind about marrying him. She didn't say she still wanted to.

Four days later, and exactly one week before they were due to sail, Henry telegraphed to say he was coming to Urbana to bring her home if she'd be brought. Those were the exact words on the paper the Western Union boy handed her. Edith tossed the telegram onto the kitchen table where her mother and Betty were playing a spirited hand of gin rummy.

Betty opened the note, smoothed it out, and read it.

"Sounds like he means business," she said.

"He's being a nuisance," Edith said.

Betty and Edith's mother exchanged a pointed glance.

When they looked at her, Edith held up her hands.

"I know, I know. I've no right to put him off. I need to . . . . what is that saying, fish, or cut bait?"

"Edie, for Heaven's sake, do you want to marry this man or not?" Betty asked. She still held her hand of cards.

"I want to marry him."

"And do you want to go to England with him? Before you answer, and forgive me for sticking my big nose in, but I think you'd be a fool to pass up a trip like that."

"I know."

"Good, it's all settled."

If only it were, Edith thought, but when Henry arrived the following evening, she embraced him lovingly.

"Darling," she said and guided him into the house where Betty and her mother stood waiting to greet him.

Introductions were made. Henry kissed Edith's mother's hand, then Betty's. Henry looked debonair in his pale blue linen suit and yellow tie. The way Betty flushed said she thought so, too.

"Edie didn't tell us you were so fancy, but then I should have figured, you being an English lord, and all," she said, and steered them into the living room. Henry sat with Edith on the loveseat. Their knees bumped.

Henry didn't appear nervous or ill at ease. He complimented the women on their lovely home and said how grateful he was for their taking such good care of Edith for him.

"How was your trip?" Betty asked.

"Surprisingly long. I've never strayed far from New England. It's quite a large country, you have. A lovely country, I might add."

Henry said he wished they could stay longer, but they must take the morning train back to Boston if they were to have any hope of then going on to New York the day after tomorrow.

"Alistair has packed for you already, I hope you don't mind," Henry said to Edith and accepted the glass of champagne Betty was handing him. She had bought it that afternoon to celebrate their engagement and Henry's arrival. It wasn't nearly as good as what Edith had become used to. She didn't mind. She looked at Betty and her mother, in their matching wing-back chairs, and was overwhelmed with affection.

"Have you chosen a date?" Edith's mother asked.

"We haven't," Henry said.

"Next June," Edith said.

Henry stared at her.

"June is a traditional month for brides. And besides, there's Mary," she said.

Edith hadn't told her mother and Betty about that particular complication and did so then.

"She's agreed," Henry said.

"What? I thought you said she was digging in against it, that you had to go ask her in person," Edith said.

"She changed her mind. My solicitor has already written to hers. The whole thing should be resolved in a matter of weeks."

"But do we still need to go? To England, I mean?"

"The passage is arranged. My parents are expecting us. As I said, I'm sure you'll have a lovely time."

Henry's tone suggested there was no room for debate.

Betty told him he was welcome to spend the night there at the house. With Edith, in her room. They were engaged, and even if they weren't, well, let the neighbors speculate about the sleeping arrangements. It was good to keep them on their toes.

Henry said he'd reserved a room at a hotel in town. He had no wish to impose.

Edith was glad. She wanted to be alone to think about what she was headed for. First, England. The idea was still delicious. Then, The Turned Page caused a quick stab of guilt until she reminded herself of all she'd been through and how capable Patricia was. Lastly, the new press, as yet unnamed. The Heartland, she thought, to honor this place she was now reacquainted with. Yes, The Heartland would do beautifully.

Chapter Four

The dress she was promised for her twelfth birthday was described in such glowing terms Edith couldn't wait for it to arrive. There were delays in the alterations that couldn't be helped, and as the days passed, Edith's enthusiasm waned. She told herself it was just a dress, nothing special, despite her mother's excitement. How her mother convinced her father to allow the expense Edith didn't know. Her mother had a canny side, to be sure. Then the dress arrived, almost two weeks after Edith's birthday, and she looked calmly at the box on the kitchen table. As she opened it, she was filled with delight. The blue satin was jewel-like, the ruffles delicate and lovely as an exotic sea creature. And it fit perfectly. Even her father's disdain couldn't dampen her joy. She hadn't expected the dress to be so nice, or to make her feel so happy and whole. For years after she compared how often she was disappointed to that one time when she was wonderfully surprised.

It was the same way sailing across the North Atlantic. An open vista was a given, but she was unprepared for the way the reach of it settled inside her and pulled her toward the horizon.

She was full of ideas for the future, and sober reflections on the past. If Henry's mind were wide, too, he didn't show it. His manner was cool, almost distant.

As they stood at the rail, loving the freshness of the wind on their faces, Edith asked what he was thinking about.

"All those lost at sea," he said. Behind them a couple of children raced back and forth, screaming with glee.

"In the war, or otherwise?"

"The war mostly, of course, but many are down there, aren't they?"

"Yes."

The smoke from Henry's cigarette was nothing more than faint wisps that had no chance against the wind. Edith admired his heightened color, and the way his sandy-colored hair, normally tidy and in place, ruffled. She stood on tiptoe and kissed him gently on the cheek. He looked down at her, surprised.

"Despite the somber subject, I find myself full of affection," she said.

"I'm glad."

But her warmth hadn't lightened his mood. He went on staring out over the water. She stared, too. It was like the prairie, she thought, the heartland she'd reconnected with, and she wondered if the pioneers crossing it felt the way the passengers on the Mayflower had, carried along by faith, hope, or the need to escape something worse than what they were likely to find ahead.

When she told Henry what she was thinking, he said, "In time, the prairie, too, will give up her dead."

"Oh, Henry, how gloomy!"

"The ocean brings us closer to eternity, don't you think?"

"It's bringing us closer to England, and me to you."

"That calls for champagne."

They enjoyed it in her stateroom because it was larger than his, a welcome act of generosity on his part. Not that his wasn't lavish to a degree that Edith found overwhelming, merely that hers had a bigger seating area with a sideboard, on which stood a magnificent bouquet of roses in the cheeriest shade of yellow she could imagine. She was truly happy and couldn't remember the last time she'd felt that way.

"You spoil me, Henry," she said, sipping her delicious Veuve Clicquot.

"It's entirely my pleasure, my dear."

Edith asked if they should invite Alistair to join them. He was traveling in Second Class, ate in a separate dining room, and strolled a lower deck.

"He doesn't join us at home. I think he'd find it odd to be asked now."

"It's funny, but I miss him. Don't you?"

"We'll see more of him soon."

One evening Henry turned in early, and Edith asked the ship's operator to connect her to Alistair's cabin. He sounded surprised to hear from her, but quickly accepted her invitation for a drink in the First Class lounge. They sat by the window, looking at the black sky suspended over the thicker darkness of the ocean. Edith had had several glasses of wine with dinner, and briefly debated the wisdom of consuming the martini the waiter put in front of her. Alistair had ordered a gin and tonic. She said she always heard the English were fond of gin.

"Not the upper classes," he said, touching his glass to hers.

"Ah. Well, live and learn," she said. The martini was excellent and very dry. Alistair thanked her again for inviting him. He'd been reading a book he didn't like much and was glad to put it down. She asked which book.

"*To The Lighthouse.*"

"You and Virginia Woolf? Who'd a thunk it?" She giggled and covered her mouth in a way Alistair's smile said he found charming.

"An Americanism, I assume," he said.

"You assume correctly. Now tell me, what don't you like about her? Woolf, I mean. And how did you decide to read her in the first place?"

Alistair said he'd gotten the book from the ship's library. Someone had left it on a table, he saw the illustration on the cover, and felt it would be apt for the sea voyage he was on. Didn't she agree? He asked her to forgive him if she weren't familiar with the book.

"Oh, I know it well. I adore Woolf." She had another taste of her drink. "I didn't know there was a library on board."

"Oh, yes. And a movie theater."

"I did know about that. I believe they're showing *All the King's Men*, which Henry has no interest in seeing. I might go alone if I can't persuade him to join me."

"His Lordship doesn't care much for film."

A party several tables away erupted in raucous laughter. Alistair looked at them with what Edith felt was longing. She wondered if he were lonely.

"It's interior, isn't it?" she asked.

"What is?"

"The book."

"Yes, yes it is."

"Is that what you don't like about it?"

"I just find it hard to read."

"Many people say that about her work."

Authors must be up against it, Edith said. They never knew if anyone would like what they wrote. Taste was so subjective. Her mother's roommate was a mystery novelist, wasn't that something? Alistair might like her better. Edith said he should look for titles by Marion Holt, her nom de plume. He asked if she could write that down, but neither of them had a pen or paper.

A man passing by their table gave Edith a long, appraising look. She happened to catch his reflection in the window, otherwise, she wouldn't have seen.

"Goodness, what's the matter with him?" she asked.

"Beautiful women are distracting."

"Who's beautiful?" Then she held up her hand to ask Alistair to remain silent. "He's just drunk, that's all."

"He still has eyes in his head."

"Drunk eyes." At this, she laughed for a few minutes without embarrassment. She was having fun. A lot of fun.

Alistair leaned back in his chair and regarded her across the table.

"What?" she asked.

"It's nice that you're enjoying yourself."

"Oh, I am, I am. I didn't think I would. I mean, sure, I thought it would be exhilarating and all to sail over the ocean, but I had no idea how comfortable the ship would be, or how lavish."

"Well, in First Class, yes."

"Your cabin isn't nice?"

"It's snug."

"Henry could have afforded to get you a stateroom."

"That wouldn't have been appropriate."

"Don't you ever get tired of being appropriate?"

Alistair finished his drink and stared into the empty glass for a moment. Then he looked at his watch.

He said he didn't mind the constraints on his life. The way he saw it, he was lucky. He'd been in the First World War, and a lot of his friends had been killed. It was hard to come back to such an empty country. He promised himself always to feel lucky to be alive, even when times were tough.

"What times do you mean?" Edith asked. She was sipping her martini more slowly for fear she might slur her words.

"I was married once. It ended badly. Our son died. He was still a baby," Alistair said.

"Oh, I'm so sorry!"

"It was a long time ago, yet one tends to remember, especially at a time like this, forced from one's normal routine."

"I didn't mean to make you sad."

"You didn't."

Edith wanted to know how Alistair came to work for Henry.

"I grew up on the estate. I returned from the war, became an under footman, then Lord Henry's valet. After he married Lady Mary, I went with them into their own home," he said.

"The one she lives in now."

"Yes."

The waiter asked if they'd like another drink. Edith said not for her, Alistair said he wouldn't mind if Edith didn't.

"Please, be my guest. It's all going on Henry's bill, anyway," she said.

Alistair looked momentarily tense. Edith hoped Henry wouldn't chide him for this later.

"They were happy? In the beginning?" she asked.

"Not as happy as you'd think. Lord Henry wanted to start a family right away, and she didn't. I shouldn't be telling you this."

"Alistair, I'm going to be his wife, so you can't betray any confidence here." Mary's abortion seemed doubly cruel considering what he just said.

Alistair's second drink arrived. Edith wished she'd ordered another one.

"They fought about it?" she asked.

"Yes. A lot."

"Henry doesn't seem like a fighter."

"She provoked him."

"That, I can see. Mary's a tough nut."

Edith realized that while she hadn't liked her at first, she came to admire how decisive she was. But perhaps her admiration was gratitude in disguise. Mary had made the bookstore possible by persuading Henry to buy it.

"If you'll permit me, and feel free to blame this on the gin, she's also a cruel woman. She was unfaithful. Several times," Alistair said.

"Oh, dear. Poor Henry."

"Yes."

"Is that why they came to America? To stop her extracurricular activities?"

Alistair paused, then said there was a man she got involved with who wanted her to sue Lord Henry for divorce. She didn't want to. The man became a nuisance, ringing up all the time, writing letters, and showing up unexpectedly. Alistair had to throw him out more than once.

"Not Henry? I'd have thought he'd have been delighted."

"His Lordship abhors violence or any sort of rough behavior."

"Which is why he did intelligence work in the war, rather than going overseas."

"Yes."

Edith was suddenly exhausted. The liquor and Alistair's revelations were draining. She asked to be excused and made her way out of the lounge toward the stairway. Alistair was at her side to escort her, and she told him he should have stayed and finished his drink. A few moments later they were at Edith's door, and she fumbled in her purse for her key. When she found it, Alistair asked if he might be of assistance, then unlocked the door for her, went inside, turned on the light, and stepped back out.

"Thank you," Edith said.

"Good night, Madame."

"Edith."

She thought his lips brushed her cheek, but later she couldn't be certain.

In the morning, Henry called to ask if she cared to join him for breakfast. She explained that she'd had a late night and wanted to sleep some more. When she woke up again, it was afternoon. It was their last day on board, and she regretted wasting so much of it in bed. It turned out not to matter because Henry's mood was grim. Conversation was impossible and Edith didn't think she could leave him to his own devices, so they sat in their deck chairs for much of the day drinking tea and watching the waves.

They spent two dreary days in London, though the weather was glorious. Edith was full of energy and wanted to walk for hours, but Henry wouldn't have it. He preferred to show her the sites from the window of a moving taxi, and even though the driver did as Henry asked, and drove slowly, causing a symphony of angry honks from other drivers, she wasn't able to take in much of anything. Trafalgar Square, Buckingham Palace, the Tower of London, and even London Bridge went by in a blur. On the second afternoon, she went alone to an exhibit of illuminated manuscripts at a nearby gallery, and the man there was snooty to her when he heard her American accent. When she complained of this to Henry, he said he would have gone with her, and Edith said she saw no point in asking him to, no point at all. She didn't even think of Alistair until later, then decided he wouldn't have felt it proper.

On the train ride to Shropshire Henry's mood worsened. Edith stopped trying to draw him out. It had been tiring trying to keep his spirits up, and she thought of her mother and all the times she prattled on idiotically to her father, hoping he'd respond with a cheerful word. She wasn't going to take up that ridiculous habit, so she told him when he had something to say, she'd be all ears, but until then, she was going to keep quiet. He apologized. He said he was letting his misgivings get the better of him. The train pulled into Whitchurch and as they left their compartment, he stopped and patted his face with a handkerchief. He was pale. Edith hoped he wasn't falling ill. He recovered himself, then took her arm as they made their way across the platform.

Alistair was already there, taking charge of the luggage. He, too, seemed to be under some strain, and Edith wondered again why they'd bothered to come all that way when they didn't have to. The weather was cooler than it had been in the city. There was an autumnal hint to things, seen in the faint yellowing of some trees and shrubs. The thin northern light fell at an angle and made her long for a cozy, happy fall, and winter.

"Oh, there's Morris," Henry said, indicating a middle-aged man in a chauffer's uniform heading their way. When he reached them, he removed his cap and nodded to Henry.

"Welcome home, milord. The car's ready for you. Alistair has it all in hand."

Edith expected to be introduced, and when Henry continued to say nothing, she extended her hand and gave her name. Morris looked confused but shook her hand anyway. He told Henry they were ready to leave unless they needed a moment to refresh themselves first. Henry asked Edith if she needed to powder her nose. Edith said she didn't. They followed him off the platform onto a gravel parking area where a late-model Rolls-Royce stood gleaming in the sun.

"Is that yours?" Edith asked.

"My father's."

"Good heavens."

"Try not to be so easily impressed, dear."

"Lest I look like the Yankee rube I am?"

"That's not what I meant."

Morris told Henry the trunks were being transported separately, that his father had sent another car for that very purpose.

"Thank you," Henry said.

Alistair would remain behind with the trunks and come along in the second car.

"Not another Rolls," Edith said.

"No, I don't think so."

Morris held the door open for Edith, and she slid into the ridiculous luxury of the car's interior. There was a glass barrier separating the front seat from the back, and Edith asked Henry what it was for. He said it allowed them to have a private conversation if they wished. She found him looking at her then as if to apologize for his recent behavior. She squeezed his hand to say it was all right.

The tidy scenery was calming, with stone fences and sheep-dotted fields in which stood a lone oak tree here and there, perfectly symmetrical, gracious, and deep green. The homes were small with stucco walls and sometimes a thatched roof. It was everything Edith imagined the English countryside to be. The large, swift-moving white clouds added to a sense of excitement. When she pointed them out to Henry, he pressed the button that lowered the glass barrier and asked Morris if they were expecting rain.

"Always likely in this part of the world, milord," Morris said. Edith detected a slightly sarcastic tone. Henry had grown up there. Wouldn't he know what the weather was usually like?

Henry raised the glass. A minute later, he produced a silver flask from the inside of his jacket, unscrewed the top, and offered it to Edith. She asked what it contained.

"Whiskey, of course," he said.

"It's not even noon."

"All the more reason."

"Well, if you're in, I'm in," she said and took a large enough swig to send some liquid dribbling down her chin. Henry gave her his handkerchief. Then he helped himself to the flask. Before he put it away, he used it to tap on the glass barrier, causing Morris to look in the rearview mirror. When Morris saw the flask in Henry's raised hand, he nodded, and Henry once again lowered the glass. Then he passed Morris the flask. Morris took a large swallow, wiped his mouth, and handed the flask back. Edith laughed.

"What?" Henry asked.

"We'll all smell of liquor when we arrive."

"Won't make a bit of difference."

"Why?"

"Because they won't bother with us at all until teatime, or later if I know them."

Edith asked how long it had been since he saw his parents. He said it had only been about a year. They all had dinner right before he and Mary left for Boston. Edith then asked how often letters were exchanged. Henry said his father didn't write, but his mother did, regularly, about every six weeks. Edith wondered why Henry never spoke of her letters, but she already understood that they both made him uncomfortable, and that it was easier for him not to bring them up.

They entered a wide lane lined with trees leading to a circular driveway in front of a large stone manor. There was a pool of water with a gaily spewing fountain in the middle of it. Henry said he used to play there as a boy, and if she cared to look sometime, she would find it full of coins he threw in to make his wishes come true.

"And what did you wish for?" she asked.

"Exactly what I got, which was to leave."

"And now you're back."

Henry had another swig from the flask.

The car stopped, and they got out without waiting for Morris to open the doors. A frail old man in a black suit and white shirt came slowly down the stairs to greet them. Henry whispered that this was Carstairs, the family butler. Edith looked him over for any sign of gladness at their arrival, and finding none, she walked past him into the front hall and looked around. The place was dark and cold. The walls were clad in wood with oil paintings perched up high, portraits of Henry's forebears, she assumed. There was a large round table in the center of the hall where a bouquet of spectacular lilies stood as a bright spot in the gloom. Overhead, a crystal chandelier gave back what small bits of sunlight managed to find it. Edith went to the table with the flowers and inhaled the almost sickeningly sweet scent. Henry hadn't joined her, so she entered the room immediately to the right, which was both wide and deep, clearly the library, with floor-to-ceiling shelves packed with books. A fire was going in the fireplace, and on a side table there were glasses and a decanter of what appeared to be sherry.

Well, someone had made an effort to welcome them, she thought and poured herself a glass. When she sipped it, she could tell at once that it was of an even higher quality than what Henry kept at home. She sat down and kicked off her shoes. She could get used to living like this.

"Mrs. Sloan?" a woman's voice asked. Edith hadn't heard anyone come in and realized whoever it was had been in the room when she entered it, seated in the wing-backed chair in front of the fireplace. Edith slipped on her shoes and crossed the room. A woman with Henry's tall forehead and soft chin extended a small, gnarled hand.

"Please forgive me for not rising," she said and nodded to the cane leaning against the chair.

"Lady Alice," Edith said. They shook hands. Alice's grip was weak. She was exquisitely dressed in a pale green suit with a heavy gold and pearl brooch near her right shoulder. As soon as they dropped hands, she gestured for Edith to take the second wing-backed chair.

"Where's that son of mine?" Alice asked. Her voice was steady but suggested her words didn't come easily. Henry hadn't said anything about her being ill.

"Still outside, I think. I just came in on my own. I hope you don't mind."

"Not at all. You can't wait for him to make up his mind about anything."

Edith wasn't sure how to take that remark. She apologized for having helped herself to sherry. She hoped she hadn't overstepped.

Alice removed a handkerchief from her sleeve and brought it briefly to her nose.

"May I pour you a glass?" Edith asked.

"That would be lovely, though my doctor forbids me alcohol. I'll tell him this was a special occasion, though I fully expect him to wag his finger at me in disapproval."

Edith set her glass on the table conveniently placed between the chairs and went back across the room to the silver tray. She poured out another glass and returned to Alice, who took it from her with a trembling hand.

"Have we come at a bad time?" Edith asked.

"Don't be silly. We were expecting you."

Henry appeared, walking quickly and in an agitated manner.

"There you are! I had no idea where you went," he said. He realized his mother was present and bent down to kiss her cheek. Alice's free hand reached out to pat his arm.

"Henry, dear, I'm so glad you've come," she said.

"Where's Father?" Henry asked.

"Oh, he's about somewhere. Walking around with Brennerman, I expect."

Henry told Edith that Brennerman was their estate manager.

"Why don't you go find him, and let him know you've arrived?" Alice asked. "I want some time alone with Mrs. Sloan. Unless you'd like to see your rooms first."

"I'd love to stay and chat," Edith said and sat down.

"Are you sure?" Henry asked.

"Of course."

Henry said he'd be on his way but wouldn't be long. He held Edith's gaze as if he wanted to convey something, but she had no idea what. He'd gone from keeping his thoughts to himself to trying to express them with gestures and expressions. Edith wished he would speak plainly.

When they were alone, Alice told Edith she hoped she'd be happy, joining the family.

"I hope you'll be happy with me," Edith said.

"If you'll forgive my bluntness, would it matter if we weren't?"

"Not to me, but to Henry, I think."

"I hoped you wouldn't say that."

Alice added their approval had always been important to him, a little too important. Not that he wasn't sure of himself, she didn't mean that.

She paused. Edith smiled politely and waited for her to continue. When she didn't, Edith sipped her sherry and studied the view through the window. The lawn was cut with a gravel path that led to a thick stand of trees. Henry walked on the path with his hands in his pockets and his head down as if keeping an eye on the ground. Near the trees to one side was a hedgerow being trimmed by a man on a wooden ladder. Edith asked Alice what type of shrub it was.

"I'm sorry?" Alice asked.

"The hedgerow, out there."

Alice looked through the window. "Privet, I believe," she said. She asked if Edith were interested in horticulture.

"No, not particularly, though my mother has quite a green thumb."

Alice asked her to tell her about her family. Edith said her father had recently died, and that her mother lived with a lifelong friend who wrote mystery novels. Otherwise, Edith was more or less alone in the world.

"And where does your mother reside?" Alice asked.

"Urbana, Illinois."

"Is that near Chicago?"

"Somewhat."

Edith relaxed. She'd been both excited and tense during their journey and now it was over. The whiskey and sherry no doubt helped ease her mood, as did the room itself, which was pleasant and tastefully decorated. The rug in front of the fireplace had rich shades of green and blue; the round card table gleamed in the sunlight; and the cushions on the couch were embroidered with a riot of flowers, roses, and lilies from what she could tell. If this were her house, she'd spend a lot of time here reading, thinking easy thoughts, dreaming about the future and what she could accomplish.

She realized that one day the house would be hers. Hers and Henry's. A marvelous place to come for long holidays in the summer.

She closed her eyes, imagining it. Alice cleared her throat, and Edith wondered if she'd dropped off for a moment. But no, her glass was still firmly in her hand. It wasn't even empty.

Carstairs entered the room and stood beside Alice's chair. He informed her that the luggage had arrived and been seen to. Did they care for tea? Alice said they were enjoying their sherry and would soon take a brief stroll. Had he seen anything of Lord Gerald and Lord Henry? Carstairs said Lord Gerald was still with Brennerman and assumed Lord Henry would find him before too long.

"That will be all," Alice told him. When he left, Alice finished her drink, picked up her cane, and stood. The library had a door that led directly outside. As they left the house, Edith was skeptical about how much walking Alice could do, but she held a slow, steady pace. The air was lovely and scented, which Edith found odd, given that it wasn't flowering season. It must be the country itself, unsullied by urban dirt and grime. Alice led them along the same path where Henry had walked earlier. They soon passed among tall oaks and maples whose leaves were dark green, causing the light to dapple and dance when the breeze lifted them. They didn't speak. Edith tended to fill in the gaps other people left when they withdrew into themselves, asking questions to keep them focused on her, or commenting on what they had most recently discussed. With Alice, she didn't feel the need. She trusted her without understanding quite why. Maybe because she needed nothing from her.

Beyond the trees was a pasture with grazing sheep where Henry, an older man, probably his father, and a middle-aged man, the manager no doubt, stood together talking just outside the fence. Their discussion was heated. Henry's father waved his arms in a gesture of frustration.

It took a moment for the men to register their presence. Henry's father removed his hat and shook Edith's hand. He didn't look much like Henry. His eyes were dark and fierce under a pair of absurdly bushy eyebrows. Brennerman had a weathered face and the kind of squint that suggested a lot of time spent outdoors, looking over long distances. He, too, removed his hat but didn't offer Edith his hand to shake.

"There you are, darling," Henry said to Edith. He asked Alice if she were all right, or if the walk from the house had been too much for her.

"I wouldn't be here, had it been," Alice said.

"Why did you drag Mrs. Sloan out here?" Henry's father asked his mother.

"Oh, go on, Gerald, I hardly dragged her," Alice said.

"I enjoyed it. It was a splendid walk. Lady Alice was very thoughtful to suggest it," Edith said. The way Henry's arm suddenly draped her shoulder thanked her for her calming tact.

He explained that something was preying on the sheep. Two ewes had been killed the previous week, most likely at night. Brennerman thought it was a wolf, though none had been sighted recently by any of the neighboring estates. Henry's father thought it was a poacher.

"They do it for sport, I tell you," Gerald said.

"At night? Where's the sport in that?" Edith asked.

Henry removed his arm from her shoulder.

"For revenge, then," Gerald said.

"Against whom?" Edith asked.

"Me, of course. Plenty of people want to cause me harm."

"Oh, Gerald, that's not true. Things have been much better since that bad business a couple of years ago," Alice said.

Henry said his father had raised the rent for his tenant farmers and that there had been a lot of grumbling about it. Someone set fire to one of the outbuildings, but it was put out before much damage had been done. A couple of chickens had gone missing from one of the coops, later found dead in the woods.

Edith shaded her eyes and took in the entire three-hundred-and-sixty-degree view. Mary told her that Gerald had sold part of his land to a real estate developer who put up modest homes before the war. The estate must be immense since none was visible from where they stood.

"How are they killed? Is there any evidence of gunshot?" Edith asked. Brennerman said no, not at all.

"Well, a person would surely have used a gun. Or an arrow. I mean, you can hardly think someone crept up on them in the dark and strangled them, or something. It's got to be a predator. Someone's dog got loose if no one's seen a wolf."

Brennerman's annoyed expression said he'd covered all that with Gerald before.

Gerald looked hard at Edith. He seemed to want to say something. In the middle distance, a sheep was bleating. Edith laughed. She said they always sounded like a parody of themselves. Didn't everyone find it was a silly sound?

"Will you come back to the house now? It's time for me to rest," Alice said to Edith. Edith wanted to stay and enjoy being outside some more but took Alice's arm and told Henry she'd see him in a little while.

As they went, Alice said Gerald was being foolish, which was nothing new. He just liked to complain and have everyone agree with him, even when he was clearly in the wrong. Alice hoped Edith didn't think ill of her for saying so. She and Gerald had been married for a long time and she was entitled to a little candor.

"And speaking of candor, how do you feel about my son? Be truthful, now," Alice said. Her pace had slowed, not because she was tired, Edith thought, but to give them time to talk.

"Well, I'm very fond of him. I'm not in love with him, and I ought to be. Or rather, I shouldn't have said I'd marry him, given that, but he seems all right with it. I suspect a brave face there. He says love could sneak up on me. He could well be right."

"Why *did* you agree to marry him?"

"I think he can help me. Not financially, I don't mean that. I have some money of my own. I mean with my bookstore. Did he tell you about my bookstore?"

"The one he bought for Mary."

"Well, for both of us, except she wasn't interested in it. When my father died, Henry sold it to me outright."

"I see."

"I'm also going to establish a press to publish poetry."

"That's quite something."

"I don't want you to think I'm using Henry in any way. I mean, other than the obvious way," Edith said. The crunch of the gravel underfoot was pleasant and reminded her of the solid lovely world all around.

They neared the house where a young woman in a simple black dress stood in the doorway they'd departed from. Alice said this was Martha, the head parlor maid who would serve as Edith's lady's maid during her stay. Edith didn't object. When in Rome, she thought. Alice dropped Edith's arm as they crossed the library and entered the foyer. Alice said she'd see Edith at teatime, if not before, and that Martha would show her to her room.

"Thank you," Edith said. Alice went up the stairs slowly, with obvious difficulty. Edith watched her go, then asked Martha where she might find her things.

"This way, Madame," Martha said.

"Please, call me Edith."

Martha led her up the stairway to the long hallway Alice had just gone down, only they went in the opposite direction to a room at the far end behind a heavy, carved door. There Edith found her trunk, two bouquets of white roses, and soft plum-colored drapes framing a window that looked over the lawn they had just crossed where Henry now walked alone, his hands clasped behind his back, deep in thought. Edith tapped on the window, but his demeanor remained unchanged. He was too far away to hear her.

Chapter Five

Edith hoped for a celebration to be held in honor of their engagement, but none took place. At dinner the first night she was the subject of several rambling toasts made by Gerald at the head of the table, still in his tweeds and rubber boots. He came in from viewing the dead sheep and went straight to his study to drink whiskey, a long-standing habit, Edith soon learned. Alice had told her beforehand they didn't dress for dinner anymore and appeared in a tasteful gray dress that made Edith's deep red one seem gaudy.

"To our very dear Mrs. Sloan," Gerald said, lifting a glass of champagne poured out by the footman, a pimply teenage boy whose uniform was too large. "We welcome you to our home and into our hearts."

Henry caught Edith's eye across the table. She looked forward to laughing with him about this later when they were alone. The bedrooms were clustered at either end of the hall; family on one and guests on the other, which meant, he explained as they went up for the night, that Edith must wait for him to join her. She was not to come to him. When she asked why he said it was obvious, she might be spotted. Edith didn't see why that was a problem. What about all those salacious house parties she always read about when people waited for the servants to turn in and then crept off to visit their lovers? Henry's sigh said he found her remark silly, or worse, and repeated it must be he who would visit her. She asked how *he* planned to avoid detection. He answered with another sigh. The disappointment she felt was sharp and made it hard to meet his eye over breakfast. By the third day, she was quietly fuming at his neglect, which extended beyond nighttime pleasures. For large parts of the day, he couldn't be found. Alistair, who managed to keep himself busy though his sole task seemed to be to take care of Henry, his room, and his wardrobe, said Henry and Gerald were going over every inch of the estate while the weather held. Edith was hurt they hadn't asked her to join them. She was a good walker and a good observer. She'd proved that the first day, hadn't she? Alistair said he would take her on a guided tour if she wanted. He knew that acreage like the back of his hand. They could bring lunch. He was sure Cook could put something together. Thus far, Edith had occupied her time with a book from the library, then tired of it and chose another. Oddly, reading didn't engage her now. Alistair's invitation was welcome.

She slipped into a pair of rubber boots selected from several near the back door, where she also found a mackintosh that was too big for her. Alistair said it might rain. Edith hoped it would. She wanted to walk hard, tire out, withdraw inside, and feel that things were normal again. She was off-balance and Henry must put her right. Being needy was embarrassing, she thought, even as she let Alistair hold the door for her. It was being in a new place that was to blame. She didn't belong here, even though that first day, sitting with Alice, she'd felt at home. Alice made herself scarce now and stayed in her room. Edith was sorry because she enjoyed her company. She asked Henry if he thought it would be all right to visit her. He answered with a shrug.

Alistair said they should walk first, then return to collect the lunch basket from the back door and pick somewhere near the house to sit and eat. Unless she wanted him to carry it along. Edith thought it was better to be unencumbered. They set out under a changeable sky. He spoke of walking these fields as a boy, then after he returned from the war (the First World War, in case Edith had forgotten) usually in troubled spirits, finding great calm in the wild pastures and quiet oaks. After his son died of diphtheria and his wife was inconsolable, he escaped here and walked for hours, even in the rain, hoping he might develop pneumonia and pass away quickly.

"That's awful," Edith said. "Poor Alistair."

Alistair stopped, removed his cap, smoothed his hair, and looked down at her with an earnest light in his eye.

"I suppose you know Alistair is my last name," he said.

"Well, I assumed as much. Henry explained that to me when I first came to stay. What is your first name?"

"Malcolm."

"Oh, I could never get used to that."

"No, I shouldn't think so."

They climbed a low hill that gave a perfect view of the house and woods. Alistair pointed northeast and said a creek ran there, though this time of year it was more of a trickle. In the winter it rushed and sometimes overflowed its banks. One year sandbags were needed to prevent the lower pastures from flooding, though efforts failed and several hundred sheep had to be moved off in a hurry. It wasn't easy, rounding them up. They were stupid creatures and panicked easily.

The wind stilled and Edith studied a darkening corner of the sky. She described tornados to Alistair, how the thought of them terrified her as a child, but then she was so often terrified. He asked her what of.

"My father, principally. He was an awful person," she said.

"In what way, if you don't feel it too personal a question."

"Not at all. I brought it up."

She said he had no patience for the ordinary mistakes children make. If she dropped something or broke a dish, he screamed at her. He always wanted quiet and perfection.

"Sounds like a hard man to please," Alistair said.

"Impossible to please."

Alistair lit a cigarette by cupping his hand around the match. He offered the pack to her. She helped herself. He struck another match, and the breeze blew it out. He tried again and brought the lit match to her cigarette. They leaned toward each other, and she could smell the soap he used that morning. She had the same kind in her bathroom.

She said when her father died, she felt no grief, but in the time since she remembered things about him that weren't completely terrible, like the way he put a pencil behind his ear when he was reading in case he wanted to make a note in the margin of the book, though she didn't like the idea of writing in books. Of course, she had, herself. In college, she often jotted down things in textbooks, usually a conclusion she'd drawn about a complex item. She found it helped secure it in her mind. Alistair asked what she had studied.

"Classics. Though I didn't learn to read Latin or Greek, more's the pity. Everything was translated into clunky nineteenth-century prose, all long rambling sentences that sometimes lost the thread."

Alistair nodded. He said he thought of going to school. Lord Henry had offered to pay for his tuition.

"That's generous of him. What would you like to study?" Edith asked.

"History, I think."

"Whose?"

"Ours. Or American. Probably American."

"I see."

In the distance, a truck bearing hay bales came slowly up the road. The sound of the driver shifting gears reached them, carried by the wind.

"Then you studied poetry," Alistair said.

"I did. In graduate school. I thought of going on with Classics, but the ancient world had lost its charm. I had a lot of literature courses under my belt, which turned out to be a good thing. It persuaded Harvard to let me in."

"Poetry is marvelous."

"It is, though not always easy to read."

"Do you know the work of Shelley?"

"Hail to thee, blithe spirit!"

Alistair laughed. "Good for you!"

"It's the only line of his I know."

They descended the hill, finished their cigarettes, and ground them out in a small tin box Alistair had brought along. He explained he didn't care to litter the field even though no sheep grazed there. They bore west toward some outbuildings Alistair said were used during shearing season. As a boy, he loved helping with that. Once, he was given a fleece as payment. His mother spun it into yarn.

"Sounds picturesque," Edith said.

"We didn't see it that way. It was just how we lived."

Edith asked him if he was in London with Henry during the war, and he said he had been. In what capacity? Butler or valet? He said both. The boundaries of service changed during that time. People filled in where they had to and did what was asked. In any case, seeing to a man or home was all of a piece, wasn't it?

"I think any woman would agree with that," Edith said.

"My wife certainly would have."

"What was she like?"

Alistair said she had started one way and ended up another, and not just from grief, from something else, some deep anger about everything, even being female. He added that she was a dedicated person and hated people who weren't equally dedicated. She grew up in the Midlands and wasn't used to Shropshire. England was a varied country geographically and culturally, he said, just as varied as the United States, though some people didn't understand that.

"No, of course not," Edith said.

"Mind how you go here." They came to an area where the ground was uneven, covered with hillocks and depressions. Edith wished for sturdier shoes. Alistair took her arm. It was slow going for several minutes, during which they didn't speak. The earth became smoother, and Alistair dropped her arm.

"I'm sorry about your child," she said.

"Thank you."

"I don't imagine one ever truly recovers from something like that."

"No, not really."

In the distance, Henry and Gerald were walking toward them. Their pace was brisk, almost animated. Edith was glad Henry was enjoying himself, but as he approached, she heard raised voices.

"Oh, dear," she said. "Can we escape?"

"I believe they've seen us, though we could later claim otherwise."

"I'm in if you are."

Alistair turned toward some trees and told her to go quickly. She went as fast as her stupid boots would allow. Soon, they were in cover. They looked back. Gerald and Henry were still walking, but not looking in their direction.

"We made it!" she said.

"I think so."

"You'd have made a marvelous spy."

"I know how to keep a secret."

He kissed her. She pulled back.

"Please, forgive me. That was completely inappropriate," he said.

"Yes, it was. Have I given any hint that I wanted to be kissed?"

"No."

She stood, trying to take in the fact that she didn't mind. Was the universe trying to tell her something? Or was she just tired of being neglected by Henry?

"I think I need to sit down for a minute," she said and lowered herself onto the shady ground. He joined her. He apologized again. He said he didn't know what had come over him.

"Yes, you do. Don't think I don't understand. That's how it is when you're attracted to someone," she said.

He said nothing. She asked again if she'd encouraged him in any way.

"No, and I had no way of knowing how you would respond. I simply took a chance, that's all."

She said she wished it were so simple. Women had to be careful. They couldn't appear to be too easy about this sort of thing. Oh, she didn't care much what other people thought, but she did have to consider Henry's feelings and those of his parents.

"Are you going to tell him what happened?" Alistair asked.

"Do you think I should?"

"I don't know. But if you do, he'll ask for my resignation."

"After all these years? That would be extraordinary!"

He said women weren't the only ones with firm boundaries placed upon them. Those in service, even in these modern times, had to follow unspoken rules.

"One of which is not making a pass at the boss's fiancée," she said.

"Precisely."

"Well, I guess it will have to be our secret, then."

He was quiet. She put her hand on his arm.

"I won't blackmail you for it if that's what you're worried about," she said. He lifted her hand and kissed it.

"I know you won't," he said.

"Then, why so glum?"

"Because I'm so fond of you and now see it's hopeless." He paused. "Forgive my asking, but is it the difference in our ages that bothers you?"

Edith reclaimed her hand.

"Alistair, I'm engaged," she said.

"Yes, but you're not in love with him."

"Why do you say that?"

"I have eyes."

Edith felt as if she were sinking into the earth, pulled down by a force far below the surface, a merciless strength against which she was powerless.

"That's none of your business," she said and struggled to her feet. For a moment, she was dizzy as the trees swam around her. She inhaled deeply and waited for the world to stand still. Alistair also stood and said he'd escort her back to the house, where they could still eat their picnic lunch if she wanted.

"I do, indeed. I can't listen to these declarations on an empty stomach. Let me eat, first, then you can try again." He said nothing. "I'm kidding. That was in poor taste, I know."

"That's quite all right. I deserved it."

They walked slowly. Alistair had rattled her. The air was soft and lovely, and she willed it to soothe her. She wondered if Henry were still walking around with his father, and what they were discussing with such energy. Maybe Gerald was telling him Edith was the wrong woman for him. Henry wouldn't care, he had enough money of his own, but she saw affection there, between father and son. Henry wouldn't say anything to hurt Gerald, even as he stood his ground.

"Do Henry's parents approve of me?" she asked.

"I have no idea."

"I thought you had eyes."

"I think it's safe to say you've impressed them favorably, so far," he said.

"Because I haven't broken any family heirlooms?"

"Because you're articulate, dress well, and have nice manners. All of these are important to the English."

"The Americans, too."

Edith said, even so, she supposed they probably preferred Mary to her. Alistair said they hadn't liked her much, to be honest.

"That must have been hard on Henry," she said.

"He was younger then, and defiant. And very much in love."

"I see."

"That doesn't upset you, I hope."

"That he loved her? Of course not. Why should it?"

Alistair didn't answer. They changed direction once again just as the wind rose. Edith smelled rain in the air. The house was just coming into view, its stone now dark under the gathering sky. It didn't look like a happy place. It should be surrounded by flowers, but the garden was at some remove at the end of a paved walk. Gardens should never have a formal feel and Edith said if she ever had a place in the country, there would be flower beds by every door. Alistair said he assumed she was devoted to living in Boston. She said not at all, only for the time being. She'd lived in both a small town and a big city and was ready for a change. The country seemed just the thing. Assuming Henry would like it, too. Seeing where he had grown up, she had to think he'd be mad for the idea.

They were on a different route from the one they took out, and when Edith said so Alistair said he was bringing them past his boyhood home. No one lived there now. The cottage had been abandoned for years. He thought Lord Gerald didn't have the heart to tear it down. He was fond of Alistair's father.

"What was he?" she asked.

"A tenant farmer."

"An odd person for a lord to be friends with."

"I wouldn't say they were friends, but they understood each other. My father was one of the few who didn't condemn Lord Gerald for selling off so much of his land. He saw the profit in it. And it made the barley we grew more valuable, as a result."

"A case of less supply and more demand."

"Exactly."

The walk had crumbled, and the bushes were overgrown. Inside, the air had an unmistakable scent of decay and neglect. The curtains still hung on rods over the windows. Drawing near, Edith detected many places where the fabric had worn thin or away completely. The glass was filthy. Delicate webs hung in the corners of the ceiling and wavered as they passed. Yellowed newspapers that must have been there for decades lay open here and there on the wooden floor, left over from belongings that were packed and removed.

"It must have been nice, once," she said.

"It was, at least as far as I can remember. I haven't lived here for almost forty years. Another family had the place after my parents went, but they didn't stay long."

He stood in the empty kitchen, staring into the sink. He turned and came her way, with an odd, almost lonely look to him.

She said it was hard to revisit childhood places and told him of returning home just before her father died. Of course, she'd lived there much more recently than Alistair had lived here, in the cottage, but it left her with a sense both of time passing and standing still as if she were caught in a picture frame her older self was viewing.

"I just wanted you to see where I came from," he said.

"Then I'm glad we came. But we should be getting back."

She walked out the door and made for the main house. The sky was knotted with clouds. Alistair followed. They didn't talk. At a relaxed pace, it took them over twenty minutes to reach the back door and the picnic basket waiting for them just inside. Alistair asked if she wanted to try to eat outside, or if the weather seemed too threatening.

"I thought we passed a conservatory. Is it locked?" she asked.

"I don't think so."

It was just around the other side of the house and full of blooming orchids. Edith said she didn't know Henry's parents enjoyed horticulture, and Alistair said Lord Henry's grandfather had been passionate about it. Lord Gerald was mildly interested and Lady Alice, too, but he suspected the gardener was the one who kept an eye on things. There was a stone table and a bench that hadn't been used for some time. Alistair used his handkerchief to dust off the bench so Edith could sit. The air was warm to support the orchids. She asked how it was managed. He pointed to a steam radiator at the end of the room that he said was fed from the main house. The water line ran underground. One winter, it had frozen, and some plants died from the cold.

She removed the mackintosh. Then she removed her boots. Alistair made it a point not to look at her feet. He took off his jacket and seemed more relaxed, a mood that was soon aided by a bottle of beer he took from the basket. There was a second one for her. She didn't like beer much and would have preferred wine, but when he offered to go into the house and find some, she told him to sit still. Beer was fine. Cook had packed a bottle opener and a pair of glasses. Alistair had the caps off quickly. He asked if she wanted hers poured into a glass, and she said she'd drink it from the bottle unless he were planning to use a glass. He said he wasn't.

There were two ham sandwiches with mayonnaise and mustard and a green salad with dressing in a small jar. The utensils were the same sterling silver that sat on the elegant candlelit table at dinner. Edith remarked that it was a fancy picnic lunch.

"Oh, Edith, you do amuse me," Alistair said, then saw she was staring at him.

"You called me Edith."

"I did. It's much easier, now that I've kissed you."

"Oh, go on."

She bit into her sandwich. It was delicious. Drops of rain hit the glass roof overhead.

"I asked Martha to call me that and she blushed and stammered," she said.

"I can imagine."

Alistair handed her one of the two heavy cloth napkins that came with the food. She spread it on her lap. Across from her, several striking white orchids bloomed in terra cotta pots lined up in a wooden planter box. The petals of the orchids were speckled and pink. She said orchids were nice flowers because they bloomed for such a long time. Alistair agreed and asked if she'd ever been given an orchid corsage to wear by some eager young man.

"Oh, Walter didn't go in for that sort of thing. And besides, the war kept our belts pretty tight," she said. She drank her beer. She enjoyed it more than she thought she would at first.

She asked if he knew of an American painter, Georgia O'Keeffe.

"I'm afraid I don't."

"She paints flowers."

"I see."

"No, remarkable paintings of flowers. Gives an intimate viewpoint. Close up."

He nodded. He finished his sandwich. He asked if she cared for salad. She didn't, but she'd dress it for him if he wanted some. He said he didn't.

The rain picked up and was loud on the glass overhead. For a few moments, the noise made it impossible to talk, so they sat and enjoyed their beer. Edith returned again and again to Alistair's kiss and confession and was deeply flattered. She didn't want to be needy for the male gaze, and suspected years of being married had stimulated that within her. Her age was also to blame, she thought. She would be thirty in two years. At that point, she would be secure in herself, not hoping for some man to give her the eye. And the press would be alive and well. The Heartland had a great future.

"A penny for your thoughts," Alistair said.

"I'm thinking about my press."

"It's an exciting idea, to be sure."

"Oh, it's more than an idea. As soon as I get home, I'm meeting with a printer to discuss his costs."

Alistair nodded. His beer bottle was empty. Edith asked him the time. When he told her she said, "I had no idea we've been gone so long. They'll send a search party for us."

"I don't think anyone will worry about us much."

But Henry was at that moment opening the conservatory door and walking over to where they sat.

"There you are!" he said.

"Hello, darling. We just had a marvelous long walk. How was your outing with your father?"

Henry said they made it to the far end of the estate and Gerald didn't want to walk back, so they asked a farmer to give them a lift.

"You must have gone miles," she said. She slid over to give Henry room to sit next to her.

Alistair stood, collected the picnic items, and packed them away. He said he'd be getting back to the house now if His Lordship didn't mind.

"We won't be long," she said.

Alone with Henry, Edith felt suddenly awkward. He took her hand and apologized for neglecting her. It's just that he was so caught up in being home again and couldn't refuse his father's daily invitation to tour the estate. They'd completed it now and he would devote himself to her for the remainder of their stay. She said she understood, and that she'd toured a bit of the estate today, herself. Alistair was a wonderful guide.

The rain lessened, then stopped. Sunlight broke out, making the flowers around them even richer and more lush.

"This is a beautiful place," she said.

"I played here often as a boy. Until it got too warm for me."

"Alistair explained about the plumbing. I bet it costs a fortune to heat."

"Everything costs a fortune here. I think Mother and Father are getting weary of bearing the expense."

"It's not a hardship for them though, surely?"

"It's not that. The place feels too big for just the two of them. Mother is so often in her room. She seems to prefer her own company most of the time."

Edith said she understood. He asked if she were ready to return to the house. His father was resting, and everything was calm and quiet.

"I could stay with you," he said. She took his meaning and kissed him warmly on the mouth. She pulled away to get back into her boots. They left the conservatory hand-in-hand, observed by no one except Alistair, standing at the back door, watching their progress.

Chapter Six

Two days before they were due to leave for London, Henry told Edith that his father had asked him to return home permanently. He'd been right about Gerald's increasing frailty, something Gerald admitted as he looked to the future now with a candid eye. He offered anything Henry wanted for him and Edith to be comfortable living there. Henry didn't need to think long before turning him down.

"I'm an American now," he said.

"Not with that accent."

She said she wished that he had mentioned Gerald's offer at the time. She should have been consulted. Henry asked if she'd seriously consider moving to England and leaving the States behind for good.

"Oh, probably not. But it might have been fun to think about. It wouldn't have been for good, anyway. For the indefinite future, maybe. There's no real permanence in anything."

"Spoken like a philosopher."

"Or a skeptic."

"The skeptics left their mark on philosophical canons."

"So did the hedonists."

"Are you suggesting something?"

"Oh, go on. Leave me alone to finish my letter."

She was writing to Patricia at the bookstore, asking her to telephone the manager of the printing press she'd connected with earlier in the summer. She hoped he could meet with her sometime during the second half of September, and said she'd be back in Boston on the ninth of that month. The air mail stationery was thin and crumpled easily, so she took care folding it and slipping it inside the envelope.

She took the letter downstairs and didn't know where to leave it to be posted. No one was around to ask. She supposed she could find Henry, but she didn't know where he'd gone.

She wandered into the library where Alistair was reading a book. He stood when he saw her.

"Oh, hello," he said.

"Hello. I have a letter to mail. I don't know where to put it."

"There's a tray on the table just by the front door, I believe."

"Thanks."

She wondered what he was reading and was too far away to read the title.

"*Pride and Prejudice*," he said when he saw what she was looking at.

"You and Jane Austen? There's an unlikely romance."

"I've read her before. Years ago."

"You're a dark horse, Alistair."

"None darker."

He smiled, something he rarely did. She wondered if he were looking forward to going home. Since their outing the week before, she'd barely seen him. He dined with the other staff in the servants' hall. She thought of asking after him a couple of times and didn't think she should.

"About the other day," he said.

"Yes?"

"I'm glad there are no hard feelings."

"Of course not. It's just one of those things. All forgotten now."

"I'm not likely to forget it."

She sat down on the other end of the couch. He sat, too.

"Perhaps not, but surely it will all pass," she said.

He closed the book and set it on the table by the couch. He said he didn't know what it meant for something to pass, because really, didn't we carry within us the recalculated sum of all of our sorrow, blended with all of our joy? He didn't mean to sound mysterious, he just meant that things remained, even if they didn't rise every day and say, look at me, here I am again. He learned that after his child died. He never recovered; grief simply came to occupy a small place inside him that most of the time stayed quiet. Until it screamed. Caring for someone had the same effect. In Edith's case, he wouldn't dwell on anything, he just accepted that from time to time his feelings would resurge.

"This makes me so unhappy," Edith said.

"It shouldn't. It's just the way it is."

"But, Alistair, I just don't understand. You don't know me, not really. I'm not a nice person. And I'm mixed up. I didn't see that before, but I do now. I just can't seem to settle on how I want to live. Part of me wants to be a successful businesswoman. Part of me wants to stay home and make Henry's dinner. Another part wants to do neither, and just loaf around, enjoying his money and putting my feet up."

Alistair lit himself a cigarette. He didn't offer one to Edith.

"Why not all three? Whenever you feel like it?" he asked.

She said women weren't supposed to occupy their roles fluidly. They had to choose one and stick with it, didn't they? Trying to do more than one thing or be more than one thing was a terrible mistake. She'd learned that being married to Walter. She had to follow his lead in everything, and when she went her own way—which in her case was wanting to continue with graduate school—things fell apart.

Alistair smoked his cigarette and considered her remarks.

"I say do as you damn well please. Why not? Who should tell you otherwise?" he asked.

"And you? Do you do as you please?"

"Within reason."

She asked what he saw for himself in the future. Would he go on being Henry's butler until he retired, or would he follow up and go to school, as he talked about? Neither? Both?

Alistair put out his cigarette in a delicate china ashtray. He pressed so hard, Edith thought he might break it. After a moment, when he still hadn't responded, she got up and went to find where to leave her letter. Just as Alistair said, there was a tray on the table by the door. It held two pieces of recently delivered mail, which meant the postman had already been by that day. One was addressed to her, care of Henry's parents. It was from Mary. She picked it up and put Patricia's letter in the pocket of her sweater, which a persistent chill in the house made necessary. She perched on the staircase, grateful for the thick carpet on the tread, and slid her finger clumsily under the seal.

Dearest Edith,

I hope you don't mind my calling you that. I realize we didn't know each other all that long, but during that time I believe we came to an understanding of sorts. We think the same way about certain things, business, for one, although I admit my interest in The Turned Page waned quickly after it became ours. Life with Henry had just gotten too ghastly to bear, which I suppose you have heard all about by now. When I learned of your travel plans, I took the liberty of writing to you where I assume you now are, unless this has been sent on to you somewhere else.

I will come to the point. You must not marry Henry. These are not the words of an ex-wife (or soon-to-be-ex-wife) but those of one who lived with him for the better part of ten years. While he is not cruel, he is weak; though not lazy, he enjoys idleness a little too much. You may have learned from Alistair the reason we came to Boston in the first place—I was involved with someone else here and that situation became intolerable. Consider, if you will, what might have made the attention of another man desirable. Happily married people don't cheat on their spouses. Henry seems to drift in a dream world where nothing holds much reality for him. I sought to stir him from it many times, but he has no interest in anything other than drinking, reading a book now and then, visiting his tailor, and dining out. The life you will have with him will be bound by this seemingly gracious lassitude. But it's ultimately a trap because whatever energy you have, he pulls you down. Any resistance you offer is met with a declaration of love.

Naturally, he is unaware of himself. In my experience, most men are. Perhaps you can enlighten him, in time. If you decide to try, I very much hope you succeed. I also wish you all the best. Please understand I felt it my duty to convey my concerns.

Mary

Edith folded the letter and put it in her pocket, just as Henry trotted down the stairs.

"Whatever are you doing here?" he asked and ruffled her hair with his hand.

"Just thinking."

"About?"

"Everything."

"Oh, dear, that does sound serious. Would you like to take a drive? That is if you haven't seen as much of the countryside as you can bear by now?"

"I'm fine. I should think about packing, though I suspect Martha's been turning her capable hand to that."

Henry sat next to her on the stairs. He put his arm around her, and she leaned in close. She asked how his father was doing today because she hadn't seen him at breakfast. Henry said he was in his study reviewing some estate paperwork. He might be irked at Henry's refusal to move home again and thus making himself scarce, but he thought it more likely that he just fell behind with processing rent receipts during their stay.

"I don't know what I would have done if you'd agreed. Though I must say this place has grown on me a lot. There's no one I'd mind leaving behind. Except for my mother, of course. And Betty. Oh, and Aunt Margaret," Edith said.

She went on to add that she supposed, if in his true heart, he did want to return to the estate, she could just as easily establish a press here as in Boston. The bookstore would be missed, though she could remain its owner, regardless.

"Aren't you a funny duck, pondering something that won't even happen," he said.

"But it might have."

"If I'd had the slightest inclination to agree, I would have come to you immediately."

Really?

The memory of him calling Walter to announce their engagement without telling her still gnawed.

She asked what he'd do when they got home.

"Do?" he asked.

"With your time. I mean, I expect to be busy with the press. You'll have to do something with yourself. Unless you're serious about buying that boat. Even if you do, you can't go sailing in the winter, I wouldn't think."

"No."

Henry removed his arm and took out his cigarettes. He lit one for himself. Edith said she didn't want one just then.

"It's odd that you should mention it, but I've been thinking I could help you," he said.

"How?"

"However you needed. Answer letters. Talk to people. I hope you won't mind my saying this, but there might be some who don't like working with a woman or are more comfortable meeting with a man. It's ridiculous, I know. And I'd only do what you wanted me to do. Nothing else. And if you don't want me to do anything, I won't. I'll find a venture of my own. I always rather fancied going into the antiques business."

"Seriously?"

"Quite."

He said he knew a lot about decorative periods. He could thank his mother for that. For instance, that charming table just there in the hall was Georgian, but the sideboard was Regency. Some people liked to keep all their pieces from the same time frame, but he never saw the point. If you liked something, you should have it.

"I can see you wandering around a store in one of your lovely suits, offering sherry to someone considering a large purchase," Edith said.

"You make it sound frivolous."

"Not at all. Boston is a wonderful place for such an enterprise, but I'm afraid you'd face stiff competition."

"I don't mind a little competition now and then. By the way, Mother wonders if you'd like to have tea with her in her room."

"That sounds splendid."

She asked if she should change her dress first and Henry said not to bother. She looked smashing, as always.

Alice sat in a chair before the fireplace and asked Edith to take the other one. She apologized for having been absent so often and explained that she'd fallen into a bad habit of liking to be alone. Perhaps she simply made a virtue out of necessity, what with Gerald being so busy all the time. She hoped Edith hadn't thought her rude. She assumed Henry had kept her well occupied. She heard Alistair had shown her around a bit the other day, bless him.

Edith could see why Alice preferred her room to all the others in the house. It was full of south-facing light. There was a bouquet on each nightstand, another on a table at the end of the couch, and a fourth on the mantle over the fireplace. The blossoms varied—some were roses, others were lilies, and all were shades of white. There were books lining the built-in shelves on two walls. Edith wished she could take a moment and browse the titles.

Alice poured the tea, arranged on the table between them. She asked if Edith had enjoyed her stay and was looking forward to going home.

"It's a case of mixed feelings, I'm afraid. There's so much to do when I return. It's been so pleasant not doing much, though you'd think I'd have had enough of that by now," she said.

"How do you mean?"

She explained what happened after she left Walter.

"I just couldn't seem to concentrate on anything, some days I couldn't even get out of bed, as if I were truly ill," she said.

"Grief can do that."

Edith sighed. How was it possible that she didn't want to leave? There was no life for her here, not really, but all the same, she'd come to feel at home. There was always someone to take care of something for her—a button sewn on, her night things laid out, her shoes polished every evening and set quietly inside the door. Henry was different here, too. He'd gotten over his initial unease at being around his parents and seemed to be thriving. They'd all settled into each other, though it was a quiet, almost closeted life. She supposed there were other people in the neighborhood they might meet and come to know better. It was odd that no one had visited, and she asked Henry about it. He said his parents kept to themselves and always had. Edith assumed they were lonely, but Alice didn't seem that way, and neither did Gerald. She thought back to the war, working in Washington, and what it was like to get up every day and join everyone else heading for some useful occupation. It was an exciting time, and it made people feel worth something. She recalled the energy she felt in school, reading her poets, and working on her thesis, followed by the dull but predictable job at the UN. Where had that woman gone? With no demands on her, she was free to think and feel what she wanted. Yet thoughts and feelings only took one so far. There was action, and deeds to be done. Those, too, were necessary for a full life.

"I haven't even done much reading here. You can't imagine how disappointed I am in myself," Edith said.

"Never be disappointed in yourself. It permits other people to criticize you."

Edith couldn't tell if this were meant as encouragement or as a rebuke. She sipped her tea. She could feel Alice watching her. Now she knew where Henry had learned his habit of scrutiny.

"Reading is a lovely pastime, isn't it?" Alice asked. "You know, when I was a girl, I was discouraged from reading. My parents were afraid that books would make me antisocial, or suspicious of other people. I think their real worry was that no man would take on a bookish wife. Thank goodness I wasn't homely, at least according to my mother." A warm light came to her eyes which suggested her memories were fond, rather than harsh.

Edith slipped off her shoes and leaned back in her chair.

Alice said Henry's brother had been a great reader, though of course, he was only a child at the time, and a child is somewhat limited by his understanding of the page's complexity. Even so, he adored being in the library, choosing a new title, and becoming lost in it. After he died, Gerald was so distraught he threatened to do away with his books, but Alice stopped him.

"And I'm not a woman given to defying my husband," she said.

"I'm glad you did."

The sun swung around and sent light into a new corner of the room. Dust motes floated gently and made Edith feel sleepy, like a cat warming itself on a window seat.

They sat quietly for a few minutes. Alice put her cup in the saucer and asked Edith if she cared for more. Edith said no, not at the moment.

"Tell me about Mary's letter, if you don't find the question impertinent," Alice said.

"How did you know I'd received one from her?"

"Not much goes on in this house that I'm not aware of. And she'd said she was going to write to you."

"You're in touch with her?"

"Yes, often."

"But Alistair suggested you weren't particularly friendly."

"Alistair is a dear man, and a loyal servant to be sure, but he doesn't know everything. Far from it."

Edith said she found the letter unsettling. Mary said things about Henry that she suspected were true, as a warning, presumably. Edith didn't understand why Mary found her welfare important.

"She's a kind woman, in her way," Alice said.

"Perhaps."

"They just weren't suited."

"Are we? Henry and I?"

"Oh, I think so. You seem to be exactly what he needs."

"And, what's that?"

"Someone to push him out of himself, and gain perspective. His father and I have been waiting for that to happen. Everything he goes through seems to settle him further in himself if you know what I mean. He becomes his own refuge. Losing his brother, the war, Mary, and even moving to America didn't seem to leave an impression."

Edith said she begged to disagree. It struck her that Henry had a deep well of sadness, and terrible loneliness.

"Yes, because he won't let anyone in. But you seem like you can get past the defenses," Alice said.

It sounded exhausting, and the pleasant mood she enjoyed fell away. She didn't want to get past anything, but to have the way forward be smooth and easy. She'd spent years coddling Walter because she thought it was her duty and because she saw her mother do the same thing with her father. She never questioned this burden placed on married women, or upon any woman involved with a man. And while she didn't question it now, because she knew it was how the world worked, she rebelled against it.

"I'm sorry if I upset you," Alice said.

"No, no, it's all right. Everything you say is true. It's just a lot to think about."

"It is, indeed."

There was a discreet knock at the door, then it opened and Carstairs entered carrying a small silver tray, different from the one downstairs, and told Alice a telegram had come for Mrs. Sloan.

Edith snatched it off the tray and tore it open.

Store badly damaged by fire. Cause unknown. No injuries. Closed until further notice. Patricia.

"Oh, my God," Edith said. Alice asked if she might see the message for herself. Edith gave it to her, and she put on the reading glasses hanging from a chain around her neck.

"How unfortunate!" Alice said.

That damned electrician, Edith thought. He must have done something to the wiring. He had a shifty, incompetent look to him. Patricia had thought so, too, but then she distrusted just about everyone.

"I must go and find Henry," Edith said and excused herself. Henry was in the library, alone, pouring himself a drink.

"One for me, too, please, and be generous," she said. She handed him the telegram. He read it.

"Dreadful business. How can it have happened, I wonder?"

Edith shared her thoughts on the electrician. She sank into the nearest chair and wept. Henry knelt and put his arms around her until she calmed. Her face was damp, and Henry patted it with his handkerchief. Then he stood and handed her a ridiculously large glass of whiskey. She stared at it, then had some. He told her not to worry. Everything could be put right. She wasn't to think about the cost. What the insurance wouldn't cover, he'd be happy to give her. Or lend her, if she preferred.

She went on sitting, wondering how the sky beyond the glass could remain so absurdly blue. Images of smoke-blackened walls, wood floors buckled from water, and piles of ash and debris floated past.

"It's my fault," she said.

"Nonsense. You weren't even there. You couldn't possibly have known."

"But don't you see? I didn't follow through. I left. And now I'm being punished for it."

"By whom, God?"

"I don't believe in God."

"By the universe, then?"

"Yes.

Henry sat in the chair next to hers and said things didn't work that way. She mustn't fall prey to magical thinking. It was tempting, he knew. In the war, a lot of people crossed their fingers or touched the amulet hanging from their necks, and performed meaningless rites with fervor, like pulling a curtain closed a certain way, or wearing a particular tie on certain days. Even he had, at times. But she must stay grounded in the world, tethered to what she knew to be true, and the truth that was there was no punishment here, just misfortune from which she would soon recover.

"Do you see my point?" he asked.

"I don't know, but I have to get back as soon as I can. Can we fly?"

"Possibly. Let me put Alistair on it."

Henry left the library. Edith put her drink down. She had to keep a clear head and pull herself together. When what felt like a long time had passed and Henry hadn't returned, Edith went to find him. He was in his father's study, telling Gerald about the fire. Edith approached Gerald's desk. He stood and told her how sorry he was.

"Thank you. What did you find out?" Edith asked Henry.

Henry said yes, it was possible. There was a flight every day from London to New York. They could pack lightly, leave in the morning, and let Alistair shepherd their trunks on the sailing they were already booked on.

"How long will it take?" Edith asked.

"The flight? A little over fifteen hours."

"It's incredible."

"Isn't it?"

Edith said nothing for a moment. Henry asked what was wrong.

"I've never been in an airplane before," she said.

"Neither have I."

"I'm terrified."

"We'll be all right. It's perfectly safe."

Gerald said during the war the RAF pilots would bring their planes down low over the estate on training runs, scaring the sheep out of their wits, and him, too, a couple of times, if they didn't think him a fool for admitting it. Alice found them a nuisance, but then she had nerves of steel. Always did. Once, a plane ran into some trouble, he didn't know what kind, something to do with the engine, he assumed, and the pilot had to make an emergency landing in the field, miles off, in a remote corner of the estate, and the poor chap made his way to the road hoping to hitch a ride from a passing farmer but there weren't any that day so he kept going, all the way up to the front door where old Carstairs gave him the once over before letting him in!

Edith didn't appreciate Gerald's tale of mechanical trouble, though he clearly enjoyed sharing it.

Two days later, they were aloft over the Atlantic Ocean. Henry found the whole thing a marvelous adventure. He asked the stewardess technical questions about the aircraft, most of which she could answer. What she didn't know, she said she'd refer to the pilot when time allowed.

He told Edith the good folks at Lockheed had things well in hand, and that his father had invested in them before the war and made a tidy sum.

Edith didn't think of herself as a fearful person but every time she peeked out the window at the undulating surface of the water below, her hands went clammy and cold. Even after several hours, she was on edge, unable to eat or drink. The stewardess came around periodically to try to tempt her with something. Finally, she took a glass of champagne. When it failed to calm her, Henry ordered her to take a sleeping tablet.

She asked where he'd gotten them, and he said he'd pinched them from his mother, who kept them for emergencies.

She was too upset to argue and did as he asked. She woke up as they were preparing to land, and Henry was trying to fasten her seat belt.

"Good lord, how long was I out?" she asked. Her head felt numb.

"I don't know. A little while."

"Did you sleep?"

"Some. Oh, look! Isn't it a beautiful sight?"

He pointed out the Statue of Liberty as the plane banked and circled back toward Long Island for its final descent into Idlewild Airport. Edith had to admit that it was an inspiring thing to see and made her hope everything would be all right, though she had an awful feeling that it wouldn't be.

They went at once by taxi into Manhattan and the Waldorf Astoria where Alistair had booked them two rooms for the night. Henry slipped the bellboy a ten-dollar bill and asked him to unlock the connecting door. As soon as they were installed, Edith telephoned Patricia at home.

There was no answer and Edith tried again about half an hour later, with the same result. She wished she had sent Patricia a telegram saying when she'd be back in the States, but the last two days at Henry's place had been tense and miserable. It was all she could do to oversee Martha packing and not break down crying again.

Henry said they could go out for dinner, but Edith wanted to stay close to the telephone, so he ordered room service. He told her to eat something, and she did. The steak was delicious, the wine superb and even the baked potato was wonderful, though she didn't normally like them. Henry enjoyed his filet of sole which he paired with a nice white wine. For Edith, he had a bottle of red sent up.

Afterward, they stood looking out into the glow and glitter of the city. It made such a sad contrast to the gentle land of Henry's estate, and when she said so he said, "It's not my estate, not anymore."

"But it will be, one day."

"Not for a long while. Father isn't as robust as he once was, but he's only fifty-six. He'll live a long time yet."

Edith tried Patricia again and was immensely relieved when she answered.

She said she had been at the store all afternoon seeing what books could be salvaged, and Edith realized she should have been trying to reach her there, instead of at home. Edith asked the extent of the damage, as specifically as Patricia could describe.

The fire seemed to have started in the basement, lending credence to Edith's suspicion that the wiring wasn't done correctly. The back room was in bad shape—the front room was all right, just a mess. The office had been spared, which was a mercy, because of the financial records. Patricia said they should start keeping a duplicate set of books, either that or one of them should take the books home every day when they left.

"How long will the repairs take?" Edith asked.

"I don't know yet. I haven't contacted any repair people. The insurance man hasn't finished, but he's almost done."

"What's he doing?"

"Putting together a cost estimate."

"I see."

Patricia then said people had been coming around to the store to see how badly off it was. Some offered to help clean up, but Patricia wasn't letting anyone in. They weren't entirely certain the ceiling was stable, but the inspector was just there that afternoon and he certified that it wasn't going to collapse.

"You have a sign up saying that we're closed?" Edith asked.

"Yes, of course."

And yet they wanted in. Edith took that as proof of a loyal following. Or just morbid curiosity.

Patricia said the establishment next door had suffered some smoke damage, and that their insurance was going to cover fixing that, too. It was a little shoe store students liked to visit because it was cheap. Edith asked if had to close. Patricia said it did.

"And they think it was the wiring?" Edith asked.

"That's the most likely cause. But one of the girls smokes, and I just can't help wondering about that."

"You said the fire started at night. After the store closed."

Patricia said she'd found evidence that someone had been in the place after hours. Nothing was taken, that wasn't the issue. But a plant had been moved slightly, and a book hadn't been put back where it should have been. Edith said she thought no one had keys to the place except her and Patricia.

Patricia said the lock on the back window had been broken for months. She may have mentioned that to the girls.

"I found cigarette butts in the basement after the contractor was down there. I assumed they were his. But now I'm not so sure."

"Why would one of them come in and go down there to smoke?"

"Maybe they went down there for something else."

"Like what?"

"Edith. You're a married woman. Do I have to explain?"

Edith asked why someone would want to have an assignation in a basement. Patricia suggested there might be some perverse romance associated with it, or they went down there out of curiosity and were overcome with sudden passion.

"Good God, this sounds like a bad novel," Edith said.

"It does."

"Get that window lock fixed."

"Already done."

"You should have had it repaired the moment you knew it was broken."

"I told you about it before you went on leave."

She had. Edith remembered that now. And she'd said not to worry about it and that she'd call someone about it soon. Further proof that this was all her fault.

"Who's the smoker?" Edith asked.

"Liza."

Edith said to say nothing. Once it was officially declared the result of faulty wiring, that would be the end of it. With the window lock repaired, no further invasions would take place.

She told Patricia she'd be home the following day. When she hung up, Henry expressed his disappointment.

"Well, it sounds as if Patricia has things under control. There's no need to rush back, is there? We missed out on touring London, we might as well enjoy ourselves here," he said.

"We missed London the first time because you were in a foul mood. The second time it wasn't possible to linger."

Henry said she was right. He finished off the bottle of white wine he enjoyed with his dinner. Edith poured herself a second glass of red and joined him on the sofa. She apologized. He made an excellent point. They should take time to enjoy themselves. How many days did he want to spend there?

"Oh, I should think no more than three. Would that do?"

She said it would do perfectly. Later, lying awake after making love, Edith reflected that she'd become an accomplished liar.

Chapter Seven

The smell of smoke and damp paper, coupled with the heat of late summer, made The Turned Page almost unbearable. On her first day back, Edith looked over every book for signs of smoke or water damage; scrubbed down walls to see if cleaning alone would be enough, or if a coat of paint would be required; measured for new curtains to replace the ruined ones in the back room; and went over all business matters twice. They had to pay a deductible of fifty dollars on the insurance policy but otherwise, the big concern was the loss of revenue while the place was closed. She'd have to cover at least two months' rent from her own funds.

She came home exhausted to find Henry reading, listening to the radio, or drinking and playing solitaire. Alistair wasn't due back for another week and Edith had been preparing their meals. She'd arranged for their laundry to be picked up at the apartment—Alistair usually dropped it off weekly at a place a few blocks away. She asked for groceries to be delivered, too. She just didn't have time to shop.

That Henry was useless in domestic matters was no surprise. All his life other people had handled things for him. Even in London during the war he'd had Alistair. But she was infuriated that he expected her to put in hours at the store and then wait on him at home. He said he was happy for them to dine out every night until Alistair returned. She said she didn't always want to go out. Sometimes, it was nice to stay home and put her feet up.

"You're right, poor dear. Let me make you something. I'm sure I can find my way around the kitchen well enough," Henry said.

"About all you can do is make a piece of toast."

His expression showed a surprising degree of remorse. He flopped down in his favorite chair and said he tried every day not to disappoint her, but somehow never seemed to manage.

"Oh, Henry, don't be like that. I'm just tired, that's all. And worried about the store. Why don't you fix yourself another drink? And one for me, too," Edith said.

He was instantly on his feet. The thought of liquor always made him move fast.

"Why are you worried? I thought the repairs were scheduled, and everything was fine," he said.

"Oh, I don't know. It's just nerve-wracking, that's all."

She sipped her drink. She said she did have some good news, though. She'd finally gone to the printers in Concord. The man was pleasant, but he raised an eyebrow when she said she'd be bringing out poetry titles. It wasn't as expensive as she initially thought, because, in the beginning, the print runs would be small, only a few copies or so. She'd have to wait and see how well things sold. He did say that while he had experience setting all kinds of typefaces, poetry would be more exact and time-consuming. Not that he was ever sloppy. He didn't mean to give her that impression.

"Concord? You took a taxi all the way out there?" Henry asked.

"Of course."

"I'd have driven you."

"It didn't occur to me to ask you. He called and said he had time this afternoon if I could get over there quickly. The person he was going to meet with canceled at the last minute."

"I see." His tone was grim.

"Henry, what is all this? I've gone back to work, and you said you were fine with the whole thing."

Edith couldn't be certain, but it appeared for a moment that he pouted. When she glanced again, she decided she'd imagined it.

He said he was fine with it; he just didn't like the idea of her traipsing all over on her own. He knew it sounded silly, but he worried about her all the time when she wasn't home.

"You're not a worrier, Henry, come on," she said.

"I am a worrier. You just ask Mary."

"Why would I do that?"

"I know she wrote to you. I assume you'll answer her letter."

"You assume incorrectly."

Edith was annoyed that Henry knew about Mary's letter. Alice must have told him, but why? To warn him that Mary was leading her down a certain path where she might turn against him? Alice was protective of her son, Edith had observed. And she wanted him to marry Edith and for Edith to point him toward living a useful life. If she'd wanted that for him, she should have raised him better, she thought.

"You would worry less if you had something to do besides sit around the apartment all day," she said.

"I visit my club quite often, as you know."

"I can't imagine that's much of an activity."

"Perhaps not, but I enjoy it."

Edith lifted her glass and put it down again. She didn't feel like drinking now. She thought about the printing press she had viewed this afternoon, and the man laying out the metal type letter by letter. It was fascinating. She wanted to telephone Clara Levy, an elderly poet she'd met last spring, and ask how her manuscript was coming along. Edith had offered a second edition of the volume Levy brought out herself a few years before, and she was in the process of adding and revising poems. Of course, Edith would still have to review it.

And that gave her a thought.

"Be my editor," she said.

"Pardon?"

"You studied English literature. You know how to read a text closely, don't you?"

"Of course."

"Well, Clara Levy is reworking her original manuscript, and before I give it to the printer it will need to be gone over and corrected."

She watched the idea take shape in his mind.

"She was such an odd bird, and I suspect I'd find her poetry quite interesting, though grim," he said. Levy's work centered on the Holocaust.

"Then it's settled."

She said he already had a desk in the library, and they could set up a second desk if he didn't mind.

"Not at all, it would be nice to have you in there with me," he said.

"Oh, no, I'd take one of the guest rooms. We don't need two guest rooms, do we?"

"What if your mother and Betty want to visit?"

"Oh, I hadn't thought of that. Well, we could put them up at a hotel, couldn't we?"

"We could indeed."

Edith then said she wanted a telephone line installed in whichever room she would take as a home office. She needed to be able to conduct business and didn't want to use the phone in the library. Henry said he'd ask Alistair to arrange it when he returned. Edith didn't want to wait. She'd call the telephone company in the morning.

Soon the pace of activity was thrilling, like stepping into a rushing stream. The store reopened and drew a healthy flow of customers according to Patricia, Jocelyn, and Liza, whom Edith briefly regarded with suspicion, then dismissed her concern. It wasn't that she couldn't imagine her sneaking into the bookstore to be alone with her boyfriend, it just didn't matter now. The repairs were done. The new curtains looked wonderful, and Edith ordered a matching set for the front room. New area rugs had been laid down, and the wooden bookcases were painted white, not an antiseptic white but a warm, glowing white, like a summer moon, Patricia said. The storage shelves in the basement, which had only recently gone in, had to be rebuilt from scratch, and the new contractor did a better job than the first man had. Edith had always believed in silver linings, and here was her proof.

Miss Levy's manuscript turned out to be a mess of typing errors and questionable word choices that caused Edith and Henry to draw different conclusions about her original intention, argue, then reconcile. Finally, Edith asked if she could visit Miss Levy to go over the document in person, but she was under the weather again and instructed Edith to use her judgment. Edith decided to put the manuscript aside until she had a chance to review other submissions. There must be some that would require less editing. The notice she put in the window asking for manuscripts resulted in more than fifty hopeful local poets dropping off boxes, paper bags, and even a wooden crate of material, most of which was typed, some of which was hand-written, hard to read, or illegible. Jocelyn and Liza were tasked with getting everyone's name, mailing address, and telephone number. The authors would receive a written letter from Edith when a decision had been made about their work, and they were not to call or visit the store and ask about it before then. Then, their pages could be collected, unless they wanted them destroyed. No one wanted them destroyed. Some responded to that question in anger. One man told Jocelyn Edith sounded like a Communist. Another wanted to know what right Edith had to think she could decide whose passions lived or died.

"His very words?" Henry asked over dinner. Alistair was back, and he'd made a scrumptious roasted chicken with potatoes and carrots on the side.

"Apparently. All this power makes me feel like a divine being."

"Oh, dear. It's all gone to your head, hasn't it?"

Edith said it had, and she'd never expected that. But Henry knew as well as she did that most of what they were asked to read was dreadful. Some were passable, and only one or two manuscripts had any shine to them at all. They settled on two, one by a man, the other by a woman. Henry felt the man's should come out first. It was full of life and assaults against the status quo. The themes of world domination rang true, even though the war was over. The plight of the ordinary man was spectacularly rendered, Henry thought, and felt this should resonate with Edith, given that she'd focused on both Whitman and Sandburg for her master's thesis. Edith said that was all well and good, but the woman's poems were wonderful, too. All that emphasis on the natural world, and the play of shadow and light. A visually oriented poet was lovely, didn't Henry agree?

He did, but her poems felt smaller, at least in his mind.

"Define 'smaller,'" Edith said.

"They're less serious, if you know what I mean."

"I'm afraid I don't."

Alistair appeared to ask how they liked the dinner. Henry said it was wonderful. Alistair said there was some fresh fruit for dessert. Edith said she couldn't eat another bite. After Alistair cleared the table and withdrew, Henry poured himself another glass of wine and offered some to Edith. She didn't care for that, either. He resumed his explanation with a patient, kind expression.

He said using the natural world as a mirror to the human condition was perfectly fine, but it was the sphere of politics where the big things happened. The *real* things, to be specific.

Edith watched him as he drank his wine.

"I don't accept that. Emotions are crucial—they're what make us human," Edith said, aware of the tightness in her tone. Henry noticed it, too, because he put his glass on the table and kept his hand on it. She'd learned this meant he was anxious, on alert, searching for the right thing to say next. She could destroy him now with a few well-chosen words, he was that dependent on her affection. But not, it seemed, on her insight.

"Let me lay out the problem as I see it," Henry said.

"Of course."

He said equality between the sexes was a beautiful idea and one worth striving for. He hoped she believed him when he said that. Women were every bit as intelligent as men and creative, and strong—in their way. But biology had endowed them with the gift of creating life and carrying it forward, and this made their sensibilities rest on different things. They were important things—necessary for the survival of the species—and this pull from nature and toward nature led them to be reflective, emotional, and deeply instinctive. They thought with their hearts, not their minds. Or, to put it another way, they listened to their hearts first, and to their minds second.

"You make us sound like animals," Edith said.

"Well, we're all animals, aren't we?"

"Only women are more so."

"You misunderstand me."

He explained that women could be empirical, rational, and incisive when called upon, but these traits didn't come naturally. How could they? And men could be tender, nurturing, and sensitive but those traits didn't come naturally to them. Did she see?

"All I see is that you're saying women are inferior. That their inner lives are frivolous because they're not as important as a man's. Let me tell you something—my father was the moodiest man I've ever known. He'd blow up for no reason. He was possessed by his emotions. And he taught mathematics, a subject requiring complete intellectual rigor. I honestly don't know how he managed, given his 'nature.' My mother, on the hand, had a first-rate mind and always kept her cool. They were the complete opposite of how you describe men and women."

She went on to talk about Walter's fears and anxieties, all seemingly immune to any logic she applied to them on his behalf. He believed people were always trying to get the better of him somehow, and that he would never measure up even when he was lauded, decorated, and celebrated. It was as if he had a black hole inside him that he could fall into at any moment. It was devasting to watch. On the one hand, she hated him for giving in to what he knew was false; on the other, she felt terrible for the way he repeatedly suffered. And the worst thing was, it created a divide between them, a barrier, that had nothing to do with gender or rearing, education, or life experience. It was just there, the way the barrier between men and women was there. In a personal relationship, the barrier might be removed over time if both parties were willing and able to work at it. In society the same thing was true, and the barrier between men and women, between what they were allowed to do, could in time be broken. It had to be. Otherwise, there was no hope.

"Edith, you can't fight biology," Henry said.

"No, I can't. But I can fight against attitudes, traditions, and practices."

"With your press?"

"Yes."

"Well, I admire your zeal."

"Laura's Brown manuscript will come out first. Then we'll publish Robert Nedleman's."

"As you please."

"And I've just had another thought, about the name. Of the press, I mean."

"I thought you'd decided on The Heartland."

"I've changed my mind. And please don't tell me that's my prerogative, as a woman."

Henry held up his hand in a gesture of surrender.

Edith's face was hot, and her hands were cold. She was enraged and tried not to show it. Were she to give voice to what she felt, Henry would merely say that her behavior proved his point about the female psyche. His eyes were on her, as always. All this time what she assumed was love on his part was merely the habit of gathering intelligence on her, trying to discover who she was, in essence, to see what she was made of. She felt like a specimen under a microscope, one from which she could never escape.

"The Hedgerow," she said.

"For the press?"

"Yes."

She watched his focus shift from her to some vague point in space. There was worry in his eyes, blended with the keen intelligence she always found there. It had been hard for him to say what he had, she realized. He was honest because he believed that's what she wanted from him. He let himself be vulnerable. She could tell him that in so doing, he was exhibiting the same traits he assumed were the unique provenance of women, but that would be cruel.

"Intriguing. A decorative, occasionally unnecessary boundary, but a boundary, all the same," Henry said.

"Exactly."

His mood brightened, and she felt a surge of affection. She stood and walked around the table. She bent down and kissed his cheek.

"What's that for?" he asked.

"Nothing. Everything. I don't know."

"Hear, hear!"

The next morning, she telephoned Robert Nedleman about his book, *Comes a Starling*. She said she wanted to publish it and would send over a contract as soon as one could be drawn up. She'd find someone who knew about those things unless he didn't mind her doing it herself. It might be better if she did it herself. They could keep everything simple that way.

"Simple, as in . . ." Nedleman said.

"You know, how many copies we'll run, what to do if you decide you don't want to follow through, or if I decide I don't want to. Or how we'll handle a dispute about royalties. I haven't thought about royalties. I'll have to look into that."

"Well, I'm no expert, but I believe the usual arrangement is for the publisher to take eighty-five percent of the sales and for the author to take fifteen percent. Or a ninety-ten split. Whichever."

"Oh, I see," Edith said.

"You're new at this."

"I am."

"Well, it's certainly a pleasure to know I'll be the first author published by a new press."

"Oh, you're not the first. You're the second."

"Well, second's good, too."

Edith promised to be in touch again soon.

To spare herself another awkward phone call, Edith wrote Laura Brown her acceptance. Two days later Miss Brown called the store and asked if they could meet for coffee or even a drink. Edith paused. She hadn't expected to be offered anything as thanks but said that sounded delightful and Miss Brown should choose.

"Oh, I'm a B-girl from way back," Miss Brown said. Edith found her throaty laugh charming.

They arranged to meet at the bar in the Copley Plaza, the same hotel where Kathleen had stayed the winter before, at five o'clock that afternoon. Edith said she'd bring along her notes on the manuscript and would go over them if Miss Brown wanted.

"Sounds swell. See you then."

Patricia opened the door and leaned in. She said a man was demanding to speak with her, one of the authors who submitted a poetry manuscript she turned down. She asked him to leave, and he refused. She could call the police if Edith thought that were appropriate.

"Is he making trouble?" Edith asked.

"No. Just staying put."

"Oh, all right. Ask him to come in."

"Are you sure?"

"Leave the door open, if you're concerned."

Edith took her compact out of her purse and freshened her powder and lipstick. Then she smoothed down her hair, which needed to be cut. In the back, it was touching the collar of her dress. Patricia opened the door again and entered, followed by a middle-aged man with a severe military-style haircut. He wore a plaid shirt and blue jeans, far too heavy for the unseasonably warm weather they were having. Edith was self-conscious about her bare arms and wished she had a sweater to put on.

"This is Mr. Fitzhugh," Patricia said. She looked at him with frank annoyance. After she left, Edith waited for a moment before asking him to sit down in the chair opposite the desk.

"I'm not here to make myself comfortable," he said.

"And I'm not here to talk to someone who chooses to remain on his feet."

Mr. Fitzhugh sat down. The buttons on his shirt strained across his stomach. His collar dug into the flesh on his neck.

He said he'd come right to the point. He drove a bus, not that that mattered, one way or another, and took night classes at BU. That did matter, at least according to his professor, who thought he had something going and was helping him. And he'd been working at home, after the kids were in bed, while the wife listened to her programs, though he didn't see the point. Radio had become the opiate of the masses.

"More so than religion?" Edith asked. Mr. Fitzhugh stared at her. She asked him if she had lipstick on her teeth.

"Why did you reject my book?"

"What's the title?"

"Bruising the Blues."

Edith remembered it clearly. Page after page of angry rants about the disrespect suffered by the working man. She and Henry had had a good laugh over several absurd passages. Something about the rage of bulls being nothing compared to the ire of a bricklayer denied a promised raise.

"It was heavy-handed," she said. She offered Mr. Fitzhugh a cigarette. He took it, lit it with a small book of matches, leaned across the desk, and lit Edith's.

"So are the times we live it."

"I agree. And while poetry can reflect the times, it must hit a higher bar."

Mr. Fitzhugh looked around the office. His eyes rested on a crystal paperweight that had belonged to the bookstore's former owner.

"What do you know about it? If you'll forgive my bluntness," he said.

Edith explained about her master's degree from Harvard.

"Okay, you pass," he said.

"Thank you."

Mr. Fitzhugh put out his cigarette, even though he hadn't even smoked half of it.

"Look, I'm sorry for the attitude, but I thought I had something to say," he said.

"You have. But that's only part of it. How you say it matters just as much. Don't hit people over the head. Be subtle. Suggestive."

"Now, you're talking dirty." He held up his hand. "Sorry, my wife says I'm a terrible flirt."

"No argument there."

Edith leaned back in her chair. She said surely his professor had said more or less the same things. Mr. Fitzhugh said yeah, he had, and it didn't make any more sense to him now than it did then.

"How much poetry do you read?" Edith asked.

"Not much."

"There's your problem. You have to learn, see how others do it."

"Swell."

Edith looked at his hands and imagined them on the wheel of a bus, holding his child, folding up the evening paper. She asked him what he did during the war.

"Drove a Jeep for the 87th Infantry Division. All over France. I got to like French food if you can't believe that. Snails, even. You?"

"Me, what?"

"During the war."

"I made maps."

Mr. Fitzhugh said lots of gals did their share. Couldn't have won the war without them.

Edith told him to come with her and led him out of the office into the front room of the store, where Jocelyn's lovely sign indicated the poetry section. Edith pulled out books by Browning, Dickinson, and Millay and handed them to him. He looked them over.

"They're all dames. I mean, ladies," he said.

"That's right. And you can learn a lot from them. You take these home and read them, slowly. Then read them again. Ask yourself what the author is trying to say in every line, and why she chose a particular word."

"I can't afford these."

"I'm lending them to you. Just bring them back when you're done."

"I can get them from the library."

"As you wish."

He gave the books back to her, thanked her for her time, and left. Edith knew he'd never read any of the titles she suggested. Or if he did, he wouldn't admit it to anyone.

Miss Brown was a refreshing change from Mr. Fitzhugh, but not what Edith had expected. She wore slacks, a button-down shirt, and not a speck of makeup. Of course, Edith had met lesbians before, or those she suspected were lesbians. There was a girl in one of her college classes, another in the mapmaking office, and a typist in another department at the UN. They didn't make her uncomfortable, just curious. Even the way Miss Brown held her cigarette, between her thumb and forefinger, was mannish. Did these things come naturally to her? Or were they a signal to show that she preferred women? When they shook hands, Miss Brown's grip was strong, almost overpowering. She'd taken the liberty of ordering two dry martinis since she'd arrived a bit early. She leaned in and told Edith in a quiet voice that the bartender had been keeping his eye on her, and not in a flattering way.

"Ever the Puritan town," Miss Brown said.

"I haven't found it so."

"Well, you wouldn't, would you?"

Edith said she'd enjoyed her poetry and was excited to be bringing it out. Had she been writing long?

"Years. It comes easily now, but it didn't, not for a long time," Miss Brown said.

"And what do you do, otherwise?"

"Nothing at the moment. I majored in English and wanted to write for a newspaper, but they wanted me to review cookbooks, and talk up garden clubs, and I just couldn't see myself doing that."

"It does sound pretty dull."

"I worked in a bank for a while, lived on a shoestring, saved up a bundle, and now just write, mostly in the evenings. I'm something of a night owl."

"Well, your work is wonderful."

"There were plenty of bad poems, believe me. And lots of people telling me I was wasting my time," Miss Brown said.

"I'm glad you ignored them. I adore your manuscript. My fiancé did, too, by the way, but not as much as I did. He's my co-editor. I don't believe I mentioned that."

"I thought you were already married. Your letter said Mrs. Edith Sloan on the return envelope."

"I'm divorced."

"I see. And already engaged. You work fast."

There was nothing offensive in the way she said this.

Edith said her fiancé was the one who worked fast, at least where she was concerned. He didn't hurry in other matters, except when it was time to freshen his drink.

Miss Brown listened politely, but Edith could see a gleam of whimsy in her eyes.

"I'm afraid I might be one of those women who can't imagine themselves being single," Edith said.

"But you were single, once."

"Of course."

"Was it so bad?"

"Not at all. I didn't think about it. It's just that my family thought I should get married."

"Mine thinks I should, too."

The chairs were comfortable. The light was pleasant in the room. The martini was delicious. It was lovely to relax and let her thoughts drift. Had she been wrong to speak about Henry like that to a stranger? Miss Brown didn't seem to mind. She seemed to think the whole thing funny.

Edith returned to the matter at hand. She wanted Miss Brown to understand that the print run on her book would be small, only fifty copies. They would be sold through The Turned Page. Edith would contact other bookstores in the area and see if they could be persuaded to carry it, too. And Miss

Brown should count on coming in to read. She thought the store could accommodate up to twenty or thirty people comfortably. Of course, she'd have to round up some chairs. She'd look into that.

"I must say, I admire your bravery," Miss Brown said and signaled the waiter for another round.

"It's not so brave to publish a woman. If more people did, it wouldn't be seen as so unusual."

"That's not quite what I mean."

"What, then?"

Miss Brown waited for the waiter to clear their glasses and put down fresh drinks. She scooped a handful of salted peanuts from the bowl on the table and fed them to herself one by one, slowly, as if she had all the time in the world. Edith grew irritated with her.

Miss Brown said Edith must have noticed how often she wrote about flowers and the parts of flowers, and how she likened those parts to human parts or endowed them with human qualities.

"Yes, of course. I found it all so lovely. You gave something that has been so frequently written about a kind of romantic flavor normally reserved for human beings. I wonder if you'd think about a new title, though. *You, Forever*, doesn't quite summon the ethos of the work. I was thinking something like *A Silent Passion* because you summon so well the feeling of things that go unexpressed. And I understand, I do, because it's so typical and expected that women love flowers, so we've all learned to keep quiet about it because otherwise, we look silly."

Miss Brown continued to eat her peanuts until she finished. Then, she wiped her hands on one pants leg.

"On the level?" she asked.

"Of course."

"The flowers aren't just flowers. They're women. Well, one woman in particular. Do you understand my meaning?" Miss Brown asked.

Edith did but hadn't until that moment. No wonder Henry had objected to the manuscript. Read a certain way, it was sexually explicit. Why hadn't she seen that for herself? She'd been too swept away by the idea of publishing it that she hadn't read it closely enough. The subject matter would cause no end of trouble unless she were clever. And resolute. That said, the imagery was stunning, and the language was first-rate, despite the subtext. Miss Brown was watching her closely in a way that made Edith feel close to panic.

"Of course. And I think people like you need a voice. I'd like to give you that voice if you still agree," she said.

"I do."

Edith complimented her on her subtlety. Some people might not see what she was driving at, and that would be helpful if there were any objections down the road.

"We'll just accuse them of having a dirty mind," Miss Brown said.

"Exactly."

Miss Brown asked if she'd excuse her for a moment so she could go powder her nose.

"Isn't that the silliest expression? I don't know why we can't just say we need to use the washroom," she said and stood up.

Edith watched her go. She felt like a fool. It was too late to back out now. She had to go forward and make the best of it.

When Miss Brown returned, she said she hoped Edith wasn't having second thoughts about her book.

"No, of course not. Just let me edit it a bit more, and then you can look over my suggestions. You don't have to accept any changes you don't want to."

"I'm just happy I'm going to be in print. But I'm not sure giving a reading is such a great idea if you know what I mean."

"Cambridge is a liberal place."

"Not as liberal as you'd think. I know a couple of guys who got arrested last year."

"Oh? For what?"

"What do you think?"

"I see, yes, of course. But . . . for women, isn't it different?"

"We tend not to carry on in public restrooms if that's what you mean, so the police aren't as likely to discover us doing what we shouldn't, or what they think we shouldn't. But there are bars we like to visit where we feel safe, and they show up sometimes. They're not exactly polite when they do."

"I imagine not."

Miss Brown asked Edith her thoughts about the design of the book's dust jacket.

"Oh, I'm afraid I haven't given it any thought at all! I need to get up to speed," Edith said.

"Do you have a designer?"

"I don't."

"Oh, well, I might have a friend who's good at that sort of thing."

"One of my salesclerks is an art student. I'll ask her."

Edith suggested Miss Brown jot down some ideas about imagery she felt would be appropriate as a guide for Jocelyn—her clerk—if she agreed.

The waiter presented their bill and Edith said she'd get it. Miss Brown didn't object. They walked out together, and Edith said she'd be in touch.

"Thank you for meeting with me. And for everything. You don't know how long I've been trying to get published," Miss Brown said, then trotted across the street to catch her bus.

Edith walked home, framing what she'd tell Henry. She wouldn't tell him about her meeting with Miss Brown. Instead, she'd tell him about Mr. Fitzhugh coming to the store and her offering him titles by women authors. He'd enjoy that. She was sure he would.

Chapter Eight

But Henry was out, at his club, Alistair thought. His Lordship hadn't said specifically. As usual, Alistair had prepared dinner. He said it was beef stew, nothing special, and asked if Edith cared for some, anyway.

She was hungry. Had he eaten? When he said he hadn't, she said to join her in the dining room. Henry wouldn't mind. He wasn't there in any case. And besides, wasn't this Edith's home, too?

Alistair didn't resist, and even let Edith help set the table. She lit the candles and looked over the bottles of wine on the sideboard. She picked out a nice Beaujolais, and as she poured it, Alistair said when he was in France in 1917, he drank lots of wonderful French wine.

"I'd like to visit France," Edith said.

"I imagine you will."

Rather than sit at opposite ends of the table, as she and Henry usually did, she sat at one end, and he sat on her right. It made conversation easier. The stew was delicious, and Edith asked if Alistair had added a dried bay leaf or two. He said he had. Three.

She told him about her day, even about the nature of Miss Brown's manuscript. Alistair leaned back in his chair with a raised eyebrow and said no wonder His Lordship had recommended against it.

"Will there be trouble if I bring it out?" she asked.

"I honestly don't know. You can always deny the subject matter."

"We thought the same thing."

Then she told him about Mr. Fitzhugh and his reluctance to read anything by a woman.

"Perhaps you can direct him to Miss Brown's book," he said.

Edith chuckled. "Yes, I'm sure he'd appreciate that."

She stood to clear the table and Alistair helped her. She offered to do the dishes, and he said no, she already did enough by allowing him to dine with her.

"I think you should dine with us every day," she said.

"I think my presence would make conversation difficult."

Edith didn't understand why but didn't pursue it. Where was Henry, anyway? It was almost eight o'clock. She told him she'd be home in time for dinner.

She went into the library to pour herself a small glass of sherry. On Henry's desk was the manuscript he was editing, *Rising Tides*, by Brian McLeish. The author was a former GI who'd been all over the South Pacific, and he wrote about the horrors of war with a neutral, chilling, dispassionate eye. Edith admired his work. She thumbed through the manuscript.

Henry hadn't made a single mark on it. There was a typo on the second page, two more on the next page, and another several pages further on. He'd told her it was going well, and he hadn't even begun! She closed the manuscript and went to the window and looked out into the twilight. People walked along the river. Cars passed on the street below. Alistair came in to ask if she required anything. She asked him if he thought something could have happened to Henry.

"I shouldn't think so. We'd have had a telephone call, if so," Alistair said. He wasn't worried in the slightest, Edith saw. He seemed glad. She had no idea how Alistair felt about Henry as a person, if he liked working for him, if he stayed only out of loyalty.

Or, for her.

"Have a drink with me," Edith said.

"I had a glass of wine with dinner."

"I know. I was there."

Alistair looked skeptically at the liquor cart.

"I'm sure Henry won't mind," Edith said.

"We did our share of drinking together, during the war."

"There you are, then."

Alistair helped himself to a glass of scotch and sat on the couch with her.

She asked if she could be honest with him about something that was bothering her. He said she should feel free. She said she just discovered that Henry wasn't working on the manuscript he said he'd tackle for her. She suspected he wasn't interested in helping her edit poetry at all, though he said he was.

"Perhaps he'll turn his attention to it soon," Alistair said.

Edith sipped her sherry. She wondered what Miss Brown was doing right then. Working on a new poem or celebrating her book coming out. Did she have a girlfriend? The one she wrote the poems to?

The door opened and a moment later Henry came into the library. His color was high, but he seemed sober. He took in the fact that Alistair and Edith were there together. She asked him where on earth he'd been.

"Devoting myself to your happiness, as always. And to that end, I have a surprise for you," he said, and poured himself a drink, though Alistair offered to.

"I'm not in the mood for a surprise," Edith said.

"Oh, you're going to like this one."

"All right, then."

"I found us a house. In the country. I met with a realtor, and he gave me a quick tour. It's perfect."

"Henry, are you out of your mind?"

Alistair excused himself. He took his drink with him.

"You said you wanted to live in the country," Henry said.

"One day, yes. I didn't mean now."

"This is a beautiful house, darling. You don't have to take my word for it, though. We can drive out tomorrow if you like."

Edith leaned back and closed her eyes. She thought again of the neglected manuscript. She'd just take it off his desk when he was out of the room. He would never notice.

She told him to sit down and tell her all about it. But, had he eaten?

"The realtor and I stopped in a diner," Henry said.

"You, in a diner? What did you order?"

"Meatloaf. It was delicious."

"You'll be an American before you know it."

He sat close to her and brushed her bangs off her forehead. He said she looked tired, and he hoped she wasn't working too hard. She assured him she was fine. Now, what about this house of his?

He said it was set back from the road, on fifteen acres of rolling hills. It was colonial style, very New England, with massive white columns in front. But despite all the formality of the exterior, the previous owners had made the interior homey. There was a large stone fireplace in the living room and built-in bookcases; the master bedroom had those, too, and a porch accessible by a pair of charming French doors. There was a small sitting area that might make a perfect office for her if she wanted it. The whole place was charming. He couldn't wait to show it to her.

"How far away it is?" she asked.

"About an hour's drive."

"Hmm."

"Hmm, what?"

"I'll need my own car, for when I want to come into town."

"Parking on Harvard Square is dreadful, you know that."

"I'll park here and walk over or take a cab. We're still keeping this apartment, aren't we?"

"Yes, of course."

"Well, then. It's all settled," she said.

"About the car, but what about the house?"

They went out the following day under a spectacularly clear, blazing blue sky. Edith told Henry about meeting Mr. Fitzhugh and Miss Brown. She hinted that she knew about the gist of Miss Brown's book all along and looked forward to the challenge of publishing it. She added that publishers had to be daring if they were any good at all. He said she could afford to be daring because she didn't need to make a large profit on the book. True, she said. Its commercial appeal would be low. That's why she'd told Laura—Miss Brown—that there would be a small print run.

"I should like to meet her," Henry said. They were passing a farm where black and white cows grazed happily in the rich grass.

"Laura? Why? Do you want to get up to speed on lesbians?"

"Honestly, Edith. I'm not as cloistered as you might think. We had our share in the Intelligence Branch, you know."

"Then, why?"

"I have a feeling you two will become friends, that's all. And I'd like to know her."

Edith hadn't thought about being Laura's friend. She hadn't had any real friends since she left the mapmaking office. Except for Walter's sister, Kathleen, of course, lost now in the wilds of rural Florida. Laura might be someone she could talk to. She seemed honest and genuine.

The farmland gave way to rolling hills dotted with large homes. This must be where wealthy people from Boston escaped to when the city became too much. Henry would have picked up on that at once. He wouldn't be comfortable if his neighbors weren't of a certain class. He wasn't a snob, he was just used to money, yet during the war, he must have been surrounded by people who didn't have any. She wondered if he'd found that odd. There were so many things she wondered about him, she realized. Mary's warning returned. Edith studied Henry's profile as he drove. She tried to project ten, or even twenty years of age onto his face. He would still be a handsome man if drinking too much didn't ruin him. Mary said he wasn't a good person, yet he was kind. How could one be kind and not a good person at the same time?

"Here we are," Henry said and pulled into a driveway lined with poplar trees. Edith at once found the landscaping fussy and artificial. The aura of fake grandeur extended to the house itself. It was a newer home but built to look as if it had stood there for a century or longer. The porch was small and dark. Based on Henry's description, she had imagined sitting there on summer evenings, having cocktails, talking about which book was coming out next. There was barely enough room for two modest chairs. What had the architect been thinking?

Mr. Lanehurst, the realtor, greeted them enthusiastically and said he was delighted to see Henry again. Edith didn't care for the fact that his palm was clammy, nor for the way he kept looking at his watch as he escorted them into the front hall.

"This way, if you please," Mr. Lanehurst said, as they were led into the living room, which was large and gloomy, and needed the wallpaper removed, and the floors refinished. Edith asked Henry if he'd considered those costs.

"Well, no. I thought I might leave that to you," he said.

"Henry, the store. My time is pretty limited."

"Store?" Mr. Lanehurst asked.

"I own a bookstore on Harvard Square. And I just established a small press to publish works of poetry," Edith said. Even in the shadows, she could read Mr. Lanehurst's expression. He found the idea amusing, almost quaint. She wanted to kick his shin.

"We'll get Alistair to help you," Henry said. Then, to Mr. Lanehurst, "That's my man. Came over with me last year. A true whiz at just about everything."

"Wonderful."

They went on, room to room. The house did have charm, particularly the rooms at the back, with southern exposure and a view of a long, sloping lawn. Edith asked Mr. Lanehurst if he thought flowers would do well there, and he said he thought they would.

"We'll hire the best landscaper we can find," Henry said.

"Oh, we don't need a landscaper, Henry. I have some ideas of my own," Edith said.

"I thought you were too busy."

"Not to plan a garden."

"Oh, Edith. You're so charmingly inconsistent!"

Edith allowed Henry to take her arm and they followed Mr. Lanehurst up the winding staircase into the master bedroom. There, she understood why Henry had fallen in love with the house. The natural light poured in. The window seats made the oversized room cozy and approachable. The built-in bookcases rose to the ceiling on either side of the fireplace. This was a special place, she could tell. A place where the only mood that could settle on one's soul was quiet contentment. She could see herself hiding out there with her books. But she would need an office, too, and she raised this with Mr. Lanehurst, who looked quizzically at Henry, who said, "That's right, an office."

"Well, we do have a lovely wood-paneled room downstairs behind the dining room, but I assumed you would want it for yourself. Of course, it could be redecorated, with some cheerful floral wallpaper, or whatever the lady's taste required."

Edith asked to take a look at it, and Mr. Lanehurst led them out of the room and down the stairs. The study gave onto the back yard, where a deer and fawn now stood, helping themselves to the leaves of a low hedge that hadn't been trimmed recently. Mr. Lanehurst saw them, too, and tapped angrily on the glass to scare them off. Edith asked him to stop. The deer weren't bothering anyone.

"Oh, I'm afraid you'll soon see what a nuisance they can be. This area is full of them. We're trying to pass an ordinance to allow hunting."

"Of the deer? Whatever for?"

"Dear, Mr. Lanehurst just explained. There are too many of them, and I should imagine the local predators don't succeed in thinning their ranks," Henry said.

"Precisely," said Mr. Lanehurst.

The study was dreary, and Edith couldn't imagine anything she could do would improve it. She asked about the room upstairs which she'd admired on their way down the hall. It wasn't large, but it was sunny, on a corner, and just generally seemed like a cheerful place.

"I thought you'd use that for a nursery," Mr. Lanehurst said.

"Oh, we won't need a nursery," Edith said.

"Won't we?" Henry asked.

Mr. Lanehurst directed Henry's attention to the crown molding, and to the box beam ceiling which carried over into the dining room and kitchen. Henry wanted to take a closer look at the kitchen, and the two went there, leaving Edith alone to stare out the window where the doe and fawn had resisted Mr. Lanehurst's efforts to drive them off.

Of course, Henry would want children. Hadn't Alistair described his disappointment that Mary didn't? Why hadn't Henry raised this before? He simply assumed that Edith felt the way he did. Here was another crucial point they hadn't discussed.

Edith snapped open her purse and got out a cigarette. She smoked for a few minutes, then couldn't find an ashtray. She opened the door from the study that led to a small, useless patio that wasn't big enough for anything except a couple of potted shrubs and tapped the ash onto the grass beyond. The breeze rose, bringing a sweet, earthy smell with a touch of something else, the coming season, she thought. There was an impression of dampness and decay. She imagined the stand of elms in the distance bared of leaves, Henry reading a book by the fire, and her handing him another drink. The wind might rise, and Henry would remark that the winter ahead promised to be colder than usual, a record snowfall was predicted, too, but there they were, safe and snug in their new country home.

The door closed quietly behind her, nudged by the wind. She turned the handle, and nothing happened. She walked along the outside of the house, looking for the kitchen, which she found a moment later. She peered through a window. The kitchen was empty. She banged pointlessly on the glass, dropped her cigarette on the grass, crushed it with her shoe, and continued her progress around the side of the house where there was another patio outside a pair of French doors. She tried both handles, and again, nothing happened. What she hoped to enter appeared to be the dining room, judging from the large chandelier hanging from the ceiling. Like the kitchen, it was vacant. Where the hell had they gone? Her next stop was the front door where she rang the bell twice and got silence for her answer.

A window on an upper floor opened, and Henry leaned out of it.

"What on earth are you doing down there?" he asked.

"I got locked out."

"We're in the attic. It's a marvelous space. I have an idea of converting it into a game room. Why don't you come up and take a look?"

"Because all the Goddamned doors in the house are locked!"

Henry brought his finger to his lips to say she should refrain from using that sort of language.

"If you don't come down here this instant and let me in, I'm going to go wait in the car," she said.

A few minutes later the front door opened, and Henry emerged. He wiped the dust from his hands and the front of his jacket. He said the attic was finished. The owners had had the idea to use it for something, and he did think a game room would be splendid up there. Pool, billiards, something like that. Edith said it would be impossibly hot in the summer months, and Henry paused to consider her remark. He agreed. Well, then they could build an addition in the back and put the game room there. Or anywhere she wanted.

"I don't care about a game room, Henry. All I want is a pleasant home with a room of my own to work in when I need to. And I think we need to discuss the issue of having children."

Henry looked through the open door to see if Mr. Lanehurst were behind him. He wasn't.

"On the way home, dearest, not now," he said.

Mr. Lanehurst joined them on the porch. He said he hoped they had enjoyed seeing the house, and he was available for them any time.

"You'll hear from me within the week," Henry said.

"Don't wait too long. There's been a lot of interest in this one already," Mr. Lanehurst said. The men shook hands. Edith smiled her best smile.

Henry asked if she wanted to stop for a drink on the way back to Boston. He'd passed a charming little place the other day. Paul Revere's Run, he thought it was called. She said that sounded lovely.

The tavern was in a historic house with genuine period detailing, like wood beams around the windows, unlike the place they just saw. The wide planked wood floor was uneven, and Henry took Edith's arm. They were shown to a quiet table by a window where the leaves of a tall oak tree dappled the light and gave a dreamy, calming effect, soon enhanced by a well-mixed, dry martini. She apologized for her earlier outburst, but it was so alarming to realize that she'd been locked out, especially when she had no idea where they'd gotten off to.

"You were gone for so long, we just decided to go up and view the attic. We'd seen everything else," Henry said.

Edith said she was certain she wasn't outside all that long, and in any case, it didn't matter. She wanted to talk about his expectations where children were concerned. She wanted there to be no misunderstanding.

"All right," he said, then waited for her to continue. Suddenly, she had no idea what to say. Then, after a moment, she promised not to rule anything out, but she didn't want to become a mother before she was thirty. She knew that sounded radical. Her mother had dropped a hint or two about her advancing age, but honestly, there was just so much on her plate right now, how could she—they—possibly manage a child?

"People do it, darling. They hire nannies," Henry said.

"Well, nannies aren't the ones having it, are they?"

"No."

He asked if she were afraid of the idea from a physical standpoint. Again, she didn't know what to say. Children were something that had never been on her radar. When Walter vaguely raised the issue, she shot him down, finding it absurd. It was as if she put it in a corner of herself, shut the door, and tossed out the key. She was afraid. Who wouldn't be? The whole idea was monstrous. Something growing inside of you, like a parasite.

"I don't think I have much of a maternal instinct," Edith said.

"You might find you do, in time. We can wait and see how you feel about it after we're married."

"Yes."

"And speaking of marriage, I have another surprise for you."

He pulled a letter out of the pocket of his jacket. Edith could see at once that it was airmail stationery.

"It's all gone through. I'm a free man," he said.

"The divorce?"

"The divorce."

She touched his glass with hers. Then she asked if he weren't the least bit sad.

"Why should I be?" he asked.

"You were together a long time. Longer than Walter and I were."

"Yes, but I knew, also for a long time, that we were mismatched. I hoped otherwise, and I think she did, too, but here we are."

Edith wondered what Mary was feeling. Relief? Regret? Was there someone in her life now? She hadn't been on her own all that long, and that thought caused a deeper reflection. This time a year ago, Edith hadn't even been back in Cambridge for a month and was missing her brief but wonderful life in New York every single day. And here she was, with her store, her new press, manuscripts to publish, and a new house to buy—unless she could persuade Henry to look at something more to her liking, which she thought would be no trouble. He was always so eager to please her.

"Well, congratulations," she said.

"Let's get married."

"We are."

"I mean now."

"What?"

"As soon as we can. After the blood tests."

"What happened to June?"

"It's too far off."

"Henry, you're mad."

She told him to take just a moment and think. If they married now, no one they cared for could come. He said the only people he cared about attending were his parents, and they already said they wouldn't make the trip over. His mother was too frail for that kind of long-distance travel. He asked who she wanted to have present. She said her mother and Betty. She'd also like to have Aunt Margaret. Henry would love Aunt Margaret, he really would, then she explained again that she was Walter's aunt, not hers, but that she was closer to Edith than she was to Walter. Walter couldn't stand her, which Edith always found odd because she was marvelous.

She stopped talking. He regarded her with a blend of humor and curiosity.

He said he would like to make her acquaintance. Then he said they should discuss the honeymoon, and she said she assumed the lovely trip they just took was that, only in reverse order. He said it was nothing of the kind, and he wanted to give her a real one, wherever she wanted to go.

"Henry, I don't want to go anywhere, I'm fine where I am," she said.

A look of frustration settled on him then.

"Because of the bookstore, I assume," he said.

"No, because we were just away for a long time, and I'm home now and want to settle in. In a year or two, when we're feeling stale again."

She realized her mistake. Henry always felt on the verge of staleness, or, at least, dreadful boredom.

But he let it go and asked if she wanted another cocktail, or if they should be on their way. Edith checked her watch. It was only a little after two. She said they were in no rush. They were free to linger. Henry signaled the waiter.

As she enjoyed her fresh drink, Edith contemplated the idea of an earlier wedding. Part of her just wanted to get it over with, though of course the way she put it was to praise Henry's cleverness in pointing out the many months they'd have to wait otherwise. It was September then. What about around Christmas? Henry considered for a moment, and said that time of year should be devoted to itself, did she see his point?

"Yes, of course!"

He said he always loved October, particulary the end of October, when Halloween drew near. Would there be enough time to summon Edith's people if they set a date four weeks from then?

"I will write to everyone immediately. And it won't be any trouble to line up a judge by then."

"Aren't we to be married in a church?"

"Oh, I don't think so."

Henry looked put out. She asked him what kind of church, since she had no idea what his religious preferences were.

"Darling, I should have thought that would have been obvious to you. I'm English. We'll find an Episcopalian church in Boston. The Catholics can't possibly have the whole town sewn up."

"Henry, I don't want to be married in a church."

"Weren't you, before?"

"No. We went to the courthouse."

"Goodness. Well, no wonder things didn't work out between you. Not an auspicious beginning."

Edith's face grew warm.

"I'm joking, sweetheart. And if you don't want a church, we'll forgo that."

"No, a church is fine."

He brightened. He was sure she'd find it quite suitable. A serious, holy atmosphere was what a wedding needed.

"And afterward? What about the reception?" she asked.

"We can have it at the apartment. We'll hire a caterer. Alistair won't be able to handle everything on his own."

"No, of course not."

She sank under the thought of all that work. She'd have to be involved, because the caterer would need direction. Of course, her mother and Aunt Margaret would help. They'd offer without needing to be asked.

Edith asked if there were anyone from his club he'd care to invite, or perhaps a former professor. He said he would give it some thought. She said she'd need to ask Patricia Wilkins and the other staff, Jocelyn, and Liza.

"Well, it will be a bevy of females, won't it? Alistair will be delighted," Henry said.

"Oh, I shouldn't think any of them would catch his eye."

Henry lit a cigarette, put his lighter on the table, and spun it one way, then the other.

"I know what he said to you when we were abroad," Henry said.

"Who?"

"Alistair, of course."

"I don't know what you're talking about."

"Darling, relax. He told me everything. He wanted there to be no misunderstanding about anything, and to reassure me that his behavior toward you would always be honorable."

Was there no end to the things people did and said behind her back? Irritation made her face even hotter.

"Did you want him not to tell me?" Henry asked.

"I had already decided I wouldn't tell you, and assumed based on that, he wouldn't either."

"Alistair is his own man, regardless of what you choose to divulge, or not, in this case. He simply felt he owed me an explanation."

"Does it bother you that I said nothing?"

"Yes. But I understand, I think. You were protecting him, the long relationship he and I have had. You wanted to preserve that."

"In a nutshell."

Edith asked if she could have just one more cocktail before they went on their way. Henry said of course, nothing would give him greater pleasure than to go on sitting there with her, improving their understanding of each other. She asked if he were being cynical, and he said no, not in the least. Edith excused herself for a moment. As she washed her hands in the lavatory, she took in her reflection. She looked like a silly young woman whose hat was slightly askew. She removed it and got out her comb from her purse. Her black hair was often a subject of curiosity between her parents since neither of them had it. Edith could see her father accusing her mother of infidelity based on that alone. But then, his ego wouldn't have allowed him to suspect her of cheating on him. Edith's skin was what some called porcelain. When she was young, she always admired ruddy-cheeked, healthy girls. She was healthy, too, of course, but people tended to impute frailty because she was so fair. Yet, it was a winning combination. She was a pretty woman, even beautiful, though it was hard for her to see that. She focused always on the length of her nose, which she felt was too long, and the blue of her eyes which was never blue enough. If her ego were sturdy, she would say she was glorious. Then Alistair's declaration would have made perfect sense.

But it did, regardless of how she felt about herself. He was a giving person, whose heart yearned for an anchor. In many ways, he was even kinder than Henry was, though it made her feel disloyal to think so. Henry wanted something in return for his generosity, even if he said he didn't. Alistair gave openly and unconditionally. She had no idea what he saw in her below the surface, any more than she could fathom Henry's attachment to her. In many ways, she was just an ordinary fool.

Henry was unhappy when she returned. He said she'd taken a surprisingly long time, so long in fact that he wondered if he should ask the waiter to have someone go and check on her. She said she was sure he was exaggerating. But in any case, here she was, fresh as a daisy and ready to resume whatever they were talking about.

"We were talking about Alistair," Henry said.

"No, I think we finished discussing him. I think we were talking about the wedding."

"We'd moved on from that, too."

"Then, let's return to it. We can't possibly have it so soon. We'll have to wait until spring. I'm sorry."

"Don't be. You're right, as always. I was just excited at the thought of bringing it closer."

"We'll have time to do it right. I promise," Edith said. They touched glasses.

Later, they would argue about the accident. Henry would admit that he shouldn't have had that third cocktail but would cite the dropping afternoon light as the reason he didn't see the deer dash in front of the car. Edith would say more than once that she'd warned him. She saw the poor creature in the corner of her eye. Henry managed to slow the car and swerve enough to avoid hitting it head-on, but the deer seemed to have broken at least one of its back legs. It lay piteously in the road, staring wildly, shoving its tongue pointlessly into the air. The driver behind them stopped and asked if they were all right. He said he would go to a gas station and call the police. Henry didn't want to wait for the police; Edith said they must, and anyway, the man might have made note of their license plate number. Henry confided that he was thinking of what to say to convince the officer that he wasn't drunk or even impaired but there was no need. The officer was a young man who looked at the deer, then shot it in the head with his revolver. He used the radio in his car to call his precinct and ask them to send a truck to remove the carcass from the road. He didn't ask anything of Henry and Edith except their names and address, which he took a long time to write in his notebook. He said deer were always causing havoc for local drivers, though it was a shame that this one had had to suffer as much as it had. Henry drove slowly and carefully back to Cambridge, where Alistair greeted them as always and listened to Henry tell the story of the menacing deer. He could see that Edith was shaken and offered her a drink. She said she'd had enough. Later, in bed, she wished she'd accepted, because it might have blotted out the image of the deer's eyes as it stared at nothing, waiting to die.

Chapter Nine

Henry stopped getting up in the morning when Edith did. He stayed in bed until ten or eleven o'clock, then spent several hours in his robe, reading and drinking coffee in the library. After that, he dressed and went to his club. Alistair passed her this intelligence when she came home from The Turned Page, where she arrived every day an hour before it opened. He didn't follow through on the house, which both surprised and disappointed her. When she asked him about it, he said he agreed with her concerns about its distance from Boston, and that they should take the matter up again in the spring.

He blamed the event with the deer for his growing malaise. He promised to pull out of it soon. She threw herself into the press and the launch of Laura Brown's volume. She sent the manuscript to the printer after making only a few changes to it. The printer, Mr. Granger, called to ask about the frontispiece. Edith said she'd get her designer right on it. Mr. Granger then said he was taking a risk bringing out that kind of book, and he hoped she knew what she was doing. She told him she was shocked at his suggestion. This was a beautiful book about the glories of nature.

At the store, Edith told Jocelyn she had another project for her if she were interested. They needed a graphic for the press, something simple, something literal. Could she draw a simple hedgerow from the perspective of someone standing at one, looking down its length, seeing it run to a natural vanishing point? Jocelyn said she could try. Then she gave Edith what she'd worked on for the dust jacket. Her sketch showed an abstract rose garden below gentle drifting clouds. These were contrasted by the title in heavy, capital letters. Since Miss Brown hadn't been able to come up with much in the way of suggestions, Edith let Jocelyn read the manuscript for herself. She didn't comment on the content except to say it was different from what she usually read. Edith admired her tact and discretion.

That exchange was cause for much glee when Laura Brown came to the apartment with her friend, Fiona, to drink champagne and gorge on Alistair's wonderful sandwiches. Edith showed Laura the dust jacket the printer had run off. Fiona said she hadn't known until then what the title was. Laura explained they debated a different title and felt that in the end *You, Forever,* was best. When she said so, Fiona blushed. Edith felt awkward witnessing their private moment.

Both Fiona and Laura were in slacks and button-down shirts and jackets. Fiona had embellished hers with a brooch on the lapel, which Aunt Margaret admired. Aunt Margaret had come to Boston specifically for the party, though Edith hadn't expressly invited her. In a recent letter, she'd mentioned that Laura's book was coming out soon and hoped to have a small celebration, and Aunt Margaret wrote back at once to say she was bored out of her wits and could use an excuse to travel. She arrived directly from the train station in a cloud of perfume, having sent her bags on to the Copley Plaza, though Edith said she was welcome to stay with them.

Henry enjoyed being the host. He was gracious to Aunt Margaret, overly polite to Laura and Fiona, and affectionate with Edith, standing often with his arm about her waist or shoulder in a way she soon found cloying. He told Laura how much he enjoyed her book, then asked Fiona to tell him all about her job teaching at Boston University.

Edith was delighted to be with Aunt Margaret again, and the two soon found themselves in a long conversation about Edith's few months in New York and all the things she missed about living there. Aunt Margaret had had several glasses of champagne at that point, which rather than slowing her down, invigorated her.

"I must tell you about Francine's boy," she told Edith. Francine was Aunt Margaret's closest friend. Edith knew sooner or later the topic of Philip—Francine's son—would come up. He and Edith had had a brief, riotous affair, which Edith was sure Aunt Margaret had guessed about or at least strongly suspected. Not a day had gone by when he hadn't crossed Edith's mind, since he was the only man in her life who had aroused such physical passion in her. Even Henry didn't come close. Thinking of it then, she blushed. She hoped anyone seeing that would suspect alcohol was the cause.

The simple truth was he'd gotten some girl pregnant, Aunt Margaret said.

"The girl he was engaged to?" Edith asked. Aunt Margaret had kept Edith informed of his doings, courtesy of Francine, who complained about him often.

"Heavens, no. They broke that off."

"Really, why?"

"Oh, the usual reason, one of them got cold feet. Anyway, Francine was delighted. The girl wasn't right for him, even I could see that."

Aunt Margaret helped herself to another small sandwich Alistair offered her. He then brought the tray near enough for Edith to take one, too, but she passed. Across the room, Henry laughed at something Laura had just said. She had her arm looped through his, and Edith wondered if the champagne were getting the better of her.

Edith asked what she was like, the girl to whom Philip had been engaged. Aunt Margaret said she wasn't much, a secretary in an advertising agency, she thought, college-educated, of course, and big-boned. Francine was surprised that he was attracted to a heavy-set girl. Anyway, the girl he got in trouble was someone else, someone he met at the home of a friend, according to Francine. The girl confronted him, and he accepted responsibility.

"He was sure it was his?" Edith asked.

"He told Francine it was her first time."

"Good lord."

"Precisely."

"So, what happens now?"

Aunt Margaret said that Francine was in a dreadful way. She hadn't felt right about leaving her, but here was Edith and her poetry press, and well, one must go on celebrating the good things in life, mustn't one? In any case, money had been offered, and there was even talk of finding a doctor, but the girl wouldn't hear of it. She was going to have the child with or without Philip's involvement.

"But, what about her parents?" Edith asked.

"The poor thing is an orphan, apparently."

"Ah."

Edith smelled a rat. This girl wanted to rope Philip into marrying her. She might not even be pregnant. Philip should insist on seeing a doctor's report before he did anything foolish, but before she could suggest this, Aunt Margaret said they planned to marry and that was that.

"What? I can't believe it," Edith said.

"He seems to have fallen in love."

She could feel Aunt Margaret watching her closely. Edith fumed. If Philip had persisted with her the way he promised to when she returned to Boston, she might be the one getting ready to walk down the aisle with him, not this scheming floozy he found God knows where.

Had she wanted to marry him? Was that it? They'd known each other only for a few days, yet here she was, thinking about it. Of course, at the time she was still married to Walter, which had been inconvenient, to say the least.

Afternoon became evening. Alistair provided more food. They switched from champagne to hard liquor. Henry didn't hold his as well as he usually did and turned sullen and withdrawn. Fiona, Laura, Aunt Margaret, and Alistair played bridge at a card table Alistair had set up. Edith and Henry stood apart. She thanked him for being so cordial and gallant with everyone and asked if he'd had enough to eat.

"If that's your quaint way of suggesting I should balance out the liquor, why don't you just say so?" he asked. He spoke quietly, and Edith wasn't certain she heard him correctly. The light in his eye said she had.

"What's the matter with you?" she asked.

"Nothing's the matter with me. Nothing at all. Only I don't like being made a fool of."

"How have you been made a fool?"

"You have these people here on the pretense of celebrating your stupid press, but it's just to prove how much contempt you have for me."

Edith put her glass on the windowsill and went into her room, hoping no one else would notice her departure. She sat on the bed and calmed herself by breathing deeply. She would fake a terrible headache and ask everyone to excuse her. Then they'd all take the hint and be on their way. But she wouldn't have to, because just then Henry could be heard telling them all to get out.

She returned to the living room to find everyone still at the card table.

"I'm sorry, but you will all have to leave now. Edith isn't well," Henry said.

"I'm perfectly well."

Everyone stood up and organized themselves. Alistair tried to escort Henry down the hall to his room, and Henry told him to get his hands off. Aunt Margaret put her mouth to Edith's ear and told her not to worry, even the best people sometimes overdid it. She promised to call her tomorrow. Fiona and Laura thanked her so much for having them, and Laura promised to be in touch. Edith saw them out, hoping Henry wouldn't follow her, then realized Alistair was there to prevent him if he tried.

Edith returned to the living room where Henry sat with his head in his hands, weeping. Alistair's eye met hers with an apology it wasn't his to make. Then Edith told Henry he needed to get to bed. To her surprise, he didn't argue or resist when Alistair helped him up from his chair. Edith asked if she were needed and Alistair thanked her and said no, he had everything under control.

Edith went into the kitchen and ate one of the leftover sandwiches. It was roast beef with a light touch of horseradish. She had a large drink of water, then refilled the glass and swallowed two aspirin tablets from the bottle Alistair kept in the cabinet over the sink.

When Alistair finally joined her, carrying in the last dishes from the party, she was seated at the table, smoking a cigarette.

"How is he?" Edith asked.

"Almost asleep."

"What the hell happened in there? Why did he blow up like that?"

"He reached a tipping point, that's all."

"You don't sound surprised."

"I'm afraid I'm not."

"I assume that means he's done this before."

"Yes."

Edith asked him to go into detail. She wasn't going anywhere. Maybe they should put on a pot of coffee? Alistair nodded and didn't budge. Edith stood up and got it going. She told him to take a load off his feet. He looked all in.

It started after his brother died, Alistair said. The whole family came undone, but Lady Alice and Lord Gerald recovered themselves quickly enough. Lord Henry had a harder time. It seemed to run so much deeper in him because he was still a child. He grew out of it yet there were difficult episodes of hiding himself away, not wanting to see anyone, even at school. Letters were sent home from the headmaster suggesting a different environment. Other schools were tried. At Eton, he developed an interest in literature, a passion really, which he continued at Oxford. Things seemed well at last. He met and married Mary, which had a further stabilizing effect, though from what he could glean from Mary's demeanor and carefully chosen words, there were occasional periods of melancholy. Some of them turned physical. Mary had a bruised eye she said was the fault of a door she hadn't seen in the dark. Alistair never saw another bruise on her, so he gathered it didn't happen again.

Then came the war. Henry was talented at intelligence work. He was given purpose, and he found himself. In many ways, he was a different man. Afterward, settling back into civilian life was hard, but both Alistair and Mary smoothed the transition, or so he thought. His late brother's birthday came, and Lady Alice wished to commemorate the event. There was to be a family tea. It would have been the brother's thirtieth birthday. Henry said he couldn't attend because he was ill. Everyone assumed he meant physically. When it was clear the trouble was in his mind, his doctor turned the matter over to a good psychiatrist who kept Henry mildly sedated. Poor Lady

Mary was nearly frantic, seeing the loss of the man she married. But His Lordship pulled through. Of course, it left a mark on him. How couldn't it? Losing oneself that way, unable to swim back to shore, as it were, must have been devasting. But then Lord Henry lost ground again and it was suggested he continue with his education. Hence, the application to Harvard.

"I always wondered why he didn't study in England," Edith said.

"Mary thought a complete change of scene would do him good."

"Only she didn't take to Yankee life."

"No, clearly not."

Edith poured out their coffee. She added a large amount of cream and sugar to hers. The clock on the wall ticked. Otherwise, the apartment was silent.

"How long do these things last?" she asked.

"Months, sometimes."

He was so strong when she was falling apart, moping around the apartment, feeling sorry for herself because Walter was being a fool about everything. Without that strength, where would she be now?

"Things seemed fine. What changed?" she asked.

"It's hard for His Lordship to have those close to him distracted," Alistair set.

"I'm not distracted. I'm focused."

"Yes, but not on him."

The light in the kitchen hurt her eyes, and she realized again how late it was. She wanted to crawl into bed and wake up somewhere else.

The man she'd met last year had been urbane, gracious, witty, and kind; also gentle, sweet, loving, passionate, the list went on. There had never been the smallest suggestion of instability. He was seldom roused to anger. But as soon as she agreed to marry him, his behavior changed. She saw that his need for stimulation, not just from alcohol, had grown. Her role had changed, too. Walter's choice of law as a profession meant he needed a certain kind of wife; Henry's indolence required the same thing.

She put her coffee cup on the table.

"I can't do it," she said.

Alistair raised his eyes.

"I can't be his nursemaid. I simply can't," she said.

"It's a lot to contend with, to be sure."

Edith stood and rinsed her cup and saucer. She put them in the dish rack. She thought of Laura and Fiona and wondered what they'd made of Henry. He'd embarrassed her on purpose. He may not have known he was doing it, but the result was the same. Thank God Aunt Margaret had taken it in stride, but then she was a wise old soul, underneath her furs and jewelry.

"What happens now?" Edith asked.

"We wait."

"For how long?"

"For however long it takes."

Edith imagined the telephone calls she would have to make in the morning, apologizing for Henry, saying he'd had too much to drink. He was just celebrating her success and got carried away. He was still fatigued from their trip abroad, that was it. Edith realized she'd fool no one with that last excuse.

They'd been home for weeks, and Henry wasn't a frail man. Not frail physically, at any rate.

Every day when she came home, what would she find? Henry's demeanor would rule everything and determine everything.

The apartment she had come to love with its tall windows, view of the river, high ceilings, and warm wood floors, now felt oppressive.

"Has he ever had to be put away?" she asked.

"Once."

"Good lord."

"Before the war. Mary arranged it. He locked himself in his study and was threatening to turn his gun on himself."

Alistair brought his cup to the sink. He kissed her on the cheek, then apologized for taking the liberty and hoped she didn't think he was trying to take advantage of the situation.

"Not at all. You're just upset. It's an upsetting thing, seeing someone lose his marbles like that."

Henry was in the doorway to the kitchen, the tie of his bathrobe pulled tight across his slim waist. He'd run a comb through his hair. His eyes were hollow.

"Milord," Alistair said.

"Sit down," Edith said.

"No, thank you. I heard voices and came to see, that's all." He turned and left. Alistair and Edith both stood. Neither of them moved, then Edith said she'd go.

She found Henry in the living room. They sat on the couch.

"You need help, Henry. We'll find you a doctor, a good one," Edith said.

"Many have tried."

"Not American ones."

"I admire your loyalty to your country."

"Admire nothing, except our ability to speak plainly."

She told him to go to bed now, and not bother her until morning. She needed to rest, and he did, too. In the morning things would look a bit brighter.

"You won't come to me?" he asked.

"No, not tonight."

She took him to his room and tucked him into bed. Then she went to her room and locked the door.

Sleep dropped quickly and hard. As she reckoned the hour from the morning's rising light, she thought it odd that she could fall into the heaviest slumber when her mind was most troubled. It was no longer troubled, though she felt bad for Henry, alone in his room, perhaps also awake, fearing the hours ahead, and the gradual loss of himself to their whim.

Alistair would keep a lid on things while she was at the bookstore, and once there, she combed through the telephone directory and made several calls until she reached one man who sounded both gentle and firm. Dr. Brannick promised to call on Henry today and Edith said she would alert their butler to expect him. He told Edith not to worry, he'd had a lot of experience with this kind of thing, especially with former soldiers, and the fact that Henry had means guaranteed he would receive the best care. There was one place he thought was first-rate. Edith said she would do her best to be present when the doctor arrived, and he assured her it wasn't necessary. It was often preferable to have the patient on his own so there would be no inclination to falsify his responses.

"But why would he lie just because I'm there?" Edith asked.

"Hasn't he lied already, by not making clear the history of his affliction?"

Edith said she understood, and after giving the doctor their address and home telephone number, offered her heartfelt thanks.

She called Laura and apologized for Henry's behavior. Laura said not to worry, her old man was usually stinking, so she knew the type inside and out. She said she'd still enjoyed the evening and got a kick out of Aunt Margaret.

"She's a sassy old lady," Laura said.

"She is."

They agreed to talk again soon.

Next, she phoned Aunt Margaret and was told no calls were to be put through before noon. When they lived together in New York, she seldom rose before then. Edith was surprised that she'd forgotten. She gave the clerk the number of the bookstore, and asked that Aunt Margaret try her there.

The last call she made was to Robert Nedleman. He answered on the seventh ring, just as she was putting the receiver back in its cradle.

"Nedleman," he said.

"This is Edith Sloan."

"Hi. What's up?"

Edith asked if he'd gotten the publishing contract in the mail. He said he had. Hadn't he returned it to her? She said he hadn't.

"Oh. Well, sorry about that. It was nice and tight, by the way, despite it being your first time. The second time, actually."

"I had a lawyer put it together."

"I figured. Lots of big words. Who was it?"

"A man named Sturgis. He helped me purchase the bookstore. Why?"

"No reason. Just curious."

He said he'd get it in the mail that afternoon. She said when she had it, she'd go over his manuscript and get suggested edits to him by the third week of December.

"Just in time for Christmas," he said.

"Oh, I hadn't thought about that, but you're right."

"When's it coming out? The contract was vague. Just said something about you having up to two years if I recall correctly."

"I was thinking shortly after the new year."

"1950. It's strange to think about, isn't it?" he asked.

"It is."

She asked if he had any questions for her and he said he hadn't. She promised to be in touch.

She smoked a cigarette, made a small pot of tea, tried to edit Nedleman's manuscript, and couldn't. She wandered out into the store. There were about ten customers, a healthy number. Jocelyn approached and said someone had complained that *Cry the Beloved Country* was sold out. Edith asked if Jocelyn had explained that it was on backorder. She had, but the customer was taking the train out to California next week and had been looking forward to having it for the trip.

"There are a million books in the world to choose from, and she has to hang her hat on that one?" Edith asked.

"He. Evidently."

Edith asked how she was coming along with the hedgerow design. Jocelyn took a folded-up piece of paper from a shelf by the register and gave it to Edith. It was a pen drawing of the perspective Edith had suggested.

"I can see that running up the spine of a book, can't you?" Edith asked.

"Absolutely."

Edith said Miss Brown loved the dust jacket and realized that Jocelyn hadn't seen it yet. She took her into the office and showed it to her. Jocelyn spread it open with both hands and said the pale green background worked perfectly. She'd worried about that. It was exciting to think her artwork would be seen by people who didn't know her. Edith said if she wanted to consider doing more designs that would be wonderful. They could even talk about an appropriate payment. Jocelyn paused. The prospect suddenly seemed more serious than it had been before, and Edith could see her struggling with identifying herself as a book designer.

"Maybe it wouldn't interfere with school too much," she said.

"You'll be graduating in the spring if I'm not mistaken. I might be able to take you on part-time then, and you could keep working here part-time."

Jocelyn's future again seemed to float across her mind. She had a boyfriend and sooner or later he was bound to propose. Since the war, these proposals tended to come on the eve of graduation or right after. Being married was another impediment to a career.

They agreed to talk more about it later.

Edith called the apartment to see how Henry was doing. Alistair said he'd had his breakfast, dressed, and taken himself out for a walk. Edith explained the doctor was coming that afternoon. What would they do if Henry didn't return? Alistair said he found it unlikely that His Lordship would simply take flight. He'd get hungry, or want a drink, and like a pigeon, find his way home. Edith took a moment to consider that she'd never heard Alistair speak disrespectfully about Henry before. Then he said he thought he heard His Lordship just then, so he had better sign off. Edith said she would be home early to get the doctor's report.

Aunt Margaret called to see if she were free for dinner. When Edith said she wasn't, Aunt Margaret said it was no trouble at all because her old friend, Mabel, surely, she'd mentioned her, was delighted to learn she was in town and insisted on having her over. Aunt Margaret had told Mable that tomorrow would work, but she'd call her right back and ask if she could come today. Edith explained about Henry and the doctor. Aunt Margaret was quiet for a moment, considering this.

"Well, heavy drinkers often fall apart after a while, though it's surprising in his case. He's still a young man," Aunt Margaret said. She told Edith not to worry, things had a way of working themselves out.

When Liza arrived at three, Edith left. The day was spectacular, full of fiery autumn light. She walked briskly, even as she longed to linger on the banks of the Charles and drink in the sounds of the river. Scullers were out, and she envied them their focus and drive. She shouldn't have left Henry alone today but stayed to hold his hand, bring him tea, ask him to further open his heart to her, and reassure him she would stand by him, no matter what.

She unlocked the apartment door and entered an atmosphere of heavy silence. Not even the kitchen clock made its presence known. Voices drifted up the hall from Henry's room. She put her purse on the desk in her office and went there. Henry was in bed, sitting up, in a clean robe. Alistair was pouring coffee from a pot he'd taken from a tray on the table by the bed. In the chair at the end of the bed sat a middle-aged man with rimless glasses who introduced himself as Dr. Brannick.

"There you are, darling," Henry said. His voice was odd. Thick, slow, and too bright sounding. Edith wondered if he were drugged. Alistair asked Edith if she cared for coffee, and she said later. She took the second chair, next to where the doctor sat, and Alistair left them alone. Edith wished he'd stay. She sensed something awful.

"I've been telling His Lordship about Elm Meadows," Dr. Brannick said.

"That's a sanatorium?" Edith asked.

"One of the best in the entire state."

"Located where?"

"Near Pittsfield."

"That's quite a distance."

"Yes, about one hundred and fifty miles."

Edith watched Henry hold his coffee cup without drinking from it. His eyes were glassy. She said it sounded lovely. She wondered if Henry would excuse them for just a moment, she wanted to speak to the doctor in private, if he didn't mind. Henry said that was perfectly fine.

Edith and the doctor went into the living room where Edith helped herself to sherry. She offered one to the doctor and he accepted.

"What's wrong with him?" Edith asked.

"Deep melancholia."

"You mean, he's sad?"

"It's more than sad. It's a state of despair we see all too often, I'm afraid."

"How will you treat it?"

"Rest, relaxation. We'll keep him calm, but lucid."

"With medication?"

"Yes. And shock therapy if we must."

Edith sat down. She said she didn't want that. The doctor said he understood her concern. It tended to sound worse than it was.

"How could it sound any worse?" Edith asked.

"There is an emerging treatment where we induce a state of shock by administering insulin. This brings on a seizure and seems to help the brain sort itself out."

Edith raised her hand to say she didn't want to hear any more.

"How long will he have to be there?" she asked.

"My colleague, Dr. Harris, can speak to you about that. He's on staff at Elm Meadows, and I'll be transferring His Lordship's care over to him. But, from my own experience, some patients improve quickly, and others take more time. I'd say in His Lordship's case, we might expect a minimum of several months."

"Can I come to visit?"

"We encourage it."

Alistair passed along the hall and returned carrying the coffee tray. He put his head into the living room and asked if either the doctor or Edith required anything. Edith said they didn't. Alistair went on his way. Edith told the doctor it all seemed to have happened suddenly. She still hadn't gotten her mind around the whole thing.

"I understand you've recently become engaged," the doctor said.

"Yes."

"And that his former wife returned to England last winter."

"That's correct. Are you saying there's some connection between these events and Henry's . . . ailment?"

"To some extent, I think."

Edith asked the doctor if the problem were that Henry didn't want to marry her and felt he must follow through, regardless. The doctor thought, sipped his sherry, played with his tie pin, then said no, he didn't think so. Of course, the prospect of a new marriage brought a certain degree of pressure, but he suspected that Henry's troubles were much more long-standing.

"That's what Alistair said," Edith said.

"The butler? Yes, he seems quite a perceptive man."

"They've been together a long time."

Edith closed her eyes for a moment. Poor Henry, putting a brave face on things, hoping he would be all right.

"I wish I'd known," Edith said.

"Would you have refused his proposal, if you had?"

"That's a very direct question."

"Forgive me. It's my psychiatric training."

"I don't know if I would have. I certainly don't want to be married to an invalid. That might sound harsh, but my life's not been easy. My father was a terrible person, who was caught in the grip of agonizing despair. My first husband lacked confidence and fell into sour moods quite often, too. I suppose I was so used to these traits in men that I didn't pick up on them right away in Henry. Or, at least the slightest hint of them didn't strike me as odd. Do you think that's plausible?"

"Completely."

They didn't speak. Alistair could be heard going along the hall again. Then he was in the room.

"He's asking for you," Alistair said.

"Oh, yes, I'll go," Edith said.

"He's requesting Dr. Brannick."

The doctor set his glass on the table and rose. He said he'd go check on Henry. After that, Alistair should pack a small bag of his things. More could be sent later.

Edith gestured for Alistair to take the now empty chair next to hers. He did.

"They're taking him this evening, then?" Edith asked.

"The doctor arranged everything over the telephone after he conducted his examination."

"Were you present for that?"

"His Lordship asked that I stay."

"And?"

"And, what?"

"Was it awful?"

Alistair said it was routine. The doctor asked Henry a lot of questions about how he was feeling. Then he was given a series of Rorschach blots. After that, they did a free association exercise—here Edith stopped him. What was a free association exercise?

"Well, I say I word, and you say the first word that comes into your mind," Alistair said.

"Sounds easy enough."

"Would you like to try?"

"Sure."

"White."

"Snow."

"Cold."

"Winter."

"Love."

"Hate."

Alistair pointed out that Edith had named things similar to the suggested word until they got to the word "love."

She asked him why hate wasn't similar to love. He said he supposed it was, at least in terms of intensity of sentiment.

"You'd have made a good shrink, yourself," she said.

He refilled her glass of sherry. She was grateful she didn't have to ask him to.

"Alistair?" she asked.

"Yes?"

"What are you going to live on?"

"In His Lordship's absence? I have his Power of Attorney. I'll pay myself and cover the usual bills."

Before she could ask, Alistair explained this was an arrangement they'd agreed on years before, when His Lordship was similarly indisposed.

"Poor Henry, poor you," she said.

Voices were heard down the hall, but they were measured and calm. God bless Dr. Brannick.

She and Alistair would be alone in the apartment. How did Henry feel about that? It probably hadn't occurred to him. And Alistair? Of course, he'd have thought of it. Alistair was more intelligent than Henry, or rather, Henry's intelligence ran along narrower lines. Alistair was a man of the world.

"Should I find my own place?" Edith asked.

"If you would be more comfortable."

"I wouldn't."

"Then no, you shouldn't."

They sat without speaking until Dr. Brannick appeared and said he was ready now to telephone for the private car that would drive him and Henry west, into the Berkshires where Dr. Harris would be waiting to receive them.

Chapter Ten

At the last moment, as he got into the car, Edith thought Henry's eyes cleared and filled with panic. Nothing else about him was different. She asked Alistair if he'd seen the same thing and he said he hadn't, and that it was unlikely, in any case, given the injection Dr. Brannick gave him after the examination.

The following day was Saturday, and Edith told Alistair to move out of his tiny room and into Henry's vacated one. Alistair said he couldn't possibly. She told him to take the spare guest room, next to her home office. He seemed willing to consider that, though he said more than once that he was used to the room he was in and saw no need to change. Finally, Edith said it was entirely up to him.

Aunt Margaret called from her hotel just after nine and Edith said she was surprised to hear from her so early.

"Nonsense. I'm always an early riser," Aunt Margaret said.

Edith asked her to come over. Aunt Margaret said she was on her way, then took over an hour to arrive and said she was distracted by a hat in a shop window, which in the end she decided not to buy. It just didn't suit her, after all.

"You look peaked, my child. Are you feeling well?" Aunt Margaret asked as she and Edith made their way into the living room where Alistair had left a tray of tea and cups.

Edith said Henry had been taken to a sanatorium. She tried to make it sound as if it weren't serious, just a hiccup in the run of things, and that he'd be back home in no time. Aunt Margaret looked skeptical. She said she had a friend whose son had cracked up and he was gone for almost a year. Of course, that situation was a bit different, she said, because the young man had fallen for one of the nurses and felt no need to deny himself her kind attentions.

"You're not talking about Philip, I assume?" Edith asked.

"I'm not. But let's talk about Philip now, if you like."

"Why?"

"Darling! You don't need to be coy with me. I could see the fireworks between you two, even if Francine didn't. Don't feel bad. These things happen."

Edith said she didn't particularly care to talk about Philip. She never thought about Philip. The twinkle in Aunt Margaret's eye was maddening.

Edith poured their tea and wondered aloud when she could visit Henry. She'd have to put in a call to Elm Meadows and see how he was getting along. Aunt Margaret said since he just arrived yesterday, she might want to wait a few days to give him a chance to settle in. And she shouldn't worry because if anything were amiss, she'd be notified.

"I still can't believe this happened," Edith said. She was flooded with a sickening blend of grief and guilt. The grief she understood. The guilt made no sense. Unless it was because she was relieved that Henry was gone.

"It may delay the wedding, even though you've not firmed up a date, have you?" Aunt Margaret asked.

"I don't care about that."

"Because you're that much in love."

"I didn't mean I'd wait forever, I meant . . . oh, I don't know."

"Darling, is it possible that this marriage isn't what you truly want?"

"I wish everyone would stop asking me that."

"It's a question worth asking."

Aunt Margaret pulled out her compact and dabbed some powder on her nose. She went on watching Edith with steely patience.

"He's easy to live with," Edith said.

"Until now."

"Well, no, there were some bumps before."

Aunt Margaret asked her to explain. Edith told her about his calling Walter behind her back.

"Oh, goodness, Walter. I forgot to tell you. He's agreed to meet me for lunch. He tried to put me off when I phoned. My own nephew! But I insisted. I said I wanted to lay eyes on him and see how he was getting along."

"That's nice."

"I'll give you a full report."

"I don't want one."

"Of course, you do." She put away her compact, picked up her teacup, looked into it, and put it back in its saucer.

"You were saying?" she asked.

Edith said Henry turned out to be dependent and needy, which was odd, because Mary, his ex-wife, had written Edith a letter when she was in England which suggested he would pull her into a lazy, easy, unambitious life.

"Well, he didn't succeed, did he? You're back at work," Aunt Margaret said.

"Yes."

"That's why he's nervous, I expect. Men like to have a woman at their beck and call. Any breath of independence just ruffles their feather too much."

"This predates me."

Aunt Margaret said that in a way, it was a blessing in disguise. Now Edith knew Henry's weak spot and wasn't stuck. She could peel away if she had to. The question was, would she?

Alistair appeared and Aunt Margaret greeted him warmly as if he were an old friend. She told him he was looking well and that she was sorry to hear about Lord Henry.

"He'll be right in no time," Alistair said.

Edith mentioned that she'd heard the doorbell and asked what it was.

Alistair handed her a telegram. It was from Henry.

Arrived safely. Rooms comfortable. Dreadfully sorry about this. Will write more later.

Edith let Aunt Margaret read it.

"See? He already sounds better," Aunt Margaret said.

Alistair asked if Aunt Margaret would be joining them for lunch. She said she already had an engagement but was free for dinner. She invited Alistair to join them.

After a tense afternoon during which Edith distracted herself with unpacking a new shipment of books and paying bills, they went to a French place by the river, recommended by Aunt Margaret's friend, Mable. The décor was overdone, and the waiters were haughty, which Aunt Margaret seemed to find amusing, but which set Edith on edge. After a drink, she relaxed. Alistair kept Aunt Margaret distracted with questions about New York City, which she was delighted to answer. When a lull fell, she described her lunch with Walter.

"You simply will not believe what he told me," Aunt Margaret said. Edith stared at her silverware. Alistair coughed politely.

"And what was that?" Edith asked.

"They've called it off!"

"Walter and Babs?"

"Her true colors have finally been seen. She's a dreadful woman. Greedy. And quite untidy, it turns out."

Aunt Margaret said Walter felt himself well out of it. Of course, he was just putting on a brave face. She could tell the dear boy was miserable. Naturally, he hoped for the chance to improve her character. Isn't that what all men wanted? Oddly enough, he didn't mention Edith. In the cab going home, when it was just the two of them, Alistair said he didn't see how that could have been possible. Edith said Aunt Margaret was no doubt sparing her feelings and had deepened Walter's downcast state for her benefit.

Days passed. Edith focused on running the store and editing Nedleman's manuscript. It was in good shape already. She telephoned Henry at the sanatorium. It took a long time for him to come on the line, and at first, he seemed not to know her. He was polite and friendly and said everything was lovely. He was coming along fine. He didn't know when he'd be home. He asked if she were well and if Alistair were taking fine care of her.

"I miss you," she said.

"You're a darling."

Then he had to go. There was a limit on how long patients could talk on the telephone. Edith didn't see why, given what they must be charging in the first place.

She and Alistair settled into a routine. They shared chores. She cooked three nights a week and he handled two nights, otherwise, they dined out. He was easy to be with, and without Henry, the high courtesy he always practiced became something softer, almost kinder, though he never overstepped. She talked to him about the store and Nedleman's book. His interest seemed genuine.

Aunt Margaret wrote from New York to say how much she'd enjoyed her visit, and that Edith mustn't worry. All would soon be well. She should feel free to come and stay as long as she liked, if the bookstore and new press could spare her, of course. And she would be happy to come to Boston anytime Edith needed company. She'd forgotten what a charming little place it was. Her late husband took her there on business years and years ago. Of course, it had quite changed since then. The war changed everything.

Laura called to ask if Edith had scheduled her reading at The Turned Page. Edith said no, not yet but she thought it should be sometime after the weather turned cold, when people would long for the glory of flowers. This made Laura laugh and say Edith should try her hand at penning a poem or two.

Miss Levy's downstairs neighbor telephoned Edith at the store to say Miss Levy had moved into a nursing home and was not expected to leave there anytime soon. Her apartment was to be let. Was Edith interested in having Miss Levy's cat? Edith didn't think she wanted the cat in the apartment but said it could live at the bookstore as long as it was well-behaved. The cat was used to being let out and navigating city streets. All Edith needed to do was put a bowl of food for it in the alley from time to time. So, Edgar joined the community at The Turned Page and instantly charmed everyone. He liked to sleep on the sill in the picture window. One woman declared it unsanitary, but she wasn't a regular customer, so Edith listened politely to her complaint and let Edgar do as he pleased. She bought him a fetching red collar with a little bell that gave a pleasant sound as he trotted from room to room. When he didn't care for the windowsill, he helped himself to the overstuffed chair in her office. She had never been a cat person, but Edgar won her over quickly. She loved stroking his soft fur and causing a riotous, beatific purr.

Robert Nedleman called to invite Edith to a cocktail party at his place to celebrate his book. It was that Saturday, and he apologized for the short notice.

"I don't know if I can make it. My fiancé is ill," Edith said.

"I'm sorry to hear it. Was it sudden?"

"No."

He said if she changed her mind, he'd be delighted. He gave her the address.

"I would love my friends to meet my publisher," he said. "And vice versa."

"You're very kind."

"I might be mercenary. You never know."

She said she promised to think about it.

At home, she discovered a letter from Henry. The writing was wobbly.

Dearest Darling Edith,

I am ashamed of myself for letting this happen, though Dr. Harris would say (and has said) it is no one's fault. That you should suffer my frailty is horrible. My regret knows no bounds. I have written to my poor parents to let them know their weak son is once again afflicted. I know Alistair is taking care of you, and I hope you will do the same. He is a lonely man, strong, but lonely. Not the kind to go to pieces. I hope you will come and see me at your earliest opportunity, though Dr. Harris would prefer I wait to receive visitors for a few more weeks so that I am properly assimilated. By which I suspect he means worn down and even more ashamed than I am now. Write to me, my darling, and tell me everything. Absolutely everything. The food is good here. My room looks over a tree whose leaves want very much to turn, rather like me, I think. Quite like me.

In deepest adoration,

Henry

She read the letter in the living room, and the moment she slipped it back into its envelope, Alistair appeared and poured her a glass of sherry. She told him he was a mind reader.

"Hardly. I heard you come in," Alistair said. He helped himself to scotch. He no longer wore his butler's uniform, but a pair of gray wool slacks, a white shirt, and a pale blue cardigan. He looked comfortable, at home. Edith asked what he'd been doing with himself.

"The usual. I took care of the laundry, cleaned the apartment, and shopped for dinner. We're having pork chops if that's all right."

"I adore a good pork chop."

Alistair sat at the other end of the couch. He asked how His Lordship sounded in the letter.

"Scattered. Cheerful, but unhappy."

"Shame."

"I miss him."

"I do, too."

Edith said she couldn't stop thinking about what Alistair told her the night it happened, about the times before when he fell into himself. There had to be a common thread. Alistair said it was a perceived loss of control.

"Control over what?" she asked.

"You, I expect."

"He broke down because he wasn't the center of my attention anymore. Is that it?"

"I'd say that he realized you knew your own mind and were immune to his influence."

"Why should he want to influence me? Why should anyone?"

"It's the way men sometimes think."

"Do you?"

"I can hardly afford to."

That was true. As a servant, Alistair was used to having no influence over anything other than what laundry service to engage and what wine to recommend with dinner.

Edith considered Henry going to pieces because she wasn't dependent on him any longer. Right after she left Walter, and she was utterly dependent, he was at his happiest.

But Mary wouldn't have been dependent on him at all. She wasn't that kind of person. The difference was that she didn't have career ambitions, nothing she wanted outside of her marriage except to ride horses. And sleep with other men. Henry would have understood about the other men, even about the one who made a nuisance of himself. He had other women. That's how it was.

She told Alistair about being invited to Robert Nedleman's place that Saturday. Alistair asked what sort he was.

"A sloppy writer, as far as I can tell," Edith said.

"Are his intentions honorable?"

"Well, making a pass at his publisher isn't a good idea, so I assume so."

Edith finished her sherry. She was getting hungry.

She discovered Alistair watching her closely.

"Don't do that," Edith said.

"Do what?"

"Watch me the way a cat watches a mouse. Henry does it all the time. I simply can't stand it."

"I beg your pardon. I was just wondering if I should escort you to this event. With your permission, of course."

"You might find it amusing. And you don't get out much. Sure, come with me. Why not?"

It rained hard all Saturday afternoon, and then even harder as they set out. Nedleman's apartment was in Back Bay, not far from Henry's club. It was a swank neighborhood, and Edith expressed her surprise to Alistair who said just because someone was a poet didn't mean he was impoverished. Look at the English Romantics. Lord Byron was a fine example of a man of means applying his talents to the page.

"They're going to love you, Alistair," she said.

The apartment was in an old brownstone, much like Miss Levy's but grander. It turned out to be a single-family home with three floors. Nedleman lived there with two other young men, both of whom were at Harvard, he explained as he took Edith's coat. He stared at Alistair, who hung his own coat up in the closet by the door.

"This is my friend, Malcolm Alistair," Edith said.

"Not your fiancé?"

"No."

"Well, welcome, one and all."

They were led through a series of small rooms into what might once have been a back parlor. In front of the fire was a group of people made up of several young men, and a woman wearing a sweater and skirt separated by a black patent leather belt. Edith found her beret affected. Her own hat was a simple velvet with jet buttons. As they were leaving for the party, Alistair said it was charming, and Edith asked if she looked like a publisher. Alistair said her pale green dress with white cuffs suggested not.

Introductions were made, and Edith found herself the subject of critical scrutiny from the group. Nedleman sensed her discomfort and put a glass of scotch in her hand. Alistair had disappeared into a corner with two people who were plying him with questions about England. The most curious gaze Edith encountered came from the woman, Joyce, who showed the effect of the martini she held with a slight waver in her stance.

She wanted to know how long Edith had been a publisher. Her accent was pure Boston, not an "r" to be found. Edith said only for a month or so.

"My goodness, and here's dear Robbie trusting you with his baby," Joyce said.

"An elegant, precocious baby."

Nedleman laughed loudly. Edith didn't see what was funny, but then suspected he was trying to humor Joyce, who had a wound-up, feral look that said she might foam over and spew invective, aided by the liquor in her system. He explained that Joyce was a novelist.

"And what are your novels about?" Edith asked.

"Liars and thieves."

"Wide subject."

Nedleman led Edith away to where a young man stood by himself, eating a handful of pretzels from a bag. He introduced him as Frank, a painter who just flunked out of art school.

"That's too bad," Edith said.

"Couldn't keep up with the deadlines," Frank said. One of his eyes was blue, the other brown. Edith found the effect unnerving, but his voice was pleasant. His sweater had food stains on it, and he smelled strongly of cigarettes. She asked him what he painted. He said nudes. Edith was tempted to ask, "Nude what?" but thought better of it.

She then found herself in the kitchen with another one of Nedleman's circle, only this one was a roommate, Barry, an engineering student. Edith asked him what it was like to be surrounded by artistic temperaments, and he seemed to have no idea how to answer, so she asked him how he enjoyed school. He said he didn't, but his father wanted him to make a career in engineering, so here he was. What did Edith do?

"I'm a publisher," she said.

"That's wild."

"I'm publishing Robert's book."

"Yeah, yeah, right, about the starlings."

"Yes."

Barry looked her over.

"I also own a bookstore in Harvard Square," she said.

"That must keep you out of trouble."

"It did until it caught fire."

She told him the story, finding that telling it softened the sore spot it still occupied. She exaggerated the damage and hinted that it was an inside job.

"You mean, someone torched the place?" Barry asked.

"No, not really. The insurance man said it was probably bad wiring, but we'd just had it done, and one of our staff is a smoker, so I put two and two together."

"You might want to fire her. No pun intended."

Edith forced herself to laugh. She said it was awful to have been abroad at the time, which led Barry to ask her about her travels and if she'd done anything of particular interest. She said she stayed at the home of her fiancé's parents and didn't roam far afield.

"Well, as my mother would say, you're a busy bee," Barry said and excused himself. She poured herself more scotch and went into the room she was in before. Alistair was talking to Joyce, who was still wavering. He was telling her something funny because she kept laughing and making herself stop. She seemed pretty drunk. From the way Alistair spoke and then paused as if to not overwhelm her with information, he thought so, too. There was an empty chair near the fire, and Edith helped herself to it. She slipped off her shoes. There was a tiny hole in the toe of one of her stockings. The stockings were new. She'd ask Alistair to mend them.

Robert appeared with a chair he brought out of the kitchen. He put it on the other side of the fireplace, sat down, and asked Edith if she were enjoying herself. She said she was. It was a lovely party.

"Not really. They're good folks, but dull as toast," he said.

"Not a nice way to talk about your friends."

"They wouldn't be my friends if I couldn't insult them from time to time."

"Well, they do say familiarity breeds contempt."

"Whose 'they?'"

"Everyone."

"A large number of people to use a phrase I've never heard of."

"You haven't?" Edith asked.

"Never."

"Goodness. It's as common as toast."

He touched his glass to hers and said he suspected she was the bee's knees.

"Hardly."

"A woman publisher, at your age, and the owner of a bookstore. I'd say that's damned impressive. Not much room for improvement."

She said there was loads to improve. For instance, she let her ex-husband talk her out of continuing with graduate school. The kicker was that he wasn't committed to her, in the first place. Robert leaned back in his chair and said to give him all of it, he wasn't going anywhere.

"Hardly a suitable subject for a celebration," Edith said.

"Isn't truth always a celebration?"

He was all right, Edith thought. Full of himself, but all right.

Robert asked about her family, and she gave the salient details. He said her father and his father sounded a lot alike.

"How so?" Edith asked.

"He's overbearing. And pushy. He wants me to follow in his footsteps and go into politics."

"What's he do?"

"He's our Senator."

"What?"

"Francis Nedleman. Republican Senator for the Commonwealth of Massachusetts." Robert said this in an overly formal and grand tone of voice.

"I had no idea, but it makes sense," Edith said.

"What does?"

"This house, of course."

"This house was left to me by my grandmother. She was a Democrat. Always got under Dad's skin."

Robert explained that he got only the house, and no money to speak of, so he had to turn his hand to whatever might pay the bills. His mother slipped him a check now and then, and he taught some courses here and there. Edith asked where he'd earned his degree and he said at Harvard, bachelor's, and master's. She wondered if they'd been students at the same time and taken some of the same classes, but it turned out he was thirty-six, which meant his tenure predated hers.

"So, you've been out for a while," she said.

"You make it sound like I'm on parole."

"The opposite. Isn't one safer in school than facing the rigors of the real world?"

"Indeed, one is, given all the rigors there are. It was tough going until I found a publisher. You don't know how many I tried."

"How many?"

"I was being rhetorical."

"Okay. But how many?"

He said at least ten. The big houses didn't want first-time authors and the smaller presses were full up. Seems like everyone who was in the war had a book in him and now they were all over the place, clogging the system, as it were.

Edith asked how he served. He was a quartermaster at Camp Lejeune. Never went overseas. Never saw action. Sometimes he felt lucky, sometimes he felt cheated. He knew his father had had something to do with not risking his own skin.

"And you?" he asked.

Edith told him about making maps, and about Walter's work in Naval Intelligence.

"Walter's the ex?" Nedleman asked.

"Yes."

"Tell me about the guy you're going to marry."

How much should she say? Robert's manner was pleasant and respectful. He didn't study her as if she were a specimen. He was easy to talk to. She told him everything.

"I've heard of that place," he said. At least one of his esteemed extended family had spent time there, more than one, but his parents never liked talking about that sort of thing, and as far as his grandmother was concerned, modern psychiatry was for the birds. If you weren't tough enough to take what life threw at you, you should get out of the way and let sturdier souls prevail.

"She sounds like quite a character," Edith said.

"Began life as a maid to a rich family, back in Ireland. Came over here. Learned how to sew, make women's hats, and opened a small shop. Catered to the better set. One of them married her, and here we are."

"Sounds easy, but I'm sure it was anything but."

Robert said Edith's glass was empty. Did she want a refill? Alistair had been trying to get her attention for the past few minutes, and she assumed he was anxious to leave, so she said no, she didn't and thanked him for the wonderful party. Robert helped her into her coat and said he hoped they'd meet again soon.

The rain had stopped, and the air smelled clean. They walked over to Beacon Street and had no trouble finding a cab. Alistair was quiet on the ride but said he had fun. He hoped Edith had, too. She had but now was famished. She assumed there'd be something to eat, but all she got was a stale bag of pretzels.

At home, Alistair made them scrambled eggs with ham and cheese while Edith made toast. They didn't talk. There was no need. They were focused on their chores, and then on the food, and later, Edith went into the library to read.

Alistair asked if she'd mind if he joined her. She said of course not. This was his home, too, and had been longer than it had been hers.

He said he was thinking of going to the movies tomorrow if that were all right with her.

"Of course, it is. You don't have to ask my permission, you know. You don't work for me," she said. He lowered the paper he was reading and looked at her with amusement. Then he said he was just reflecting on the party they'd been to, and that woman, Joyce.

"She was pretty tight, I think," Edith said.

"Quite tight. You know she made an inappropriate suggestion to me."

"What did she say?"

"That I looked like I'd be fun to roll in the hay with."

"You're not serious."

"I'm afraid I am."

"What did you say?"

"I pretended I didn't hear."

Edith said that was the gentlemanly thing to do. She wouldn't remember a thing about it later.

She asked what movie he was going to see.

"I was thinking about *The Big Steal*," he said.

"I love Robert Mitchum."

"Because he smokes marijuana?"

"Does he?"

"It was in the news last year. He was arrested."

"Goodness."

She picked up her book and found her eyes moving over the words without taking them in. She put the book in her lap. She thought about going to see Henry. He'd only been gone about a week and a half, but it felt much longer. She told Alistair what she was thinking and asked if he had any interest in making the trip with her. He said, of course, but only if she drove. He still wasn't used to it, and always needed an aspirin afterward.

"We'll need hotel rooms. I don't think I can manage that round trip in a day," she said.

"That can be arranged."

"I'll call over tomorrow and see what that doctor has to say."

Edith returned to *Member of The Wedding,* which she found less good than *The Heart Is a Lonely Hunter,* but she stuck with it. Alistair said he was going to turn in, and Edith thanked him again for going to Robert's with her.

Then she was alone, enjoying her book at last and the silence of the apartment until Henry again intruded on her thoughts.

Chapter Eleven

The lovely autumn leaves had blown off the trees and added to the grim mood Edith suffered as she drove to Elm Meadows. They got on the road early so they could see Henry right after lunch. Dr. Harris suggested this was a good time for him to receive them. After that, they would check into the hotel rooms Alistair had reserved, and eat dinner with Henry, or on their own, depending on whether Henry was too fatigued to see them a second time in one day.

She thought the passing scenery would occupy her mind, but it didn't after the first half-hour. Laura's reading was to take place the Tuesday before Thanksgiving and Edith fretted that a date so close to a major holiday meant attendance would be poor. She shared this with Alistair. He said he didn't think so, and in any case, if only a few people came, that was still more than knew of her before. They would offer coffee and cookies. Alistair was going to bring in plates and cups. Henry had several sets of china at home. Edith said not to bring anything really good quality in case someone was clumsy handling it.

Edith suggested that Laura read the least controversial poems, those not about flowers, in other words, then chided herself for not being more daring. Was she afraid the store would get a bad reputation? And wasn't she in the publishing business to push boundaries? Still, her instinct was to take things slowly and give people a chance to get used to a more progressive atmosphere. Even so, she was terrified it would backfire on her. Alistair said when he was worried about something he engaged in a simple exercise: he asked himself what the worst outcome could be, then looked at it calmly. In this case, Edith said the worse outcome would be her store would be boycotted and she would get arrested on a morals charge. Alistair said in that case, he would come down and bail her out.

Aunt Margaret wrote from New York to say a date had been set for Philip's wedding and Francine, though still beside herself, was getting used to the idea of not only having a daughter-in-law but becoming a grandmother. The fact that Philip's intended was an orphan made life so much easier. The poor thing grew up in one of "those places" run by the state and came out unscathed as far as Francine could tell. Aunt Margaret had warned her to keep her eyes open for signs of deep trauma, however. Edith wished she'd been given that advice herself, before accepting Henry's proposal.

Then she thought about Walter breaking it off with Babs. He was probably doing fine on his own. Of course, in time he'd have to get himself a new wife. His future as a promising young lawyer would require that. Some attractive, energetic, educated woman with no ambitions other than to be his helpmeet.

Someone who didn't care about the pleasures of the bedroom, yet who was willing to have three or four children.

Alistair commented on the lowering sky and said rain was surely on the way. Edith hoped it wouldn't snow since she hadn't brought her overshoes. Alistair said she mustn't concern herself. If their stay were extended by a day or two due to inclement weather, it might be an opportunity for her to relax and take time to sort out her priorities.

"You mean, Henry. He's the only priority that isn't clear," she said. Leaves blew ominously across the road. It was dark enough to require headlights, and she switched them on. Rain fell in fat drops, then became heavier. She'd never liked driving in rain. She could feel Alistair's unease in the seat next to her.

"Do you still plan to marry him?" Alistair asked.

"You're very direct."

"I meant no offense."

"None taken."

She slowed the car down to forty miles an hour. She didn't want to have an accident, on top of everything else.

"I don't think so," she said.

"You don't think you'll marry him?"

"No."

She said it was clear and she'd been avoiding it for days. She knew from the moment he fell apart that Henry needed much more than she was willing or able to give him. He wouldn't be in the sanatorium forever. He'd come home and she'd have to move out. She loved the apartment, but she'd find another one easily enough. It wouldn't be as nice, and that was all right, too.

"He means to settle money on you," Alistair said.

"What are you talking about?"

"He told me the day the doctor came. 'If I'm truly going off the rails again, then I instruct you here and now to make provision for Edith should things sour between us.'"

"Oh, poor Henry!"

Edith couldn't read Alistair's silence, and she began to wonder again what his feelings for Henry were. Of course, he was loyal, but he, too, could be ready to move on. Would he leave him to his own devices, though? Could Henry successfully live alone when he was released?

Edith asked Alistair exactly that.

"You're suggesting I resign?" he asked.

"Of course not. I just can't help thinking that you might care to live your own life, without Henry. I know you go back years and years and all that. But the day might soon come when you could put aside loyalty to him and be loyal to yourself."

"An American concept."

"Oh, come now. Don't give me a speech about duty. You've done yours. Be your own man."

Even the briefest glance at his expression said she'd put her foot in it with that one. She apologized. Alistair lit himself a cigarette and offered one to Edith.

"Thank you," she said.

Alistair said of course he'd been thinking about his future now that His Lordship was ill again. He suspected that if Edith were to break off her engagement, Henry would return home to England.

"And you must decide if you'd go with him," she said.

"Precisely."

"Any hints?"

"There's nothing for me in England anymore."

"Ah. Well, good. I would miss you."

The rain continued, and the road was winding. Edith slowed down again. She hoped they wouldn't be late, but if so, it couldn't be helped. It would be all right what she had to tell Henry, assuming he didn't already know. What about the ring? Of course, she'd have to return it. If she just slipped it off her finger and gave it to him, it would spare her the necessity of saying anything else.

The rain abated. Alistair drew her attention to a small patch of blue overhead.

"Just enough to make a pair of pants," he said.

"What?"

"That's what my mother used to say."

They went the remaining miles in silence.

The sanatorium was comprised of several red brick buildings that dated from the last century. The grounds were immaculate with neatly combed flower beds that must be splendid in spring. The drive was wide and gracious. On either side of the main building stood a tall elm tree, hence the name, Edith assumed. Their branches were lacy against the sky. It didn't give an impression of illness or human struggle, but then how could it? These were inanimate objects that only bore witness, then decayed slowly over time.

They were met by an air of gaiety inside. Banners and balloons had been hung. The nurse at the reception desk explained that one of the residents was celebrating a birthday.

People sat alone, or in small groups. Some were young, most were middle-aged. No one was elderly, and Edith wondered cynically if they were denied access to the common area, especially when visitors were expected. The women wore simple dresses and cardigan sweaters. The men had slacks and pullover sweaters. They'd been gotten up to look like they were spending a day at the library or some other worthy, quiet pursuit. Cheerful orchestral music danced from speakers on the walls. The lighting was soft, the carpet thick, and voices were calm and pleasant, yet there was something insidious about the atmosphere that Edith couldn't name at first.

Despair, she thought, bordering on terror, despite being drugged and assisted with every daily task.

Alistair stood with his hat in his hand, surveying the scene. His face was as impassive. Edith thought she must look agitated, or about to become so because the receptionist offered to bring her a cup of tea. Edith said she wanted to see Dr. Harris and then Henry. They were directed to wait on a sofa in front of a coffee table that had gardening and home decorating magazines neatly arranged. Alistair picked one up and flipped through it. Edith said she felt she was about to lose her mind.

"Calm yourself. Never give yourself away," Alistair said, quietly.

"Stiff upper lip, and all that?"

"Quite."

They waited, then waited some more. When Edith checked her watch, she saw they'd been ignored for over thirty minutes. She told Alistair they had wasted their time coming, no one was going to meet with them, and just as he put his hand lightly on her arm to say to give it just a bit more time, Dr.

Harris appeared. He was younger than Dr. Brannick, with a brusque manner. He was all business, despite his red bow tie.

"I'm sorry, I was detained," he said. Edith and Alistair stood. The doctor shook Alistair's hand, and Edith realized that in the eyes of the world, or at least Elm Meadows, Henry belonged to Alistair, not to her.

Dr. Harris said they could speak in his office and led them down a wide hallway lined with photographs of trees, bushes, and bridges, but no people, which Edith thought made sense. If you were a patient here, you wouldn't want to think about people. If you did, you'd then turn to all those who were out there, living their lives, facing each day confidently, and following through on well-laid plans.

She must have made some noise or sniffed because she found Alistair's hand in hers. She looked up at him and when he caught her eye, his glance was friendly and reassuring. She let go of his hand. She didn't need to be treated like a child.

The doctor's office was large with a wide picture window looking out over the front lawn. The families of committed patients would feel all was well, with a view like that. That good possibilities remained, that things would improve. People got better, didn't they? Henry had gotten better each previous time. But he'd never been in one of these places before. It must be weighing badly on him.

Dr. Harris pulled out a heavy silver cigarette case and offered it to Edith and Alistair, who each helped themselves. Edith leaned back in her chair and blew her smoke at the coffered ceiling.

"I'm afraid he can't see you. He's taken a bit of a bad turn," Dr. Harris said.

"What do you mean?" Alistair asked.

"He's catatonic. Won't speak."

"Maybe he has nothing to say," Edith said. In the corner of her eye, she noted the sudden swivel of Alistair's head in her direction.

Dr. Harris looked at her critically. Edith hated him, she decided.

"He's fallen further into himself. We must discover the cause," Dr. Harris said.

"Oh, I can tell you that. I'm the cause. He disappointed me. He can't bear it. I don't know why. Men disappoint women all the time and don't go all to pieces. Heaven knows, my father never batted an eye at his cruelty. And my ex-husband always did just as he pleased, without a care in the world as far as I was concerned," Edith said.

An uneasy silence followed, yet Edith didn't regret her words.

"You need to talk about these men in your life," Dr. Harris said.

"I just did."

"More in depth."

"No, that's not for me. I'm not one of those talky girls. I prefer to get on with things."

"All right then, let's get on with Mr. McCormick. I feel the time has come for more aggressive treatment. Dr. Brannick noted your distaste for shock therapy if I'm not mistaken. He also raised using insulin. I advise the use of insulin over electroshock. But I need your permission."

"It's not my permission to give, is it?" Edith asked.

"No, it's up to Mr. Alistair. Medical decisions are covered in the Power of Attorney if I'm not mistaken."

Alistair said that was correct but that he had to consult with Mrs. Sloan before doing anything further. He also needed to know the risks involved in such a procedure.

"Well, to be blunt, the risk is death. It rarely happens, but there have been one or two patients who don't recover."

"One, or two? Surely you must know which," Edith said.

Again, the critical stare.

Alistair asked if there were any chance they could see him, just for a moment.

"I feel it wouldn't be right. He's at quite a disadvantage. We don't want to cause any further distress, do we?" Dr. Harris asked.

"No, I suppose not," Alistair said.

"I'm sorry you had to come all this way," Dr. Harris said and stood. Edith and Alistair did, too. Dr. Harris shook Alistair's hand, then gave him a sealed envelope. Alistair opened it in the car.

"The cheek. It's a bill for Henry's first month," he said.

"Saved himself the cost of mailing it."

Alistair asked if she were hungry and she said she wasn't. They checked into the hotel. Edith's room was drafty and cold, so she lit the fire that had been laid in the fireplace. She tossed her book on the nightstand, combed her hair, and kicked off her shoes. It was early yet, just past noon, yet the moment she lay down on the canopy bed, she fell asleep and didn't open her eyes until the knocking on the door went from discreet to insistent.

"Coming!" she said and sat up. At first, she didn't recognize where she was, then with a feeling of falling down a deep hole, recalled the visit to the sanatorium.

Alistair was at the door with a bottle of wine and two glasses. He said the manager had procured everything for him. Edith told him he was clever and invited him in. There were two chairs before the fire that had died down and left glowing embers. They sat. He opened the wine with a borrowed corkscrew and served them. Edith asked if his room were comfortable.

"It is, but the radiator is on too high, and I can't seem to turn it down," he said.

"It was cold in here when I first arrived. Funny."

They drank and didn't talk. Then Alistair asked if she wanted to go back to Boston that afternoon. They could get underway as soon as she liked. She said no, she was tired, despite her long lie down. They should have dinner, relax, and leave first thing in the morning.

"Very well, just as you say," he said.

"But what's your pleasure? It's not just up to me."

"My pleasure is yours."

"Oh, Alistair. You'll have to speak up for yourself if you want to get along with me."

"And I thought we were getting along just fine."

"You're teasing me."

"I am."

Edith thought about Henry, sitting in his room, roaming the desolate landscape of his mind. Now his mind had locked him in. She thought she could have gotten him to talk if she'd been allowed to see him. Dr. Harris knew that, too. That's why he refused it. The longer Henry stayed ill, the more money he made.

She told this to Alistair.

"You don't trust him," Alistair said.

"I don't." She closed her eyes, then opened them. "I just want what's best for Henry."

"Let's let the doctor do his job, then. I feel things will come out all right, in the end."

"You're an optimist."

"I've found the alternative too difficult."

When Alistair returned to his room, Edith changed her dress for dinner. Though the other one was fine, she didn't want to wear what she'd worn to the sanatorium. Her choice was good. Black velvet with long sleeves and a high neck matched the spirit of this dreadful day. Yet she added a small diamond brooch to her left shoulder. A little light to push back the darkness, she thought. She wore the same hat she'd worn to Robert's party, though earlier she had on a simple black cotton one.

Alistair hadn't changed his clothes. Men didn't bother with that, but then she realized Henry would have. Henry was vain. She'd never seen that in him before, and now, as they were shown to their table and took their chairs, she thought vanity contributed in part to his current condition. Most people didn't have the luxury of going to pieces and having someone on hand to put them back together. It wasn't vanity, though, just being used to being taken care of, knowing that if you displayed distress, someone would rush to soothe it.

The meal was average, the wine better than what Alistair had brought to her room. They spoke little, and neither minded. Edith wanted to focus on the weeks ahead and not worry about Henry. There was nothing she could do for him, in any case. Breaking the engagement would have to wait. She ought to remove the ring, though. She'd take it off when she got to her room.

Despite the nap, Edith turned in early, desperate for a long blank sleep. Insistent knocking on the door once again woke her up. Alistair was there, in his dressing gown, saying he heard her crying out. Was she having a bad dream?

"How did you hear that?" Edith asked, tying the sash on her robe.

"My room is next door."

"You must have imagined it."

"I'm sure I didn't. I was reading, not yet asleep."

She told him to come in. She went into the bathroom and drank some water. She dragged a brush through her hair. Alistair was at the window, looking out into the dark, smoking. She'd failed to draw the curtains.

"There's a moon," he said. She went to look. A slim silver crescent hung above the trees. She could see the lights of the sanatorium in the distance. She was certain Henry was awake, then realized she couldn't possibly know that.

Alistair asked what she'd been dreaming about. She said she had no memory of it, she never did.

"You have a history of nightmares?" he asked.

"Walter said I did."

"Well, this whole visit hasn't been pleasant for anyone, so I'm not surprised."

"I have a bad feeling that he'll never come home."

"I have it, too."

She asked him to see what he could do about getting a fire going. He stooped to look into the fireplace and said they needed some rolled-up newspaper.

"I'll call down for some," she said.

"You don't want someone to find me in your room."

"Oh, who cares?"

"Edith. You must be sensible."

"If I were sensible, I wouldn't be here, would I?"

She sat in one of the two chairs before the cold fireplace. He told her not to cry and offered a clean handkerchief from the pocket of his dressing gown.

"Ever the thoughtful butler. Sorry, valet, whatever," she said.

"I'm more than that."

"I know."

"I don't think you do."

He sat, too, and put out his cigarette. He said it was getting late, and they should try to get some sleep. It would be a long drive back to Boston in the morning.

"Will you be all right now?" he asked.

"I don't know."

They stood up and he embraced her. She was too tired to protest and was grateful for his warmth.

"Let me stay with you," he said.

"More trouble than it's worth, you know."

"I can handle trouble."

She admitted to herself she that was lonely. Why not? She didn't want to think about anything except being held and comforted, and all the rest of it, too.

When she woke in the morning, he'd gone back to his room and she wished he hadn't.

Chapter Twelve

Alistair gave his permission for the insulin treatment. Edith made no further objection. She said she understood why it was needed, and if it would help poor Henry come home more quickly, then, by all means, it must be done. Dr. Harris wrote to say it would be some time before they knew if it had worked. He counseled patience. Edith told Alistair it was easy to be patient when that kind of monthly fee was at stake.

They didn't talk about the night in the hotel. Sometimes she found Alistair looking at her in a way that said he remembered it quite clearly and wasn't at all embarrassed. She wasn't embarrassed, either, she just didn't want to sleep with him again. Not yet. Not until Henry's fate was settled, one way or another. When she discovered that she still wore his engagement ring, she realized it was helpful. Better to pass in the world as a woman bound for marriage than one on her own.

Letters came from Lord Gerald and Lady Alice that Alistair dutifully sent on. Edith asked why they didn't send them care of the sanatorium. Alistair said he wondered about that, too, and thought they hoped Henry would return to Boston soon and didn't want their correspondence delayed by having to be forwarded back from there. Edith wondered if Dr. Harris let Henry read the letters, or if they were collecting in a drawer somewhere. Alistair sent Gerald and Alice a telegram saying they had visited Henry and he was well. Edith asked why he lied.

"To spare them, of course. They're so far away, they must be frantic sometimes, worrying over him," he said.

"That's kind. I'm ashamed I didn't think to do that, myself."

"Your mind is elsewhere."

That was true.

Laura's reading was two days off. Edith had no idea how many people would attend, but everything was in place. Alistair would be on hand, and so would Patricia. Liza and Jocelyn were heading home early for Thanksgiving. Edith hadn't given any thought to Thanksgiving and told Alistair she didn't want him to do anything much.

"No turkey?" he asked.

"Oh, I don't know. It's such a silly holiday."

"I thought we'd just have a quiet dinner. Without turkey."

"I can make something."

"I'm in the mood for something French. I was going to try my hand at beef Bourguignon."

"It takes a few hours to put that together."

"That's no problem."

"We'll do it together. And mourn what will have been a disappointing author event."

At this, Alistair told her to take a moment and sit down. They were in the kitchen. Alistair was preparing tea, and since it was Sunday, Edith wasn't at the store, because it was closed.

Alistair said he understood her anxiety, but she must show confidence, even if she didn't feel it. When he first went into service, not everyone was kind to him, and sometimes he was set up to fail. But he thought well on his feet, and it showed. That's why Henry's father took him on after he came home from the war. In those days, just after his son died and his wife was sinking under the weight of her grief, a challenging job that kept him occupied was a blessing, and he gave it everything he had. Edith must do the same now and not even consider anything except success. Her future was in the bookstore, the press, and the authors she supported. If she refused failure, then she would not fail. That's all there was to it.

"Oh Alistair, where have you been all my life?" she asked.

"Waiting for someone like you to come along."

"I should fall in love with you."

"You should."

Edith stirred her tea. She said she couldn't possibly, not until she came to terms with her feelings for Henry.

"And what are they?" Alistair asked. He was parting his hair on the other side, Edith realized and wondered if that had anything to do with her, though she couldn't begin to say what.

"I'm fond of him. Very fond. He was good to me in many ways," she said.

"But you're not in love with him."

"No."

"Were you in love with your husband?"

"I thought I was, but no."

Alistair drank his tea. The sleeve of his sweater rode up and revealed one of Henry's cufflinks, black onyx, and gold. She couldn't mention it, not after accepting so much of Henry's generosity herself.

"Have you ever been in love?" he asked.

"I think the closest I've come is infatuation."

Alistair nodded.

Edith said she was hard-hearted and there was no getting around it.

"I wouldn't say that," Alistair said.

"What *would* you say?"

"That you've been ill-served by the male sex."

Edith nodded, as her mind drifted. She wondered what poems Laura would read. Edith had left the final choice to her. She could telephone her and ask unless that seemed too pushy.

"From your expression, I'd venture to guess you agree," Alistair said.

"What? Oh, no I was thinking about the reading. I'm sorry. Yes, I suppose that's it."

The reading was set for seven o'clock and at six, Edith was flooded with a sense of dread. She'd been at the store since it opened at eleven. Patricia brought her a sandwich around two when Edith said she forgot to eat breakfast again. Patricia was being kind, almost clingy these days, ever since Edith told her about Henry going to Elm Meadows. His illness put them on par, since Patricia's uncle was in a state of slow but steady decline. Now Patricia felt free to share even more details of his day-to-day suffering than she had before, and Edith found it hard to listen. But she was polite. She didn't give Patricia much to chew on where Henry was concerned, saying she had little information, which was true. The sandwich was salty roast beef that sent Edith to the water cooler in the office several times during the afternoon.

Patricia had rounded up folding chairs which she'd arranged in three rows of ten. Even without the circular display table, now in back, they took up most of the room and made it feel crowded and small. Laura would sit on a chair in front. Edith wanted a lectern, but no one knew where to get one, then Alistair suggested contacting someone at Harvard, a secretary in the English Department, who might be able to lend them one from an unused classroom, but by then it was too late. In front of the windows, a table with a white tablecloth held two coffee pots and a slew of china cups, clumsily stacked. Edith expected them to topple at any moment yet didn't rearrange them. There was also a pitcher of cream and a sugar bowl. Edith had a moment of panic when she saw there weren't any spoons, but Alistair was just then bringing them in from the car. He told her she looked tense, and she said she was about to take flight around the room like a mad owl.

Laura and her entourage arrived at six-thirty. Fiona was along, of course, and there were four new faces, all female, all roughly the same age, which Edith assumed was their late twenties. Laura introduced them to Edith, and Edith didn't take in any of their names. She offered them coffee, which one woman with flowing blonde hair and a heavy jacket accepted happily, then took a small bottle of scotch from a pocket and added it to what Alistair poured out for her. She offered him some, and he poured it straight into a cup and drank it. Alistair and the blonde made enough cups of Irish coffee for everyone there, including Edith, who declined, saying she needed to keep a clear head. Laura didn't have any either, though Edith told her she looked like she could do with some. She was dressed in a black suit. Her stockings were opaque, and her shoes were heavy with wooden heels that slammed on the floor. Edith spoke encouragingly to her with an optimism she didn't feel. Laura thanked her for bucking her up. She knew she was being silly. It's just that she'd waited so long for this day to come. Now it was here, and she was quietly falling apart.

"It's all right to be nervous," Edith said and put her hand on her arm.

Patricia was straightening the chairs again. She was nervous, too, Edith realized.

People trickled in. Some took coffee, some didn't. Some looked at the books for sale before finding a seat, and most just sat down. Robert Nedleman was among them. He introduced himself to Laura as a fellow Hedgerow author. She stared at him in terror and then said it was a pleasure to meet him. He took Edith aside and said he hoped he wasn't that much of a wreck when his turn came. Edith excused herself as Walter walked through the door. She went to him.

"What on earth are you doing here?" she asked as quietly as she could manage over the rising din of people talking all around her.

"I saw the notice in the newspaper of course. It's quite an event. I didn't think I could miss it."

He wore an expensive suit. His hat, which he now held, was new, too. His wing-tipped shoes gleamed.

"I hoped Henry would be here," Walter said, surveying the crowd. "I wanted to give him my regards."

"He couldn't make it."

"To the first author reading of your press? How slight his sense of honor."

"Are you drunk?"

"Only a little."

Walter moved off and said hello to Alistair, who didn't look keen to speak to him but was courteous and offered him a cup of coffee. Walter said no thanks, and found a chair in the last row, near the door.

The audience was mostly young, but some were white-haired. Edith prayed everyone was broadminded. She tapped a silver spoon against an empty coffee cup to quiet the group, and when silence fell, she introduced Laura Brown as one of Cambridge's finest young poets, making her debut with The Hedgerow Press. As she said this, Edith realized she should have had a flyer about the press made up, talking about its artistic goals and how it intended to serve the local literary community. Laura took her seat, Edith withdrew to the coffee table where she looped her arm through Alistair's, causing Walter to look at her quizzically, and the crowd continued its silence while Laura waited and waited to open her book. Finally, she did.

"Open like the spring blossom

Let me touch your silk

My love is your sun and with its strength,

Your beauty will never fade,

Your petals never wither."

The poem continued in its vein of passion and yearning. After the last line, "I enter you in endless delight," was read, there were murmurs from the audience. Laura took it in stride and read another poem that described tears as a waterfall coursing over the hard rocks of another's heart. The next one featured a description of gathering clouds that compared them to ineffable loneliness; another suggested a circling hawk possessed the spirit of grievous loss. She read for seventeen minutes and signaled the end by gently closing her book and putting it in her lap. There was some applause. Edith had said before that if Laura wanted to take questions from the audience, she could. That she stood up and thanked everyone for attending meant she didn't want to.

Five copies of Laura's book were now displayed at the end of the coffee table. Patricia had taken care of that during the reading. Each was autographed. People picked them up, flipped through them, read the dedication (which was to Fiona), and put them down. One elderly woman wanted a copy, and Patricia escorted her to the cash register. The woman said she was buying it as a gift and asked if they had suitable wrapping paper. Patricia apologized for having only brown paper and string. The woman said not to bother, she could wrap it herself at home.

Robert approached Laura and complimented her work. The women she came in with surrounded her lovingly. He assessed them and seeing that his chances were nil, politely excused himself and returned to where Edith stood with Alistair, a coffee cup in her hand from which she was sipping scotch.

"I'd say that was racy," Robert said, and indicated to Alistair he'd take a cup of scotch, too.

"It was. But it didn't seem to shock anyone too badly," Edith said.

"It's Harvard Square."

"Still."

A man asked Edith where the history section was, and she pointed it out to him. A young woman wanted to know if there would be another reading, and Edith said yes, then introduced her to Robert.

"You?" the woman asked.

"I."

She was heavy and plain with smudges on the lenses of her eyeglasses. She looked at Robert as if she wanted to bake him in a cake and eat him. He turned away, and the woman took her cue and wandered off.

"Don't you think you were a bit rude?" Edith asked.

"Not at all. She interrupted our conversation, and I indicated I wished to resume it, that's all."

"Were we having a conversation?"

"No. But, would you like to?"

Edith laughed and finished her scotch. She became aware that Alistair was looking disapprovingly at Robert, so she asked him to follow her into her office where they could talk.

Walter, who'd helped himself to an Irish coffee, tried to catch her eye as they went. Edith shut the door to the office.

"I'm in if you are," Robert said and kissed her.

"Stop that! That's not why we're here."

"I beg your pardon. I misread you."

"Yes, you did."

He sat down. "Oh, well. Can't blame a man for trying."

Edith sat too and asked Robert what he thought of her revisions. He said he hadn't looked at them yet, and she said the book was going to press at the start of next week and time was running out.

"I'll get right on it," he said.

She asked what he thought of Jocelyn's dust jacket. He said it was great, but the starling wasn't to scale. Edith said that was the point.

"Right," he said.

The office door opened, and Walter leaned his head in. Alistair was behind him, trying to redirect his attention.

"That went off quite well, don't you think? And she's not bad looking for a man-hater," Walter said.

"Go home," Edith said.

"Who's this clown?" Robert asked.

"Her ex-husband," Walter said.

"I can see why," Robert said.

"Listen, pal, there's no need to get smart."

"Someone has to."

Robert stood up. Alistair and Walter were both in the office at that point, filling the space with the smell of alcohol. Robert hit Walter squarely on the jaw, causing him to reel backward into Alistair. When Walter lunged, Alistair grabbed his arm and Robert got the other. They maneuvered him out of the office and across the store to the door. Walter said he needed his hat. It was on the windowsill where Edgar had been resting before when the store was still quiet and empty. He'd vanished. Edith picked up the hat and put it on Walter's head. It was crooked and for a moment she felt sorry for him.

"This is what she is," Walter said. "Just a tease, dressed up like a respectable woman."

Edith opened the door and Alistair pushed Walter out. He straightened his hat, then his tie, and went on his way in a well-controlled stagger.

"He was tight when he got here, wasn't he?" Robert asked.

"That's a safe assumption," Edith said.

"What's he got to prove now? You're divorced, right?"

"Yes."

Alistair walked away and began putting the dirty cups into a crate packed with newspaper to bring back to the apartment.

"I shouldn't have slugged him," Robert said.

"It was necessary."

"Well, I better be on my way before he decides to call a cop on me."

Robert shook Edith's hand, then kissed her cheek. He said he'd talk to her soon.

The only people left were Laura and her group, seated in a cluster, drinking. Laura looked at Edith and asked who that man had been, and Edith said her ex-husband, who never had great manners. Alistair asked Edith if he could have a moment, and she said sure, why not?

They returned to her office and Alistair said he'd come straight to the point. Was she involved with Robert?

"That's none of your business," she said and lit a cigarette. The start of a wretched headache was taking root behind her eyes.

"I believe it is."

"Why? Because we slept together?"

Alistair closed the door.

"Because of how I feel about you," he said.

"I can't help that."

Edith watched him calm himself. He could give Walter a lesson or two.

"I apologize," Alistair said.

"No need. And no, I'm not involved with Robert and don't plan to be. He's fresh, that's all."

"Did he take liberties with you?"

"Of course."

"The swine."

"Oh, Alistair, you're something else."

She held out her hand and he squeezed it. He said he thought the reading had gone well, better than expected. Edith agreed.

There was a knock on the door. Alistair opened it.

Laura said they were all heading out and wanted to buy Edith a drink. Would she come?

"I'd be delighted!" Edith said.

Alistair said he would stay and help Patricia close up. What time should he expect her home?

"Not 'til the wee hours, Pop," one of Laura's friends said.

On top of what she had at the store, Edith was soon drunk, but she was having great fun. She wasn't used to being in the company of women, and Laura's friends were great, especially Dottie, who designed clothes. She told Edith that with her figure and some custom-made outfits, they could go places. She admired Edith's black belted dress but said the buttons down the back were all wrong. They shouldn't be cloth-covered, but jet, or even rhinestone. After that, they took separate cabs to another bar, and another after that. When Edith woke up, she was on a couch under a blanket, with her balled-up coat as a pillow. Her head was awful.

The room she was in had pale green walls with paintings hung everywhere. The curtains were open and thin daylight fell on the dusty wood floor. A dog was barking outside somewhere. She sat up, then stood and went into the kitchen, which was just off the room she'd slept in. After opening three cupboard doors, she found a glass and turned on the faucet. She drank two glasses of water, then patted some on her face.

"Good morning." It was Fiona, looking as bad as Edith felt. Her makeup was smudged around her eyes, and her hair was tangled. She wore a man's plaid bathrobe that fell well below her knees. On her wrist was a heavy gold bangle that caught Edith's eye. Fiona saw where she was looking and said it had been a gift from her grandmother, who hoped she wouldn't turn out the way she had. And that was *after* she'd met Laura, but her grandmother didn't know anything about that.

"I don't suppose you have any aspirin lying around, do you?" Edith asked.

Fiona took a bottle out of the pocket of her robe and explained that she'd grabbed it from her room when she heard

Edith rattling around. Edith helped herself to two tablets and more water, then returned to the living room to wait while Fiona made coffee. The dog stopped barking. The telephone rang and went unanswered. Edith looked at her watch and was shocked to see it was past ten. Finally, Fiona appeared with the coffee and Edith gratefully took her mug. When it cooled enough to be tasted, she found the lack of sugar alarming but said nothing. At least Fiona had brought out a pitcher of cream, but it curdled the minute Edith poured it in. She drank it, anyway.

"I was pretty tight last night," Edith said.

"We all were. That's okay. You have to celebrate the good things."

"It *was* a good thing. She did well."

"Who was that guy that got thrown out?"

"My ex-husband. Didn't I mention that?"

"You probably did, I don't remember." Fiona sipped her coffee. "Tell me all about it."

"What?"

"Everything. How he came to be your husband, then your ex."

"It's a dull tale."

"I doubt it."

Edith took her time. She went back to the beginning, when she met Walter in high school, dating, moving to Washington for the war, and getting engaged. The part about her dropping out of graduate school was easier now as if it had happened to someone else. Talking about Henry was easy, too, until she brought the story current.

"What do you mean, he went away?" Fiona asked.

"To a sanatorium."

"Yikes."

Fiona said she recalled that he was agitated at the party, there at the end, but assumed he'd had one too many. Men got nasty when they drank too much.

"They do, indeed."

Fiona's brother went bonkers after the war, she said. Her parents didn't have a lot, so he went to live with an uncle in Wisconsin. He was discovered sexually assaulting a sheep.

"Are you serious?" Edith asked.

"Completely."

"So, what happened then?"

"The uncle said he wouldn't have a pervert on the place, he didn't care how many Japs he'd killed, and sent him home."

"Goodness. Where is he now?"

"Living with a friend in Vermont. A sculptor. He helps out, but I'm not sure how."

"As long as the sculptor doesn't keep sheep."

"Exactly."

Edith asked what she taught at Boston University. She was sure she'd asked her that before when she came to the party, but she couldn't for the life of her recall.

"English literature. The Romantic poets, to be specific."

"That's wonderful. Where did you get your degree?"

"UCLA."

"That's a long way away."

"I needed a change of scene."

Her tone suggested that a failed romance was the cause.

Edith asked where the powder room was. She said she must have used it last night but couldn't remember a thing.

"You were singing in the cab," Fiona said and indicated a door next to the kitchen.

"I was? Heavens."

Edith went and splashed more water on her face. She pulled a comb out of her purse and used it to put order in her disastrous hair. She returned and asked Fiona if she knew where she left her hat. Fiona didn't know.

"Pity, it was a nice hat," Edith said.

Fiona yawned and rubbed her eyes. She looked at Edith blearily. Then she focused.

"You seem to have quite a way with the gentlemen," she said.

"What makes you say that?"

"Well, they were all there last night, paying court."

"They weren't."

"Oh, come now. I'd be jealous if men interested me at all."

Edith sat down. She said everyone seemed to fall in love with her and she just didn't understand it. Not one bit.

"You're not exactly hard to look at," Fiona said.

"But in love? That takes a lot more. I can't begin to explain it."

"They're not in love, they're just lonely. Everyone's lonely these days."

"I suppose you're right."

Edith said she should call a cab. Fiona pointed to the telephone on the table. Edith used it, then thanked her, and told her to give her best to Laura when she surfaced.

Alistair was waiting for her in the living room. As always, he was tidy and well-pressed, but there were circles below his eyes. He asked if she'd enjoyed her evening. She said she had, what she could remember of it. She said she woke up at Laura and Fiona's place, and lost her hat, in the bargain.

Alistair said there was a telegram from Dr. Harris. The first insulin treatment had been successful, and Henry was lucid and calm.

"Oh, I'm glad," Edith said.

"Yes."

She asked Alistair to bring her some coffee. He gestured to the pot on the table, then poured her some.

It was better than what Fiona had made. Alistair had a nice way of doing everything.

The aspirin was finally taking effect and the absence of pain let her think clearly. She thought about the reading. She'd counted fourteen attendees, just under half what they had room for. Next time, when it was Robert's turn, there were sure to be more. A male author would garner greater interest, she thought.

Walter had his nerve to show up like that. She hoped he learned a lesson and wouldn't come back. She could write to him and tell him to stay away, or she'd call the law on him. He wouldn't want his employers to know he roughed up someone at the bookstore owned by his ex-wife.

"What?" Alistair asked.

"Oh, I was just thinking about that poor sod."

"Which?"

"Walter, of course. Wasn't that funny when Robert slugged him?"

"It was. And wholly deserved, I think."

"Walter never could hold his liquor."

"He's a foolish man."

"He is."

Edith said she needed to sleep a little more. When she got up, she'd see about making that Boeuf Bourguignon for Thanksgiving dinner tomorrow, if he'd gotten all the ingredients. He said he had, and that he'd be happy to help her. But what should they have for dinner tonight? Edith said scrambled eggs and toast, their reliable standby. His smile was full of warmth and gladness, and she knew it wasn't because of what she suggested, but for the days ahead, living together alone, without Henry.

Chapter Thirteen

Henry wrote that the Thanksgiving meal offered him at Elm Meadows had been passable, not nearly as fine as they had the year before when Edith first came to the apartment. He remembered that occasion with great fondness, and sincerely hoped Edith and Alistair had had a lovely day. He said he was feeling better, but still prone to brooding, which Dr. Harris assured him would soon pass. He hoped she was well and sent all his love.

Edith couldn't detect his true mood. His words felt forced. She let Alistair read the letter, and he agreed.

She wondered if they should try another visit and Alistair said they should wait until Dr. Harris could guarantee they'd be seen. It was a long way to go for nothing.

"Not entirely nothing," Edith said, then regretted her words when the color rose in Alistair's face. Since that night in the hotel, he hadn't suggested they sleep together once, and neither had she, though she thought about it. It was impossible not to think about it. She didn't do well being celibate. That

Alistair was the oldest man she'd had sex with both intrigued and made her uncomfortable. He wasn't as fit as Henry, but just as energetic. She asked him his age afterward. He was fifty-one, old enough to be her father, he said.

"You could never be my father," she said, then added that it was a bad idea to go to bed with a woman with a father complex.

"From what you told me about him when we were abroad, he sounds like the one with a complex, not you," Alistair said. Edith appreciated his kindness.

Aunt Margaret wrote to invite Edith and Alistair to New York for Christmas unless, of course, Henry had returned to them, in which case they should all come. The city was magical that time of year, she said.

When Edith mentioned the idea to Alistair, he said he hoped Henry would be well by then. Edith felt they both knew better than that. Henry wasn't nearly ready to return. Though the catatonia was behind him, he'd lost ground again, according to Dr. Harris Brannick's most recent report.

Something dire weighs on him, and I cannot find its source, but I will continue undeterred in my efforts, he wrote.

Edith felt it wasn't one thing, but many. In her layman's terms, life had gotten too hard for him to bear. At first, she had nothing but sympathy, but over time she'd grown cynical. With all that money and privilege, to do with as exactly as he pleased, plus the incredible advantage of being born male, all he could do was fall apart. Where would she be, if she let herself go? But then, she had, hadn't she, after she left Walter? The difference was that she bounced back. She was resilient, Henry wasn't.

Her mother also invited her home for Christmas and said if she couldn't come, she and Betty would plan a trip to Boston in the spring, when the snow was gone. Edith liked the idea of the holidays at Betty's and told Alistair she might go. But what would he do there alone?

"I should manage, I expect," he said.

"It wouldn't be fair to leave you here."

"Fair has nothing to do with it."

He stood to clear the dinner plates and put his hand lightly on her shoulder, something he often did now.

Robert telephoned the store twice to invite her for a drink and both times she turned him down. After his book came out, she said. Until then, it was best to keep things on a purely professional footing. He was bright and cheerful and said he'd look her up then. His reading was scheduled for the middle of January, right after classes resumed at Harvard, and they both hoped a lot of students would come.

The nursing home where Clara Levy had gone wrote to say Edith had been invited to visit if that were convenient.

Edith hadn't thought much of Miss Levy in the last several weeks and felt guilty about not moving forward with the manuscript she'd agreed to edit. She told herself she was too busy with Laura's reading and dealing with Henry, though, in truth, it was Alistair who did most of that. Edith was ashamed to realize she hadn't written to Henry in over two weeks, when she'd been writing him every second or third day. She dashed off a cheerful note full of nothing substantive and left it in the hall with bills Alistair was sending out.

Seeing them reminded her that she had no idea about the state of Henry's finances. There was money, but how much? She went to the library where Alistair had taken over Henry's former desk and asked if she could see bank statements and the checkbook. He opened the drawer and gave them to her. She sat on the couch and went through the papers. Henry had over ten thousand dollars in his checking account. A savings account held close to forty thousand dollars. An investment company in London managed two accounts with the equivalent of over two hundred thousand dollars each, and the interest from these was paid monthly into the checking account. Since Henry owned the apartment free and clear, Alistair withdrew only what was needed to pay expenses, including his modest salary. That sum was just over five hundred dollars a month. Even with Henry's care at Elm Meadows, which cost nine hundred a month, more accumulated each month than went out. She sat, staring into space, trying to take it all in.

"His Lordship is a wealthy man," Alistair said.

"Filthy rich is more like it."

She said she hadn't grown up poor, though her father kept her mother on a tight leash, financially. It turned out that he'd hoarded money for years, to start a new life for himself somewhere, probably without her mother. The kind of money Henry had was overwhelming, though, of course, he was used to it, as were Gerald and Alice.

Alistair said they hadn't always been wealthy. They were never poor, but the real money came from Gerald's wartime business ventures, betting on automobiles and modestly priced housing developments. After the money came in, they lived much as they had before, except they were able to fix up the family estate, which had grown a bit shabby over time.

"And what about you? Do you have money saved?" she asked.

Her question seemed to make him uneasy. She reminded him that they were having a frank conversation about Henry's affairs, so it didn't seem such a stretch that he be truthful with her now about his. Unless he didn't want to, of course. She'd understand if he felt she weren't entitled to know.

"Don't be silly. I have several thousand dollars put away. For the proverbial rainy day," he said.

She asked Alistair the scope of Henry's Power of Attorney. Alistair said it covered everything.

"So, you could make off with the whole lot, if you wanted," she said.

"I hope you're not suggesting that."

"I'm not."

"Good."

Then she said she had another question, one that might be uncomfortable for him. How much was she going to get if Henry didn't recover, and had to stay away for good?

"He left that to me to decide," Alistair said. He lit himself a cigarette he took from Henry's cigarette case.

"Well, how much would you give me? I'd like to know. I'd counted on not having to worry about money if I married him. In a way, and I know this sounds vulgar, it was part of the bargain."

"How much would you think was fair?"

Edith got the feeling that he was making fun of her, and she grew irritated. She told herself to calm down, and get a straight answer, one she could hold him to.

"Fifty thousand dollars."

"Edith."

"I don't think it's that much," she said, her face hot.

"It's not nearly enough, given what you would have gotten had you married."

"I'm not entitled to that."

"His Lordship would disagree."

"Well, if you'll forgive me, he's not quite in his right mind, now, is he?"

Alistair said that it was a matter of choosing a reasonable figure and then drawing up the papers. He was prepared to move forward now if she wanted. She said she preferred to wait until Henry was released from Elm Meadows. Alistair thought that was reasonable.

"What about his parents? Will they object? Pose a problem?" Edith asked.

"I shouldn't think so."

"I feel so bad for them. I've been wondering if I should write and tell them he'll be fine, but I don't think I'd sound persuasive."

"I understand. It's not easy, is it?"

Edith could see how worried Alistair was about Henry, and she was touched. She asked him to be honest with her again. Did he think Henry would recover? Alistair sat and smoked his cigarette. After a long silence, he said he didn't know. He'd always known before, or rather, he'd always been confident.

The previous episodes resolved much more quickly. Edith asked if Dr. Harris could be extending it artificially, keeping Henry in a state where he wouldn't make much progress. Alistair thought that unlikely. Henry's problems were real and deep-seated. Edith had seen that for herself.

"True."

It was hard to think about it again, how he yelled at her with a steely look in his eyes that had only ever held concern or tenderness.

"Sometimes I realize I'm angry at him," she said.

"I, as well."

"Are we dreadful?"

"I think we're human."

"I want him to come home. I miss him. The way he used to be."

"Sometimes I find myself just wanting to erase all that's happened."

Edith went into her home office and considered the amount of money that would land in her lap when Alistair followed through with the legalities. While the reason she'd receive that sum made her uneasy, the things she could turn it to filled her with excitement. She would hire a full-time designer for dust jackets and take on more manuscripts. If she set herself a goal of ten titles a year, the press would begin to make a name for itself.

But who to publish, after Robert? Henry said he would pull from the manuscripts they'd received others that had merit. He never had, as far she knew. She also didn't know where they were now, and after about twenty minutes of going through his desk, and scouring the study and living room, she found them in the top drawer of his dresser. For a moment, she was infuriated with him for being so lax. Each of these authors was owed a decision one way or another, and here he'd hidden them from her. Then she was cross with herself for losing track of them. Patricia said an author had telephoned the store just the other day, against the stated submissions guidelines, to ask when he'd hear back. She'd put him off in her usual pleasant, brisk way, and told Edith she had a feeling they'd hear from him again.

She took the pile into her office and went through them. She'd seen several before and had decided against them, and those she put on the floor. On others, Henry had made notes on the title page, "dull," "awkward wording," and "arrogant." She noticed his remarks were harshest against the female authors, which was frustrating because only about a fifth of the submissions were from women. She separated these and went through them. Henry was right. There wasn't much here.

From the men, there were two contenders, both about war and repatriation. One author focused on the physical damage done in armed conflict, the other on ravaged souls. She preferred the latter and would offer publication to that author first. Bernard Cavelli. She imagined him living in Brooklyn and driving a taxi for a living, but then her assumptions usually proved false.

When she arrived at the store the next day, she found a letter from Kathleen.

Dear Edie,

Walt said he came to your author reading. I don't mind telling you he found it surprising, to say the least. He said the author is a lesbian and didn't bother to hide the fact in her pages. Now, I'm not one to judge, but, Edie, what are you thinking? Of course, the dear boy is probably exaggerating. He does that. Anyway, just wanted to let you know. How's life with the British peer? All's fine here. Dennis has soured on tung nuts and wants to bail out. I've rather taken to Florida, especially the climate, so I told him I'd bust his chops if he tried to uproot me again.

She wrote about missing her job in Chicago and was thinking of offering her deep knowledge of bookkeeping and accounting procedures to the local college, assuming she could talk her way in. In Edith's experience, Kathleen was good at exactly that. She closed the letter by wishing Edith a happy birthday the following week. Edith hadn't thought much about that and didn't want to now.

She put a piece of paper in her typewriter to let Mr. Cavelli know about her decision. Patricia knocked on the door. Someone was there to see her. A police detective.

"What?" Edith asked.

"That's what he said."

Edith's first thought was that something had happened to Henry, or even to Alistair, but then realized that made no sense. She told Patricia to show him in.

Detective O'Connell was in his forties, Edith guessed, and needed to go on a diet. She asked him to sit down, and he remained on his feet. He didn't remove his hat or offer her a cigarette when he lit one for himself.

"Your name?" he asked.

"Edith Sloan."

"You the owner of this establishment?"

"I am."

He said he'd come straight to the point. Someone had reported her to the local precinct. Something about an inappropriate book being sold at her store. He was considering arresting her on an obscenity charge. He named the book and asked if there were any copies around.

"Yes. Four," she said.

"Give them to me."

"And if I don't?"

"I'll arrest you."

"You said you were going to do that anyway."

"I said I was considering it."

"Well, perhaps I should retain an attorney."

"Perhaps you should."

Walter was the only lawyer she knew, besides Sturgis, who had drawn up the publishing contract. Walter would have a field day with this. She'd never live it down. Better to let herself get hauled off and throw herself at the mercy of the court, rather than ask for his help.

Edith stood up and told the detective to wait there. He looked at her sharply.

"You wanted the books, did you not?" she asked.

"I did."

"But you think I might just make a run for it."

"Not in those shoes."

Edith had worn particularly high heels that day. She went into the store and gathered up the copies of Laura's book. Patricia was watching her with terror from her post behind the cash register. Edith was grateful the store was empty. She hoped it would stay that way. It wouldn't help business for her to be observed being led away in handcuffs.

O'Connell had helped himself to a chair in her brief absence. Ash from his cigarette had fallen onto the rug. Edith dropped the books on the desk and slid the ashtray in his direction. O'Connell picked up a copy and looked at the copyright page.

"Hedgerow Press. Never heard of them," he said.

"They're new."

"You, I assume?"

"You assume correctly."

"Very enterprising."

He flipped through the pages, stopping to read one or two. He closed the book and read the text on the back cover.

"Her first book, eh? I'd call that little lady a big risk-taker," he said.

"I'm afraid I don't know what you mean."

"Come on, sweetheart, I wasn't born yesterday."

"Clearly not."

At this, he laughed. He told her she was all right. He wanted her to understand he was just doing his job. Complaints had to be followed up on. Edith asked who'd made the complaint.

"It was anonymous," O'Connell said.

Edith had a terrible feeling it had been Walter.

She said there was nothing obscene or even remotely distasteful in Miss Brown's poems, as he could see, though given his profession, his acquaintance with the fine art of poetry was no doubt limited.

"I used to pen quite the flowery line, in my day," he said.

"And what day was that?"

"Let's stick to the book."

"And what exactly *is* the problem?"

"Someone at the reading found certain lines suggestive. That's the long and the short of it."

"Do you find anything suggestive here?" Edith asked.

"I couldn't say. I'd have to look it over more thoroughly."

"Then how can you arrest me unless you know whether the material is obscene or not?

"I'm not arresting you. I'm just here to have a friendly chat."

Edith lit a cigarette. She sat while O'Connell kept flipping through the book. She hated the look of it in his meaty hands. She asked him if she could offer him a cup of tea. He stared at her, then said he never drank the stuff.

Edith had finished her cigarette and just lit another when he said fine, she won.

"There's nothing overt here, nothing I can put a finger on," he said.

"I told you that."

"Couldn't take your word. Had to see for myself."

"And now you have."

He closed the book and put it on the top of the pile. Edith asked him what would happen to the books. He said she could put them back on the shelf anytime she wanted, but before he went, he wanted to give her a piece of advice. She looked like a reasonable young woman. She should find a nice man and settle down. Running a bookstore was fine but making a home for someone was much more important. And she should think about what she published from now on. Stick to kids' books or something like that.

"That's good advice," she said.

He didn't want to hear any more complaints. And no more suggestive readings, okay?

"Certainly."

He stood up and straightened his hat. Then he left.

Patricia fluttered in and asked what on earth was going on. Edith told her.

"I bet it was that woman, the one with the sour face and that stupid little hat. You know, with the fake cherries on it," she said. Edith drew a blank.

Then she asked, "Oh, you mean the one who brought her knitting?"

"Yes."

"She looked like a dreadful person. I hope she comes to hear Robert read and that he picks the juiciest poem."

"You said his stuff wasn't dirty."

"Did I? Oh, well, it's just his mind that's dirty."

Patricia didn't follow that up.

Edith said she had an appointment and wouldn't be back that day.

She found a cab and gave the driver the address of Miss Levy's nursing home in South Boston. It was in a run-down neighborhood a block away from a dry cleaners and a bar. Restful Manor indeed, Edith thought as she got out and slipped the cabbie a five-dollar bill. She told him to keep the change. The day was cold, and she'd foolishly worn her lightweight coat. She walked quickly, which her stupid high heels made difficult. A gust of wind blew bits of paper and cigarette butts along the sidewalk in front of her. Children ran past yelling joyously. An old man sat in a rocking chair on his porch, a blanket draped around his shoulders. There was a metal gate leading to the chipped concrete stairs of the manor.

Poor Miss Levy, Edith thought. She'd certainly come down in the world.

This impression was underscored by the intense smell of ammonia inside. The woman at the desk had a pale, puffy face and a sullen, stupid gleam in her eyes. Edith said why she was there. The woman said visiting hours were on Monday, Wednesday, and Friday. Today was Thursday. Edith said she didn't care. She was asked to come and here she was. The woman stared at her. Her name tag read Miss Dillard. Edith removed her gloves and lit a cigarette. Miss Dillard looked at Edith's sterling silver cigarette case, her silver lighter, and Henry's engagement ring. She said Miss Levy was in Room 204, down the hall to the left, the last room on the right. Edith thanked her and went on her way.

The door was ajar and tinny orchestral music played on the radio inside. Edith knocked, got no answer, and pushed the door open. Miss Levy was propped up in bed, a shawl around her shoulders. The confident, dyed black hair she had when Edith met her before was now white. Edith said her name, and Miss Levy opened her eyes. Her face was sallow, her eyes bright.

"Have I come at a bad time?" Edith asked. Miss Levy shook her head and beckoned her with a gnarled forefinger. Edith removed her coat and hung it on the hook nailed to the door. She sat in the folding chair next to the bed.

"Mrs. Sloan. How nice it is to see you again," Miss Levy said. Her voice was faint.

"I'm glad you asked me to come. How have you been?"

Miss Levy gestured around the small room as if to say she was in much the same condition as her surroundings. The only furniture was a dresser and a nightstand on which sat a crystal paperweight Edith recognized from her apartment in Cambridge. A faded print on the wall of a pastoral scene was also familiar.

Miss Levy explained she'd fallen and taken a long time to recover. Her doctor said living on her own was no longer possible, and so here she was.

Edith nodded and found herself staring out the narrow window. The view offered a sliver of sky and the back of a brick building with faded lettering that said Tosco Tobacco.

Miss Levy wanted to know about Edgar and how he was getting along. She heard Edith had taken him in.

"He's quite the independent bachelor. He comes around when he wants to visit, but otherwise, he keeps himself occupied elsewhere," Edith said. Miss Levy smiled weakly. It seemed to require effort to do so.

"I'm afraid I have nothing to offer you at the moment. To ask for a simple cup of tea in this place is to submit a request of inordinate proportions," she said.

"That's perfectly all right."

Miss Levy asked after the store, and Edith told her about the fire. Miss Levy nodded as Edith described the mess she returned from England to find. She wanted to know how Henry was and recalled with pleasure their brief meeting. Edith said Henry had gone away for his health and she didn't know when he'd return.

"I'm sorry to hear that. And he's such a young man," Miss Levy said.

Edith told Miss Levy Henry's affliction was mental, not physical, and at this Miss Levy made a slight nod. She said she'd known people who couldn't cope. It was hard to witness and must be dreadful to bear.

"We're engaged," Edith said.

"Are you now? That's wonderful news!"

Miss Levy looked closely at Edith, who volunteered nothing more, though she wanted to share every detail about the whole mess she found herself in.

Edith told her about Laura's reading, the nature of her work, and the visit from Detective O'Connell. Miss Levy shook her head. She told Edith it was a fine thing she was doing, giving voice to those who lived in both fear and silence. Edith said Laura Brown wasn't a fearful person as far as she could tell, except when it came to reading her work aloud before strangers.

Miss Levy looked wistful, and Edith thought she wished she'd had a chance to do the same.

"There's something you should know," Miss Levy said.

"All right."

"My book will be published posthumously."

"I beg your pardon?"

"I haven't long, I'm afraid. Only weeks. I have cancer of the liver. Too much high living when I was young."

She spoke without a trace of emotion. Not even her eyes held the smallest light of concern.

"And I wish to change the title. *Redemption* is preferable to *Holocaust*. Wouldn't you agree?" she asked.

"Absolutely."

Edith didn't have the heart to say the manuscript was in terrible shape, and while she was saddened by Miss Levy's news, it meant she had more time to work on it now.

A nurse entered Miss Levy's room carrying a tray with a bottle of medicine. She put the tray down on the nightstand and poured out a green liquid into a small glass. She handed the glass to Miss Levy. She didn't look at Edith while she worked. Miss Levy took the glass, drank the medicine, made a face of disgust, and gave the glass to the nurse.

When the nurse had gone, still without a word, Miss Levy said, "I don't know why they bother keeping me alive. A truly pointless endeavor."

Miss Levy picked up Edith's hand. Edith was too startled to say anything. Miss Levy said her book had found a good home, and she knew Edith would give the world a better version of itself.

"It's a beautiful work," Edith said.

"Thank you."

Edith said she was honored to be publishing it.

"There's something I want you to include. I have it written out here somewhere." Miss Levy took a crumpled piece of paper out of the pocket of her bathrobe. She seemed to tire suddenly, and the color drained from her face. She gave the paper to Edith.

I dedicate this, my first and only collection of poems, to Edith Sloan with the deepest affection and heartfelt thanks.

"Oh, Miss Levy, that's lovely," Edith said and felt her eyes tear.

"Add the name of your press. What did you settle on?"

"Hedgerow."

"Ah, I see. Take this down."

Edith looked for a pen in her purse. It was blue lacquer with her first name engraved in silver, given to her by Henry the summer before.

"I dedicate this, my first, etc. to Edith Sloan and the Hedgerow Press with deepest, etc."

"I'll take care of it."

Miss Levy closed her eyes. After a moment, Edith realized she'd fallen asleep. She got into her coat and left the room quietly.

She walked for blocks along the main road past cheap bars and restaurants, waiting for her tears to stop before she hailed a cab.

Chapter Fourteen

With the holiday season in full swing, sales at the store were robust. The last Christmas of the decade brought a glow of optimism, and everyone seemed cheerful. Patricia didn't mind being on her feet all day, and Liza, who lived locally, put in extra hours when her semester ended. Jocelyn worked on the cover for Miss Levy's volume. Edith gave her some sample poems to give her an idea of what to evoke in her design. She clearly had trouble with it, given the crumpled pieces of paper Edith sometimes found in the office's wastebasket. Edith let her work at her desk when she wasn't there. Jocelyn had said before that her living situation was crowded and private space impossible to find.

The visit to Miss Levy had left Edith in a bad way. She thought of Henry constantly. Dr. Harris reported no progress and no loss of ground. Henry was in a holding pattern and there was nothing to do but wait. There were no letters from him, and none recently from his parents, either. It was as if Henry had been spirited away from all of them, and dropped down in a soft, vague place with no doors or windows. When Edith shared her thoughts with Alistair, he said he looked at it the same way. He had debated ordering his release against medical advice and bringing Henry home.

But, what to do with him then? Edith was busy all day and she didn't think it fair that Alistair take on Henry's care by himself. They could hire a nurse to live in. At this, Edith recalled the nurses who tended her father in his final days and shuddered. She knew the situation was different, that Henry wasn't dying but trying to recover, yet she couldn't bear the thought of having them underfoot. She said it was better that he stay at Elm Meadows until something changed. Alistair agreed. Edith sensed he didn't want Henry to return yet. He was finding himself, making a life that didn't focus on serving someone else but working in partnership. He and Edith shared chores though he always said she didn't have to cook and clean. She laughed at that. She'd been a housewife, hadn't she? While she was at work, Alistair read or attended free lectures at the public library. One, in particular, excited him. An archeologist who'd worked in Egypt spoke about his discoveries there, and Edith could see a longing for travel in his eyes. She told him he should do as he pleased and go where he wanted. Why not? Henry would hardly begrudge Alistair a trip or two. Alistair said it wouldn't be right to leave Edith on her own, and though she protested, she was grateful. She didn't feel right, these days. She was unsettled and nervous. And Robert was becoming a nuisance. He wanted to become romantically involved and she had no interest. When she reminded him that she was still engaged, he said sure, but wasn't it only a matter of time before she broke that off? He called every few days or sent a witty note to the store. Once, he even dropped in and Edith told him not to do that again.

She wrote to Aunt Margaret that she couldn't get away for the holiday, and Aunt Margaret's return letter expressed disappointment but was full of her usual gossip. Philip hadn't married after all. The girl turned out not to have been pregnant. It came to light when she pressured Philip to move up the date of the wedding. When he'd asked to know why, she couldn't give a reasonable answer, so he confronted her, nicely or so Aunt Margaret hoped, and the girl broke down. She said she'd fallen madly in love and just couldn't live without him. Well, she seemed to be doing that just fine. Francine hadn't specified, but Aunt Margaret suspected money had changed hands, enough to get her out of Philip's hair for good.

Edith also wrote to her mother to say she wanted to remain in Boston over Christmas in case Henry's situation changed. Her mother wrote back and promised again to come out with Betty when the weather warmed. Since Edith wasn't coming home, they planned a trip to Florida. Her mother didn't like the idea of such a long train trip but looked forward to feeling the sun on her face.

She hadn't answered Kathleen's letter and wasn't sure she would until the New Year. She couldn't match Kathleen's level of self-determination, and every sentence she framed in her mind made her sound silly or desperate in comparison. She knew she wasn't being fair to herself, but again, she felt uneasy in a way she never had before. She was losing confidence and wished she understood why.

The weather turned nasty, and snow fell every other day. Edith worked from home rather than brave the cold. Alistair offered to drive her to the store and pick her up at the end of the day, overcoming his reluctance to get behind the wheel for her convenience and comfort. His offer made her burst into tears, and she told him he was kinder than anyone deserved. He gave her a glass of sherry to steady her nerves, then brought her a bowl of delicious chicken soup. She was ashamed of her outburst and avoided him for two days until he tracked her down in the kitchen and asked what he'd done to offend her.

"Oh, Malcolm, you didn't do anything at all. I'm just a fool and my foolishness is finally catching up with me." She was dressed in a dull brown dress, her least favorite, which seemed the best thing to put on that morning, given the gloom she felt the moment she woke up.

He told her the only foolishness she was guilty of was doubting herself again. She needed to buck up and stop fretting. He'd do anything he could to help her, only she wouldn't let him. It was disheartening, if he were to be honest. Disheartening, indeed.

"I'm sorry. I know I've been selfish. I just feel like something has settled in me that I don't understand and can't get rid of," she said. She lit another cigarette. She was smoking more than usual and had developed a recurring cough.

"You'll be fine if you make your mind up to it," he said.

She said she wished everyone would stop saying that. Alistair apologized and said he was going out to another lecture but would be home in time for tea.

While he was gone a letter from Henry came, addressed to her. She debated reading it, given her rotten mood. It would be unfair not to, so she took it into her office and slid the opener under the seal. It wasn't his handwriting, which he explained in the first sentence by saying his nurse was taking dictation.

I do find it strange to share such intimacies with a relative stranger, though I now hasten to add that Miss Dean is not as much a stranger as she once was.

Here, Edith paused, disturbed to discover she was jealous.

Never fear my darling, I have eyes only for you.

Edith shivered.

He—that is, Miss Dean—wrote that he was being well taken care of. He continued to enjoy the food there, though his tastes had grown more modest in the time he'd been away. On Wednesday he had enjoyed a particularly hearty pea soup. The idea made him chuckle to recall when he considered how his mother might react to him saying so. As for his father, he could see clearly in his mind's eye those bushy eyebrows raised in disapproval.

He said he thought of her often.

You must know this is so. Miss Dean bears witness to the frequent mention of your name, dearest Edith.

And now I come to a difficult point as I instruct my dutiful scribe to impart to you the news that I am releasing you from your engagement. My condition improves so slowly that I deem it would be a gross injustice to deny you the freedom to love elsewhere. Please know in my heart this pains me greatly, and it is only for your happiness that I take this step. Write to me and tell me how you are, for your words comfort me greatly in this lonely place. If you cannot bring yourself to correspond with the man who dangled the prospect of a blissful marriage before you, only to renege on his offer, I understand completely even as I pray it isn't so.

Your devoted Henry.

P.S. Please feel free to keep the ring. It's the least I can do.

She challenged the misery flowing through her. Wasn't this easier? It spared her telling him she didn't want to marry him. But soon her suspicious nature got the better of her as she wondered about Miss Dean. Had she put him up to it? Had she worked her charms on him and found him a willing subject?

And why couldn't he pen the words himself?

The answer to that came when Alistair returned and opened the other letter that had arrived, which was addressed to him. It was from Dr. Harris who said Henry had had a violent outburst and attacked an orderly who was escorting him to the arts and crafts room. He'd loosened one of the man's teeth and blackened his eye. Naturally, Henry had been put in restraints which was thought preferable to sedating him. Dr. Harris had had to act quickly and thus hadn't had time to obtain Alistair's approval, for which he was asking now. He wanted to assure both him and Mrs. Sloan that this was for the best. Henry now had something tangible to work toward by behaving himself. As soon as he could be trusted, the straight jacket would be removed.

Alistair asked Edith how Henry was supposed to prove he wouldn't attack someone while it was impossible for him to use his hands and arms. They had only his word. Edith told him what Henry had written to her. Alistair poured her a drink and lit the fire in the library where they had convened.

"You don't seem happy about it," he said.

"I don't know what I feel, but I suppose I should be relieved."

She said she couldn't help thinking that Miss Dean was somehow behind it all and that she'd turned Henry's head.

"Oh, I shouldn't think so. She's hardly a feast for the eye," Alistair said.

"What do you mean?"

"We met her at the sanitorium, don't you remember?"

"No."

"Perhaps you'd gone to powder your nose. She came into Dr. Harris' office to ask if she should bring us coffee. She's fifty if she's a day, and hardly possessed of a girlish figure."

"Oh, Malcolm, you're making that all up."

"I'm not, I swear."

The thought of Henry falling under Miss Dean's romantic spell was laughable, though these things did happen. When she said so, Alistair asked what difference it would make in the end, since Edith had already decided not to marry him, and Henry now no longer expected her to.

"You're right, as always," she said. She drank her sherry quickly and asked for another one. Then she said it tasted off and he should open a fresh bottle. He said he would, of course, and wouldn't be a moment. While he was gone, Edith lit a cigarette and leaned back, drawn in by the fire's rising flames. Now that they were no longer engaged, it felt wrong to live here. The time had come to ask Alistair to give her the lump sum he'd mentioned and buy a place of her own.

Alistair returned with a new bottle which he poured into the decanter. He said to let it breathe a moment and then he'd refill her glass. She told him what was on her mind.

"I can write to the investment company in London tomorrow," he said. "Or if you prefer, send a cable."

"A letter is fine."

"I wish you wouldn't."

"Wouldn't what?"

"Go."

"I'm not gone yet, but seriously, how can I stay after Henry returns?"

"He might not return."

Alistair got himself a glass of scotch, then sat in a chair by the fire. Edith studied his profile. It was unremarkable but pleasing.

He said he'd been doing a great deal of thinking. It was time to be his own man. Edith wasn't the only one Henry had promised to make a settlement on. Alistair stood to receive a generous sum, too, regardless of whether Henry remained at Elm Meadows. This had all been arranged during the war just before Henry took the post with the Intelligence Branch. He and Alistair made a deal, a gentlemen's agreement, if you will, that should anything happen to him, Alistair was to take whatever he thought fair from Henry's assets. Later, they put it in writing. Alistair had that document in his room along with his other personal papers.

"Someone might challenge it," Edith said.

"I remind you; I have his Power of Attorney. And in any case, only his parents would raise a fuss, and they won't, I assure you."

"But where will you go and what would you do?"

"I'm afraid that depends on you."

"Oh, Malcolm, don't."

He begged her to listen. He felt at home with her, and he hoped she felt at home with him. That's all he was asking for, that they make a home somewhere together.

"You overlook the possibility that I might fall in love with someone," she said.

"You haven't yet, have you? Though I suspect before too long that dashing Mr. Nedleman will turn your head."

"He's a dreadful nuisance."

"You would sleep with him, though."

"That's a direct and somewhat inappropriate remark."

"Yes, it is."

She asked him for that second glass of sherry. He gave it to her, and she found it tasted better than before, but not quite the same as she was used to.

"I suppose I would," she said.

An odd light came into Alistair's eyes.

"You think I'm loose, don't you?" she asked.

"I think you approach sex the way a man does."

"Is that bad?"

"It's unusual, that's all."

"I hope you don't mind."

"I don't."

Edith wished she knew what he thought, but then that would be another burden, wouldn't it?

As the next days passed, Edith's mood eased. She enlisted everyone at the store to decorate with banners and stickers in the windows. She put Henry from her mind, though she knew she must reply to his letter before too much longer. Finally, she dashed off another cheerful note saying that she understood his decision perfectly and appreciated his candor, though, of course, her heart was sore at the thought she would never be his wife. As she wrote those words, she felt relief and guilt, those old familiar twins that ran her personal show. She had never loved him but enjoyed his company, both in and out of bed. She thought of the night she spent with Alistair and wondered if it would ever be repeated. Why did men have such trouble with the casual attitude she took to sex? They expected her devotion after a simple exchange of physical pleasure. Despite Alistair saying he was fine with it, she could see that he wasn't. Like the rest of them, he wanted more than she had to give.

Detective O'Connell dropped in to see if she were keeping her nose clean. She invited him to look around the store and decide for himself if anything were salacious or inappropriate. He said he already had a good look and thought everything was a-okay.

He stood in her doorway, filling the office with his cigarette smoke, and asked what she did in her time off.

"I'm studying to take up the veil," she said.

"All right, all right, that was out of line. Message received." He said he might drop in again, unannounced, so she should keep on her toes.

After he left, she put her head on her desk for a moment. She was tired, all the way down to her fingertips.

Alistair bought a Christmas tree and was decorating it when Edith got home. It was in the library and Edith thought it would have been better in the living room, which was larger, but said he shouldn't move it. She was touched by how hard he tried to create a happy atmosphere and offered to help hang ornaments. He was grateful for her help. When she climbed the stepstool and reached up to place a smirking angel on a high branch, she got dizzy. Alistair put a firm hand on her elbow and helped her down. He brought her a glass of water and she said the episode had passed quickly. She went back up the stepstool several more times without incident. When they finished, they toasted their efforts with sherry. She told him about the detective dropping in again. Alistair said it sounded like he hadn't properly embraced the holiday spirit and Edith laughed.

"Do you attend church services on Christmas Day? Or the evening before?" Alistair asked.

"I'm an atheist."

"As am I."

Alistair said Henry used to go before the war. Mary was keen on going, too, though she never went at any other time.

"It's funny, how people pick and choose how devoted to be. I think you should be all in, or not at all," Edith said. Her back ached and she was glad to sit and let Alistair fuss over her. He asked what she wanted for dinner. She said scrambled eggs were all she thought she could manage.

"You don't eat enough, you really don't," Alistair said.

"I'm fine."

"You look peaked. You have for weeks."

"It's my own fault. I wanted to throw myself into work, and I did. I just didn't think it would all be so exhausting."

He asked if she were going to change the title of Miss Levy's manuscript, as she had been requested to.

"I don't see how I can. The poems are all linked by subject, and the Holocaust is that subject. I don't know why she wanted to abandon it," Edith said.

"People just want to forget what happened. She doesn't want her book to be an unpleasant reminder."

"Art should remind, or at least make people think. Where politics always fails, art steps in."

Alistair lifted his glass to toast her words.

Edith said she hadn't done any Christmas shopping, and time was running short, particularly if she wanted to send something out to her mother and Betty. Alistair asked what sort of gifts she had in mind for them.

"My mother's mad about gardening, so I was thinking a book about that, though she knows more than she could learn from someone else. I thought Betty might like a nice fountain pen to edit her pages. At least, I think that's how she works. She might not. She might just use her typewriter, striking through what she doesn't want."

Alistair said he forgot to mention, but he'd read her book, *Death is Never Quiet.*

"Oh? How did you like it?"

"It was wonderful."

Edith had recommended it and brought it back from the store. She asked if he thought Betty were giving Mrs. Christie some competition.

"Oh, I should say she's more like Dorothy Sayers. At least, for my money."

"I like the way she takes such a cool approach in her storytelling, letting the facts speak for themselves, yet there's always such simmering tension just below the surface."

"Indeed."

Edith let her mind wander. She didn't like the detective showing up like that. She might write a letter to the newspaper or ask Robert to get his father involved somehow. That would only draw attention to herself, wouldn't it? Yet, she couldn't fly under the radar and succeed. She realized that when she offered to publish Laura's book. She could state her case and let the court of public opinion decide. She was being unfairly harassed because she was a woman in a male-dominated field, at least that's the tack she'd take. Would Robert help her? He'd have to see his welfare was somehow at stake. If she were attacked, he would be, too, by association. Or she could lie low and hope his book would be well-received and not looked upon with suspicion.

Alistair asked what was on her mind and she told him. He said he could see the benefit of a publicity campaign, but the risk was some people might see her as naïve by not realizing the true nature of Laura's book. He advised focusing on the next title and the one after that. She said after Robert would be Miss Levy's collection, and she was beginning to realize the stir that might cause.

"I'm not cut out to be a voice for the downtrodden and overlooked," she said.

"Who better?"

"What do you mean?"

"You're an educated, articulate, attractive young woman."

"Thank you. But all those traits make people take me less seriously. If I were middle-aged and ugly, they might listen."

Alistair conceded her point. He said what she needed was a partner, another face for the press. He would love to offer his services.

Edith felt grim. She said that's what Henry was supposed to have done before he got depressed. She agreed Alistair would be helpful in that role, though. They should talk about that sometime soon and get specific.

The next day when she returned from the bookstore, Alistair said he'd received a telephone call from Dr. Harris suggesting that Henry might return home for the holiday and then go back to the sanatorium. He was no longer under restraint and the doctor was confident his condition was stable. Edith didn't know how she felt about having Henry back, even temporarily. She still missed him, but her life had moved on. Sensing her ambivalence, Alistair said it would only be for about a week, and he would do everything His Lordship required so Edith could tend to herself.

"I suppose I do need tending, don't I? But so does Henry, clearly, and this is his home. We can't refuse him, can we?"

Alistair said he'd write to the doctor and say they were looking forward to Henry's visit.

The day after, Henry called Edith at work. The connection was bad, and she had to raise her voice. Though the door was closed she feared being overheard.

"Darling, I can hear you now," Henry said. He spoke slowly but he didn't sound drugged.

"How are you?"

"I am quite well. The doctor wants me to come home for a little while."

"Yes, so I understand. We're getting everything ready for you."

"Well, that's just it. You see, I don't want to come at all, but the doctor is insisting."

Edith leaned back in her chair, slipped off her shoes, lit herself a cigarette, and asked him to tell her everything.

He said he was faring better, she wasn't to worry about that, but the idea of that long car ride and having to change his routine again was unsettling. It didn't worry him so much as make him tired. Did she understand?

"Yes, of course. But the doctor seems to think this is best," Edith said.

"That's because I expressed enthusiasm for the idea. It was the only way I could get out of that damned straight jacket."

"Oh, Henry! It must have been awful."

"I deserved it. That man wasn't doing me any harm."

"I must say, I have trouble seeing you taking a swing at someone."

His silence said she'd spoken badly.

She heard voices in the store and the sound of the cash register ringing. Someone said, "Merry Christmas," and was answered cheerfully with, "Same to you!"

Henry said he regretted coming to the sanatorium but since he was there, he would like to remain until he truly felt up to any small change in his circumstances.

"I see. Well, just tell him you don't want to come, that's all. Put your foot down."

"That's all well and good, but should I do so, he'd merely say I don't know what's best for me."

"Do you want me to speak to him? Or ask Malcolm to?"

"Malcolm?"

"Alistair, I mean."

Henry paused. The line crackled. He breathed into the phone.

"No, no, I will try my hand and see if I can't persuade him to leave well enough alone," he said.

"Very well, my love. Let me know how that goes."

"I will."

He said if she liked, she could drive out to Elm Meadows. They could have that dinner they weren't able to have earlier. She said that sounded wonderful.

She put down the phone and found the idea appalling, even if Alistair came with her. She would go, though. It was her duty. She owed it to him.

Christmas cards arrived from Henry's parents, Edith's mother and Betty, Aunt Margaret, and Kathleen. Everyone seemed so cheery and optimistic about the approach of the new decade. Edith wanted to feel optimistic, too, and couldn't.

Alistair asked if she'd had any further thoughts about going over to see Henry. She said she would go two days before Christmas. Alistair was welcome to come but shouldn't feel the need to.

"I wouldn't let you drive all that way alone," he said.

The next day, as Edith was packing a small bag, a letter from Henry came by special delivery telling Edith not to come. He needed to be on his own for a little longer. He was sorry if he had ruined her plans. Edith sat on the bed next to her neatly folded slips.

"Oh, Henry," she said and put the letter in the nightstand drawer. She lay back on the bed and fell asleep. She woke to the sound of Alistair knocking gently on her door. He wanted to know if she were all right.

Edith got up, pulled a comb through her hair, and went into the hall. Alistair had a drink in his hand, and Edith realized she'd slept until the late afternoon.

"I'm fine, thanks. Just took a nap," she said.

"You should see a doctor."

"Oh, Malcolm."

"You should. I can make an appointment for you."

"Don't be silly. I can make my own appointments."

They went into the living room. Edith told him that the trip to Elm Meadows was canceled at Henry's request.

"It's not like His Lordship to decide something and then change his mind," Alistair said.

"That doctor is confusing him about what he feels. Which is why I don't like doctors, by the way."

"The doctor you need is for your physical health, not mental. There's quite a difference."

"I suppose you're right."

On Christmas morning, Edith and Alistair exchanged gifts. He was delighted with the cashmere scarf she gave him, and she said the perfume he chose suited her perfectly. And that was saying something because perfume was hard to buy for someone else.

Nothing came from Henry. Dr. Harris had asked that no gifts be sent to him, either. It might make him feel guilty for asking Edith to cancel her visit. On the table in the hall, waiting to be taken to the post office at some future date, was a lovely pipe she'd gotten him, wrapped in cheerful paper and a big red bow. She moved it to his desk in the library.

The week between Christmas and New Year's was slow at the store, and the bad weather kept people away. Edith didn't mind. She worked in her office there, ordered a batch of new books, paid bills, and went over Miss Levy's manuscript. She found studying it away from the apartment made her eye wiser.

She and Patricia closed the store at three o'clock on New Year's Eve. Snow had been falling since the night before. Edith watched the flakes swirl maddeningly from the window of the taxicab. The doctor had squeezed her in at the last minute and she was on her way home with a vial of vitamins in her purse. She pressed her cheek against the window and was grateful for the feel of the freezing glass on her skin. The stoplights were hung with garlands. The cab driver was cheerful and chatty. Edith didn't register anything he said. His driving was terrible. She left him a big tip, though. Wasn't it the season to be merry?

Alistair was out. The silence of the apartment gnawed. She removed her coat, hat, gloves, and snow boots and went into the library. Alistair had just restocked the liquor cart in the living room, bless him. She should tell him how much his help had meant and would always mean. He'd accept the compliment politely and go on his way. Or sit with her, if she asked. Even if she didn't ask. He no longer seemed to need permission to enter a room and make himself comfortable.

She plugged in the Christmas tree lights and they came to life. The red bulbs seemed garish, and the blue felt sad. The white were cold and cruel. The yellow overly cheerful. The green was just green, like her emerald. She twisted it around on her finger. It still fit perfectly, but then why wouldn't it?

She lit the fire and sat. She wanted a drink but thought she should wait for Alistair. Then she heard him in the hall putting away his coat and hat. A moment later he was in the library, looking at her with concern but gladness, too. He was always glad to find her wherever she was, whatever she was doing.

"Is it still snowing?" she asked.

"It is. And the streets are full of cars, and it's getting to be quite a mess."

"Then it's a good thing we're here, at home, with lots of food in the refrigerator."

"Indeed."

He poured himself a glass of scotch and asked if he could get her anything. She said she'd have the same. He brought it to her and sat on the couch.

They enjoyed their drinks. She asked him if he were looking forward to 1950 the way everyone else seemed to be. He said he always looked forward to the calendar turning over and didn't find the approach of a new decade to be particularly important, though he understood why so many people did. The current decade hadn't been wonderful. It had been dreadful, ghastly, really. So many lives lost. So many lives ruined. It was depressing to consider, which is why he didn't, as a rule. Except now, of course. Since she asked.

"You're babbling, Malcolm," she said.

"I believe I am."

"I'm pregnant."

He put his glass on the coffee table, leaned toward her, and stared as if trying to see within her the truth she'd just revealed.

"Is it mine?" he asked.

"It has to be. And I don't want it. I told the doctor so. He said he wouldn't help me, but when I pressed, he said he knew someone who might."

"Edith, no. You mustn't even think that."

"You have it then if you're so keen."

"I would, for you."

He took her hand. He said he never thought there would be a second chance for a child after his wife left him. There hadn't been other women since then, well, one or two but those had only been sexual relationships, nothing deeper. At this Edith looked at him questioningly but kept quiet. He said he knew he was older than one should be and hoped it wouldn't be a problem as time went on. He wished, with all his heart, that she would have the baby, love it, and let him help her raise it.

"Oh, Malcolm. What in the world am I going to do with you?" she asked.

"Marry me."

"How many proposals can one girl get in a single year?"

"I'm being serious."

"I know you are."

It was beginning to sink in now as the shock faded. At first, she'd called the doctor a fool, then a quack. He was an older man, in practice a long time, and probably had heard every kind of reaction a woman could have. She cried when he told her there was no mistake. They'd follow up with a laboratory test, but his physical exam put her at about eight weeks along. She blamed the absence of her period on stress, as well as her upset stomach and grinding fatigue. Pregnancy hadn't crossed her mind, and it seemed to her she'd been in a state of deep denial. And why had she stopped paying attention? She hadn't taken her diaphragm on the trip with Alistair to visit Henry for obvious reasons. With Henry locked up in that madhouse, any sort of private romantic encounter was impossible. She couldn't possibly have anticipated Alistair's visit later that same night. Or could she have? Had she willed that to happen? Had she willed everything, including Henry's illness? But that was stretching it.

She let go of Alistair's hand and drank more of her scotch. The doctor said to take it easy with alcohol. Of course, when she went home, she could have a drink with her husband to celebrate. Naturally, he assumed the existence of a husband. She made the appointment under the name Mrs. Sloan. His resistance to her saying she couldn't go through with it infuriated her. She didn't care about legalities. She cared about autonomy over her own body.

She'd heard stories of shady abortions. Women died from them, sometimes. Or they were damaged and couldn't have children afterward. That didn't strike her as a terrible outcome, though the process by which that happened was awful to think about.

She looked at Alistair, who was gazing into the fire. Was he dreaming of a future son? Of a life with her by his side?

"We'll have to tell Henry everything, as soon as we think he can stand hearing it," Edith said.

"Are you saying yes?"

"I don't see that I have much choice."

"There's always a choice."

He said if she wanted, they could wait until she was certain the pregnancy was healthy. That way, she wouldn't feel as if she made a mistake.

"You mean, wait to see if I miscarry," she said.

"In essence."

"The doctor seems to think I'm as healthy as a horse. 'Smooth sailing' were his very words. At least, until I asked him to get rid of it."

Alistair said sometimes blessings arrived when we least expected them. If she didn't view this child as a blessing now, he was certain that she would, in time.

"And if I don't?" she asked.

"Then he—or she—will still have me."

She'd begun the year as Walter's wife. Then she left him and moved in with Henry. She divorced Walter and accepted Henry's offer of marriage. Henry broke under his private strain and went away. Now, she was pregnant, and Alistair had just proposed. Things were moving too fast, and she could do nothing to slow them. The child within her would keep growing. Anything she did to stop that would harm her, too. They were joined now.

She picked up the first copy of Laura's book, the one the printer sent over after the frontispiece had been settled on. The dust jacket concealed the embossed hedgerow on the spine, so she removed it and ran her finger over the image. She had created this all by herself, and it would fare better in the world than her child ever would.

"Malcolm, I'm scared," she said.

"Women have babies every day."

"And ruin them."

"You'll ruin no one."

"Tell me in a year—five years—if you're ruined. Then you'll see."

She put the book back on the table and ran her hand over her stomach. The idea of being fat was appalling. Her ankles would probably swell. The doctor said she was probably due around the first of July. Summer must be a terrible time to have a baby.

Alistair was talking and she made herself listen. He said she should rely on him, that he would help her with anything and everything. They'd engage someone to care for the baby so she could be at the store. They'd find a new place to live, anywhere she liked.

"I think it's best not to make promises right now," she said.

"I intend to keep any I make."

"I didn't mean you."

Alistair said she should look upon this as a chance for her to have a family—for them to become one. He'd lived long enough to know the value of that. It would give him something to both look forward to and fight for.

"I'm not here to give meaning to your life, Malcolm," she said.

"True. But you're carrying my child. That provides all the meaning I need, for now."

She said the best she could do was try to be good to him, and later to their child.

"That's all I ask," he said.

She walked over to the window. The city was cloaked in darkness, and the river was a black ribbon running through it. Snow swirled in the weak glow of a streetlight.

1950. That was reason enough to hope. After all the world had been through, it was still here, spinning in space. She was here, too, her dreams intact, for the most part.

She looked into the night, thought of the being within her, and hoped that one day they would become friends.

THE END

About the Author

Anne Leigh Parrish lives in a forest in the South Sound Region of Washington State. She is the author of thirteen previously published books which include short stories, novels, and poems. She has recently ventured into the art of photography. Find her online at anneleighparrish.com.

About the Press

Unsolicited Press is based out of Portland, Oregon and focuses on the works of the unsung and underrepresented. As a womxn–owned, all–volunteer small publisher that doesn't worry about profits as much as championing exceptional literature, we have the privilege of partnering with authors skirting the fringes of the lit world. We've worked with emerging and award–winning authors such as Shann Ray, Amy Shimshon–Santo, Brook Bhagat, Kris Amos, and John W. Bateman.

Learn more at Unsolicitedpress.com. Find us on Twitter and Instagram at @UnsolicitedP.